D1824408

Queen of HEARTS

SHERYL WRIGHT

BELLA
BOOKS
2018

Bella Books, Inc.
P.O. Box 10543
Tallahassee, FL 32302

Printed in the United States of America on acid-free paper.

First Bella Books Edition 2018

Editor: Katherine V. Forrest
Cover Designer: Judith Fellows

ISBN: 978-1-64247-019-2

Other Bella Books by Sheryl Wright

Don't Let Go
Stay with Me

Acknowledgments

While writing is a solo pursuit, turning a manuscript into a reader-worthy book takes a team. I have to tell you, I'm extremely fortunate to have an exceptional team on my side. The women at Bella Books are professionals and more. I'm lucky to consider them mentors and friends.

To Katherine V. Forrest, author and editor extraordinaire, who I make work way too hard, but has shockingly decided I might be worth it; publisher Linda Hill, a patient and caring friend; Jessica Hill, who answers all my foolish questions with kindness and insight; and Laina Villeneuve, fellow Bella author, who comprehends the weird compulsion to write and cheers me on. Let me wish you each, in my language, the only gratitude suitable: *Nia:wen' kó:wa.*

About the Author

I didn't start out wanting to be a writer. I wanted to be an astronaut. Being born in 1961, a girl, and not American, convinced my parents I had lost my little mind. So, to keep the peace, I set my sights slightly lower, deciding on the earthlier altitude of a pilot. (If we ever meet in person, ask me to tell you the cosmonaut story.)

Flying was my joy. It was my air. I needed it to breathe. On the eve of the millennium, I suffered a Surgical Misfortune. I learned that phrase from reading a lesbian medical-themed romance, not from anyone responsible for the situation. Emotionally, it was like falling from the sky and waking up lost in the wilderness. Like Edgar Allen Poe's epic poem *Evangeline*, I was forced to make my way from my beloved home through the inhospitable boreal forest. I did so, not on horseback, but by words. One word at a time. I was teaching myself how to breathe again. It was slow going, but word by word I began to find my way and come to terms with my new reality. In time the words I'd written for myself become ideas to build on—stories to share. Without realizing it, I was learning to breathe again, not with jet fuel, but by using paper and ink.

In the early days of my writing, I was like a potter up to her elbows in clay, experimenting and discovering my craft. It took time before I reached a place where I understood not just my strengths and weaknesses but what I loved. Authors sculpt their works like potters, turning out everything from cheap earthenware to fine Wedgewood. While I would love to boast of skills needed to turn out a literary masterpiece, I find I'm better suited applying my skills to the craft in a more approachable way. Think of a potter at a craft fair. Someone with unique and colorful creations you can surprisingly afford to buy. That's the author I strive to be. I live to create stories which are fresh, sometimes quirky, sometimes challenging, but always from the heart. You can reach me at: info@sherylwright.com.

Dedication

For Dawn

CHAPTER ONE

"*What?* No! No way! Have you lost your mind?"

"Allyson, really?" Pamela Parker questioned with an insincere grin. "It's not like you'll last long, so what's the problem?"

Connie, eighteen years younger than her brilliant and successful sister, gave her the look of death before turning her attention and her doe-like eyes back on their cousin, pleading, "Allyson, please! We can't proceed without four queens. It's the premise of the whole show. Come on Ally, I need you, and I promise to make up for this. Please," she begged again.

"Think about our investment," Pam offered, more kindly than her insult that Ally would fall at the first elimination.

Pam and Ally had been born only weeks apart but how different could two cousins be? Growing up, Pamela Parker was pretty, smart, outgoing—The Everything Girl. And still was. Her cousin Allyson Parker was—well, her mother had spent most of the girl's childhood making excuses for her. It wasn't like she hadn't any achievements of her own. Pam might be some highfalutin' attorney in Chicago, but Allyson was successful too, just on her own terms. She was a pilot and ran a helicopter charter company out of Toronto. No, she wasn't a conventional beauty like Pam. No, she wasn't a partner in the biggest law firm in Chicago. No, she would never rake in the big bucks like her cousin. But she managed her trust fund with brilliance and had invested so wisely she could claim the same income as Pam if she were the type to compare tit for tat. But that wasn't Ally.

"It's not being eliminated first that worries me. It's the opposite. What if I'm *not* eliminated first? I have a company to run, and we just acquired a commuter airline. KC and I already have our hands full. I can't dump everything on her."

Pam started to laugh. It was that arrogant laugh that made Ally angry and had since they were kids. Before she could think of some stinging retort, young Connie intervened. "Look, I know this is a lot to consider, but we're screwed if you don't. And Pam is right about one thing. You each invested a hundred grand in this project. If we start production without four Primaries, the network will pull its contract. I'll end up on the TV and film convention circuit trying to flog this and with everyone knowing we bailed on our network agreement. I'll never sell another show. And as for directing, well, I'll be the example they use in every film school of what not to do."

Allyson groaned, but Connie was right. If they didn't find and vet a new Primary for this ridiculous reality TV production Connie had created, her money was gone and the kid's career was over. She slumped back in her chair, defeated. "What do I have to do?"

* * *

Connie stood on the broad, grand entry to Glendennon Castle Academy for Young Women, the Toronto location for most of The Queen of Hearts shoot and the backdrop for the show's opening scene. Beside her, Tommy Proulx, Fashionista and Toronto International Film Festival goddess, had been tapped to act as narrator and on-camera personality. "Everyone's ready, Tommy. Are you?"

"Oh sweetie, I was born ready. Are you?"

Connie just smiled.

"Don't be nervous, honey," he offered with a side hug. You've blocked everything out perfectly and the women, oh the women! My goodness, they're raring to go. So, let's get to it, baby girl. The day's a-wastin'."

Connie smiled again, returning to her place beside the camera operator and the sound tech. She set the bullhorn down; she didn't need it for this unless she had to call cut and that would piss her off. They had rehearsed this opening most of the previous day. The only thing different this time was instead of a stand-in for the four queens walking over to be introduced to the contestants vying for their hearts, the true Primaries, the actual four queens, would each make a spectacular entrance and be introduced to the women for the first time. She wanted this shot to work without retakes. She needed her audience to see the look on the women's faces. See their interest and be able to speculate on just which Primaries would be selected to compete for the heart of each contestant.

This was the big reveal and the detail that had sold her show to the network. They loved how she had turned the whole bachelorette thing on its head by creating a show where the women had some choices and power. Four Primaries or queens would be introduced and given time to get to know the contestants before the women began whittling down the pool. From that point, the show would run pretty much along the same format as any of the reality TV bachelor-style competitions, with contestants focused on their favorite bachelorette or queen. And she had incorporated one more hitch: contestants could switch allegiances at any time. Again, putting the pressure on the bachelorettes, or queens as she had named them, to up their game too.

Taking one more look across the wide grand lawn of Glendennon Castle, she sucked in a deep breath. This was it. Beside her, the assistant director called, "Quiet on the set! Roll sound."

"Speed."

"Frame."

"Action!"

"Welcome to historic Glendennon Castle and the *Queen of Hearts*!" Tommy began his intro, explaining in simple terms and with great enthusiasm how the game was played. Then he turned to the two uniformed valets standing as side-boys and waved grandly for the doors to open. The contestants exited the grand foyer one at a time, allowing Tommy to capture each woman and introduce her in a few words.

Connie knew she'd have to edit this section with an eye for time, but that wouldn't happen until they were down to the final six and knew on whom to focus. For now, it was Tommy's show, and she let him have fun and take the time he needed. Once all the women vying to earn the affection of the Queen of Hearts had been introduced, she called "Cut!" before moving to the group and helping Tommy get them lined up. Now they looked more like a group of alumni lining up for a class shoot. Not happy with that, she took some time, moving women from spot to spot until she and Tommy were pleased with the on-camera look.

Back beside the camera operator, she called "Action!" again, then waved to the wrangler responsible for getting the Primaries, the four women bachelorettes competing for the love of one of these stunning women, on the move. Thirty seconds later a super car, a Mosler MT900S, ripped past the ornate entry gates, racing up the drive, skidding around the oval to the grand entry, and squealing to a stop. Some of the women in the line of contestants jumped back, but the driver, obviously skilled and confident, had never placed them in danger. A hush fell as they waited expectantly for the first of the Primaries vying to be the Queen of Hearts to step from the extravagant supercar.

Rene Santos-Dumont, a tech millionaire and *Queen of Hearts* Primary number one, opened the low-slung door, easing her lithe, six-foot frame from the vehicle, dressed in racing leathers that fit like a second skin. Her short-cropped black hair and designer shades added to her adrenaline-fueled grin as she strode with purpose to where Tommy was standing and boldly offered her hand. There was no question this woman liked to be in charge, and she was hot if you liked the lean, fearless-butch type. Judging by the reaction of the thirty contestants in line, some very much did.

Tommy was aghast. "What an entrance! Heavens me, I can hardly breathe!"

"It's exciting to be here and wow, what a group of women," Rene offered, with a slightly wolfish grin as she tipped her head in admiration of the contestants. Tommy spent a few minutes interviewing Rene for the audience and the contestants. Then he moved her to her mark as the camera panned back to the big entry gates and Connie signaled for the next queen to make her entrance.

Instead of some high-performance supercar ripping up the grand drive, a timeless Rolls Royce ambled up, looking very much at home against the classic design of the Castle's grand lawn. Reaching its mark it stopped majestically, and they waited breathlessly as a uniformed driver circled behind the classic ride and opened the rear door for its passenger.

Virginia Hazelton-Jackson, the young and infamous lesbian debutante, emerged with feline grace. She wouldn't need an introduction to anyone who read the gossip rags. She offered her hand to Tommy in that classic manner of ladies expecting it to be kissed. Tommy, always the perfect gentleman, bowed before taking her hand and doing exactly that.

Connie, curious to see the reaction of the contestants, noted that a few looked to almost swoon over the blond beauty. *Perfect.* While Tommy began his mini-interview she signaled for the next entry. This one would require a longer lead time. Connie had staged the cars just outside the gates and out of sight of the women, but this one had needed to be miles away to keep the noise from interfering with the sound.

Right on time, Tommy moved Virginia to her mark just to the left of Rene and smiled while the cameras turned toward the entry gate. As the women and cameras panned back and forth, waiting in excitement for the next queen to arrive, the sound of a helicopter grew louder and louder until it passed just over the ornate gates, hovered over the lawn, and finally set down a few hundred feet from the grand entry. Some of the women wrestled with their hair or dress to keep them from being disheveled, but it wasn't really necessary. The sleek executive helicopter was just far enough away to prevent any real upsets. Two women dressed as side-boys made their way to the chopper, ducking as they moved under the spinning blades. Opening the rear door, a tall, statuesque brunette stepped down from the helo, accepting the arm of the castle guard. Once clear of the rotor arch, the helicopter lifted off and quickly sped away, taking its noise and whirlwind with it. By the time this next queen was at Tommy's side, all noise had vanished, and they could chat on-camera normally. "Let's welcome Pamela Parker to the *Queen of Hearts*," Tommy gushed. "Pamela, what an entrance! Tell us, is that how you normally travel?"

Poised and confident, the tall beauty was a natural on-camera. "Not always, Tommy, but when it makes sense why not skip the traffic altogether?"

Tommy practically snorted in delight. "I can't tell you how wonderful it is to have you here. Now, I know all about you, but let's share a few tidbits for these ladies and our audience at home. Tell us about your practice. I understand you're a criminal defense attorney and partner with a prestigious firm in Chicago. What inspired you to take up the law?"

"Oh Tommy, since I was a little girl I've wanted to help those less fortunate than myself. I can't tell you what a privilege it is to save the wrongly convicted from a life in prison. Every day I meet young men and women who are victims of circumstance. The small part I play in helping them regain their freedom gives me the inspiration to work harder and help as much as I can."

"You say it's a small part you play, but if I were in the shoes of some of your clients, I would thank my lucky stars to have you on my side."

"I was raised to understand that those born to privilege have a responsibility to society. Some of my clients are accused of heinous crimes they didn't commit. If saving their lives and ensuring they get the chance they deserve takes everything I have, then it's well worth it."

"Said like a true champion of the downtrodden. Brava!"

While they chatted on, Connie signaled for the last queen. Secretly she worried that her cousin's arrival would be a bit of a letdown after the building excitement, but she also knew she could cut the digital recordings any way she wanted and, if she kept Ally in the last slot, it would give the network something to cut if they decided to increase the commercial break.

Moments later the same helicopter approached. Already the women were speculating. Luckily for her, many of them had sound packs on, and she had several cameras fixed and mounted around the grand entry to pick up their reactions. Yes, the speculation was on, and she could use it.

When the helicopter landed a second time the side-boys opened the rear passenger door, but no one was aboard. They looked confused, as did all the women. While Tommy speculated for the audience, the helo's main rotor squealed to a halt, and the sound of the engine died too. Moments later the pilot stepped from the sleek machine. Dressed in a sapphire-blue flight suit and pristine white helmet, she walked toward Tommy and the women with the two castle guards trailing her and still looking confused. When she reached Tommy, she removed the helmet and ruffled her short curls back into order before offering her hand. "Allyson Parker. Pleased to meet you."

Tommy, aghast and practically beside himself, let out an excited squeal, "Oh my God. You were flying that thing?"

She smiled at him, her grin lopsided and cute. "It's what I do."

Aware of who the fourth queen was and what to do, Tommy welcomed her quickly then turned back to the camera. "There you have it. Ladies, please meet your four queens, Rene Santos-Dumont, tech millionaire; Virginia Hazelton-Jackson, debutant and heir to the Jackson family fortune; Pamela Parker, defender of the people of Illinois; and Allyson Parker, pilot extraordinaire." He eased Ally into place then stepped toward the thirty women contestants. Moving to his next mark, he was in front them all and ready to explain the rules. One of the women dressed in the ornate costume of a castle guard moved to his side with a silver serving tray in hand.

"Ladies and our wonderful home audience, let me explain how the competition will work. As you see, we have four women competing to find love amongst you beauties, but there's a hitch. Only one will become a finalist and the Queen of Hearts. You women will be choosing the one whom you most want to get to know. To begin with, we will assign a card to represent each of our four queens, and each contestant will receive the four cards representing all four queens. When the time comes, you will each cast your votes, eliminating one queen at a time, until only one remains. Yes, these queens will have to compete against each other for your affection!"

Tommy turned to the second uniformed woman as she began handing each of the thirty contestants four oversized playing cards. The logo of the program was printed on the back with standard card deck queen illustrations on the front. Once the contestants had their cards, Tommy called for the four Primaries to choose a card from the four on the silver tray.

Rene was first and drew the Queen of Clubs. She smiled and held it up for all the women to see.

Virginia was next and drew the Queen of Spades. She took it with grace, holding it up for the others to see.

Pam was next and drew the Queen of Hearts. When she held it up there were a few cheers, so she blew a kiss to the excited group. That left the Queen of Diamonds for Ally. She thanked Tommy and displayed her card unnecessarily, but as directed. There were no cheers, just polite applause. Without prodding, Ally took her place back at the end of the four-woman line for the cameras while Tommy waxed on about the competition to come.

"Cut!" Connie called with the bullhorn. "That was perfect, women. Now let's move to the ballroom for the meet and greet. Contestants first. Primaries you're with me."

While Tommy corralled the contestants toward the entry door and the grand foyer, Connie marched to the Primaries. "Excellent work, women. All right, this is how the next part will work. I'll take you one-by-one to the Ballroom Terrace. Once there we will tape you having your initial meeting with each contestant. You get two minutes to sell yourself to these women. Make it short and sweet. It's going to take most of the day to shoot this scene so if you're not on camera, get your kiesters to the green room." Connie pointed to the women dressed as castle guards. "The PAs will show you to your rooms and keep you on schedule."

"Who's up first?" Virginia asked.

"Queen of Diamonds, Queen of Spades, Queen of Hearts, then Queen of Clubs. Any other questions?" When there weren't, she clapped her hands like they were pre-schoolers who needed to be rushed. "All right then, chop, chop, we have a schedule to keep."

When the four turned to follow the production assistants costumed as historical Irish Borderland guards, Connie called to Ally. "Not you, Diamond. You're with me."

Ally stopped, looking confused. "Don't I get to change?"

"No time," Connie insisted.

"What about my hair? You don't want me to go around all day with helmet head, do you?"

Connie, eighteen years younger and a few inches taller than her cousin, reached over and gave the short dark curls another tousle. "There you go. Hair fixed."

Ally wasn't pleased, but what the hell could she do? It wasn't like she had expected to last, but she did expect to be given an even chance. Judging by the response, or non-response, to her arrival, she was pretty sure she was already out. Might as well give the women time to confirm their disinterest. *This is worse than getting picked last in high school!*

* * *

Erin Bogner walked with the other women to the ballroom, listening intently to their gossip and speculation. Word was out that Ally Parker was a last-minute replacement and she was surprised to see how quickly she'd been dismissed. She knew of Ally, but had never met her. As Pamela Parker's legal assistant and secret spy, she was long familiar with the stories of Pam's adventurous cousin and had seen all the photos of the three of them, sisters Pam and Connie and cousin Ally, that rested on the office credenza. No, Ally wasn't a great beauty like Pam, but she did feel they weren't giving her a chance. She knew the two had always been competitive, but this was unfair and certainly not right for the defender of the people, as the host had called her. When she got her chance to speak privately with Pam, she would bring it up. Just when that would happen was a good question.

In the ballroom, contestants fussed around the craft services table pretending not to be interested while they scoffed down the gourmet offerings. It had been like that last night. They had arrived by limousine in groups and been given tours of the castle-turned-girls-school. Erin knew of the place, having heard stories from Pam. All the Parker girls had attended this Glendennon Castle Academy for Young Women, an exclusive boarding school in the English style. Originally the production had been scheduled to take place at Purple Mountain Ski Lodge, but even off-season the place was packed, and they had lost their spot to a movie-production company with deep ties to the skiers' paradise. With only days before the production was scheduled to begin shooting, Pam and Ally had called in favors to get the closed-for-the-summer castle opened for them. In her mind, Connie was lucky to have them both come to her rescue, and Erin couldn't help but wonder just how much they would each have to shell out to this year's alumni fundraising drive.

Across the ballroom, one of the production assistants who had led them on the tour yesterday walked Ally across the room and out onto the terrace for the next scene. That seemed unfair too. You would think they would at least let the woman get changed. She knew all about the wardrobe selected for each of the queens because she'd helped Pam choose hers. Connie had provided a list of every scene, and the attire desired, and Pam had wasted no time shopping the best of Michigan Avenue for new clothes just for this occasion. Erin didn't have to worry about wardrobe with the production company supplying the designer dresses and most of the outfits they would need. Because Erin had no intention of winning, she hadn't jumped into the fray to get the best of the lot like the other women when the dress racks were rolled out last night. For the opening scene, the production designer had selected dresses and a few slacks suits in all the colors of the rainbow. Later it was clear Erin regretted her indifference when she was forced to accept the only dress left on the rack that would fit her, a tangerine that emphasized her freckles and red hair and would make her look like a walking carrot. It was also clear to Erin that Ally was praying to all the gods to get this part over.

* * *

Ally planted her bottom on the silly rattan loveseat as ordered and let the makeup person manhandle her with a tight grip on her jaw.

"I'll need at least twenty minutes if you expect me to cover this scar and even out the tan lines from her sunglasses."

"Leave the scar," Connie ordered. "Just even out the tan lines and get rid of the shine on her forehead. We don't have time for a makeover, and besides, we want the audience to see her the same way the contestants do."

"Fine," the makeup woman said. "That will give me more time for the others."

As she quickly applied makeup, Ally fussed, "I don't like it. It's making my face itch."

"Don't touch your face," Connie warned, with iron in her voice. "You can scrub it off as soon as we're done." Turning her attention to the PA, she ordered, "Get the first one ready for her entry. We shoot in two, people. Time's a-wastin', and we only have so much daylight. Let's go!"

Ally forced herself to sit still and not let the itchy makeup drive her nuts. *Just get it over with, and you're out of here.* It felt like only seconds had passed when Connie called "Action!" and the first of the contestants walked out. Ally began to stand and offer her hand when Connie called, "Cut!"

"Allyson, for frig sakes, keep your ass on the couch."

"But, it's rude not to stand."

"And it's rude to contradict your director." For a moment there looked to be a test of wills going on, then Connie explained, "It's how we blocked the shot, okay? So just do it this way for me, okay?"

"Okay," Ally agreed without joy. *Oh, this just gets better and better.*

The production assistant had already moved the first woman back to her starting mark, and Connie wasted no time. "Action!"

She sauntered her way to Ally's side, pausing for the camera before slipping into the spot beside Ally. She offered her hand with practiced grace, then proceeded to tell her life story in two minutes flat. Ally had yet to get a word in when Connie called, "Cut! That was perfect. Okay, folks, reset for the next contestant, let's go!" she said, rushing them.

The next two hours passed pretty much the same for each woman. Some were more polite with Ally and asked a few questions, but nothing to indicate they were interested. By the time they finished shooting the scene, her face hurt from smiling and her heart was aching from the clear disinterest from so many pretty women. Yes, she was plain looking. Yes, she didn't get to change out of the unflattering flight suit and show off her trim figure; yes, she wasn't a beauty like Pam, or glamorous like Virginia, or a hot, dangerous butch like Rene, but she wasn't a complete loser. *Was she?*

"Great job everyone. Okay, Ally, you're done. Why don't you head up to your room and get ready for tonight's ceremony?"

"I have to get the helo back to the island."

"*What?*" Connie looked like she would blow a gasket.

"Relax, I'll be back. KC's going to do the drive home traffic report. I'll just get the helicopter back and drive right back."

"Why can't KC fly you back?" she demanded.

Ally shook her head. "Will you stop worrying? I'll be all of two hours. Now go shoot your other queens in the heart, and I'll be back."

Connie just grunted, "Famous last words!" before turning her attention to setting up the next sequence with Virginia, who had just joined them.

One of the PAs still in the costume of the Borderland castle guard, minus the sword, had her flight helmet. "I'll show you out."

"It's okay, I know my way around here, and I can bypass the ballroom."

That bit of news pleased the PA, who promptly returned to take care of some other concern.

Ally walked with her head down. They had made it plain they expected her to be the first queen eliminated, but she didn't expect it to hurt this much. Trying to console herself, she remembered back to when she was a student here. She'd been a favorite because of her skill on the lacrosse field, but Pam had always been the one the girls on the team swooned for. If they didn't want to have her, they wanted to be her. Ally had accepted that back then and resigned herself to the preferences of the group. At least everyone loved her when the school won lacrosse games. It was even like that up north when she would take her turn flying during the firefighting season for the company contract. Her business partner, KC, was not the most attractive of women, but she was the life of the party and all the lesbians, the women firefighters and fire jumpers, fell for KC and her larger-than-life personality. When it was Ally's turn to fly fire patrol they loved her too, at least when she was in the air and saving their lives. On the ground, not so much. Considered too cerebral and not a lot of fun, she didn't get the same attention, much less action, KC would see every season.

She took her time with her pre-flight knowing her head wasn't in the game. It was time to forget about the Queen of Hearts and all the women who didn't go for her. It was time to concentrate on her job and make sure her aircraft was airworthy, and that's what mattered. Finally, in the air, she began to relax. Flying was what she was good at. Flying was what she was amazing at. It might not make women swoon, but it did save lives. That had to count with someone. Pam might get all the credit as a champion of the falsely accused, but Ally's vocation was exciting, dangerous, with far more immediacy. Too bad no one was interested in getting to know any of that.

CHAPTER TWO

Rene Santos-Dumont took Erin's hand in hers, "It's a pleasure to meet you, beautiful."

Erin smiled for the camera while the hair on the back of her neck stood on end. If she thought Virginia was over the top trying to play the femme-fatale, Rene was her perfect opposite playing the super-butch card. It was too bad too. Rene was a good-looking woman. The suit and tie she had changed into from the leathers she arrived in were not off the rack, but they lacked any femininity. Then there was the woman herself. Between the wolfish grin and the overt familiarity, cuddling into her like they knew each other, Rene just gave Erin the creeps. Erin knew some women loved that kind of confidence or forwardness. While she was waiting her turn, many of the women ahead of her had returned to the ballroom all gaga over the woman. Erin suspected the million-dollar car sitting in the front drive, and Rene's purported personal worth, might be influencing their opinions. She didn't care though. It was her job to nose around the contestants and learn what she could for Pam.

When Rene asked about her, where she was from, what she did for a living, she explained on cue that she was a legal assistant and from Wisconsin. That wasn't a lie. She *was* from Wisconsin. She just didn't live there anymore. It was something Pam had come up with, worried the women would naturally be curious to know if their paths had crossed if they both said they worked in Chicago. She listened as Rene shared a funny story about her single pass through her home state, then thankfully the director called "Cut," and she was marshaled back to the ballroom to rejoin the other women. At least Rene had asked her something. Virginia had been a complete diva, never so much as asking her name. Pam, of course, had a whole routine they had planned, so that was easy, although having her boss's arm around her did feel weird. Then there was the cousin, Ally. That had been her first one-on-one, and she had been so nervous, her legs shaking as she made her entry walk for the camera. Thankfully, Ally was more down-to-earth. While Erin had worked for Pam for more than five years, she only knew Allyson Parker by reputation, hearing many of Pam's stories of their teenage adventures. Of course, Pam was always the hero of those stories and Ally the voice of reason. Today she had been a gentlewoman, giving Erin her personal space, asking her more about herself than the others had. For their two minutes, she had concentrated on Erin and her only.

Ally's face had lit up when Erin explained she was from Wisconsin. "Wisconsin's amazing! I used to go to Oshkosh every year for the EAA Air Show."

"Really? I grew up not too far from there. My hometown is small. It's a good thirty miles east. And right on Lake Michigan."

"Let me guess, Sheboygan?"

More than surprised, Erin couldn't keep the shock from her voice. "No, but you're so close. I'm from Manitowoc."

"It's great growing up on the Great Lakes. Isn't it?"

"I would have disagreed until I went to college. After four years in Minneapolis, I knew I had to live and work somewhere closer to Lake Michigan, I missed it that much."

"Cut!" Connie called. "Great work Erin. Okay, let's keep it moving, folks."

As one of the costumed production assistants scooted her back to the ballroom, Erin chanced a look back. Ally was smiling and gave a friendly wave. So much nicer an experience than the two that followed. Finally done with all her screen calls for this scene, Erin headed for the food. She expected it to be picked over, but the caterers had everything topped up so she grabbed a plate, intent on filling up now, since she didn't know when they would eat again. With her plate piled high and her water bottle in hand, she made for one of the few folding chairs that sat unclaimed. As she sat, another of the contestants joined her, a slender, vivacious brunette.

"This is so exciting! I just love it. What about you?"

With her mouth full of chicken salad, Erin smiled politely, trying to swallow without choking. Finally, she answered, "Yes, exciting." She didn't know what else to say, then remembered she wasn't a contestant as much as a spy. "What do you think of the Primaries?" The woman looked confused, and for a moment she panicked remembering that was the pre-production term, not what they were using today. "Queens, I mean queens. What do you think of the queens so far?"

"Aren't they incredible? I mean wow, Rene and that car! I had goose bumps when she drove up, and what about Pamela, she's the lawyer, right? My mother always says to stay away from lawyers but boy oh boy, I've never seen one who looked like that!"

Before Erin could think of what more to say, other women began pulling their chairs over and sharing in the conversation. It did make it easy for her just to sit back, eat her lunch—or was it an early dinner now? She had no idea. They had all been relieved of their watches, cell phones, tablets, and any other electronic devices. A few had even been asked to relinquish their sex toys. Connie, the director, was adamant they not consider self-relief. She wanted them excited and if they got a little edgy, more the better.

"I like the quiet one," one offered.

"She's okay," another said, "but that flight suit...I mean, really? Couldn't she think of something else to wear?"

"What else would you wear in a helicopter?" another asked.

"No, I mean, she should have taken the time to change, like the other queens. And good God, do something with that hair."

"She was nice," another defended, "But lordy, lordy, that Virginia has everything you could ever ask for."

"Are you talking 'bout her figure or her money? You do know who she is, don't you?" While some of the women made as if they knew, the speaker elaborated for the rest. "She's the heiress to the Jackson Cosmetics Company. She must be worth billions. You can't tell me a pilot or even a lawyer has that kind of money."

Erin made a note of the women who took an interest in Virginia's pending fortune and dismissed Pam and Ally for the same reason. It was all she could do to stifle her laugh. If they only knew.

* * *

Allyson stood in the hangar watching KC maneuver the power cart towing in the executive Jet Ranger they had borrowed in place of their bird painted with the Channel One logo and colors. The Billy Bishop Airport was one of the few truly inaccessible facilities once the Tower closed, situated on the western edge of the Toronto Islands chain. Before World War II, the field had been the home of Toronto's first major league baseball team, the Maple Leafs. In 1940 the old wood stadium was torn down and repurposed as an airfield to house the displaced Royal Norwegian Air Force. Today, modern hangars crowded the harbor channel along with the quaint one-time WWII headquarters and tower, now turned air terminal and administration offices. In Ally's mind, the airport manager had the best office in the world, ensconced in what was once the old wood-framed and brass-trimmed control tower.

If it was an easy airport to find, it was horribly complicated to reach. Between the lakeshore condos on the north side, the bird sanctuary to the southeast and the gay nude beach that ran parallel to runway 33 and right up to the threshold of runway 08, one's approach had to be taken carefully.

With their flying day in full swing, Ally knew she had to risk Connie's ire and make sure KC had everything under control before she drove back out to Glendennon Castle. Once the borrowed helo was parked in the hangar and the power cart returned to its charging station, KC and Ally headed for their tiny operations room. They shared this space with the pilots from the local commuter airline and weren't surprised to find a few there, completing their flight plans for the day.

"Hey guys," KC offered genially. "How come so late?"

"Still waiting for Sierra X-Ray Foxtrot to arrive. They got held on the ground at LaGuardia."

"What's that about?" Ally asked, trying to sound casual.

They shrugged, either not knowing or uncomfortable sharing company gossip with the two charter pilots. Instead, the First Officer changed the subject. "How's the traffic?"

"Chock-a-block," KC warned. "For what it costs you in gas to drive out to your parents' house in Hamilton, you could probably find a place in town to share with one of the guys. I mean, that traffic alone would make me crazy."

"Yeah but my parents are right on the lake, and we have an indoor pool." He said it like it made sense.

Trying to help, KC offered her usual, "I don't think a pool is the chick magnet you imagine. Maybe what you should do is suggest they buy one of these new condos facing the lake for when they come into town?"

"There's an idea," the other pilot said, perking up at the suggestion. "If they buy a condo, talk them into something big enough for me too. I'd dump my girlfriend and leave Scarborough forever for a chance to live down here."

"Nice," Ally commented. "I'm going to tell her that."

He laughed. "Like you wouldn't dump a girl for a chance to live down here. Wait, where do you live?"

Ally shook her head, but KC, always open with information and ready to share, did so. "I live in Port Credit. Not right on the beach, but just a few doors down. But Ally here lives over there." She signaled east as if from the windowless room they could see where it was she was pointing. "Right on the lake and on the south side of Queen's Quay."

"South?" they both asked in confusion.

"KC," Ally growled.

"What? You live over there in what used to be the Admiral Hotel. Pretty cool, huh?"

The other pilots nodded, finishing up their flight plans and offering their farewells. Ally knew they would endlessly speculate. Who lived in a hotel? She knew they would ask about it and the gossip would be relentless. *Who lived in a hotel? People who own a major share, that's who, you dorkwads!*

Once they were out of hearing range, Ally wheeled on KC, only to witness her mischievous grin. "You're a pain, you know."

"'Course, I am. It's my specialty. That and reporting the traffic. About which by the way, we have an offer to consider. The network reporter was a no-show this morning. Well, he did show up, but only about an hour after I took off. I whipped back in and picked him up, but for the first hour I had to wing it and do the reporting thing. Actually, they tricked me. I thought I was just giving the details to the anchor off-air, and she was just asking questions to get all the details, but it turns out they aired the whole thing, and they want me to do it again."

"Wow, that's huge. Congrats."

"I know! But here's the thing. They want to talk with us. Maybe do a little training for the on-air stuff, you know, stuff like that. What do you say?"

"What do I say? I..." She had to think about it for a minute. "Right now, I have to get my ass back to Glendennon. I don't know how much longer they'll need me, but I'm stuck for now. If you're comfy doing this reporting thing, then go ahead and get the new terms worked out."

"Good. Listen. I can handle the network. Why don't you stick your nose into the delays our crews are facing at LaGuardia? We can't afford to have them wasting hours on the ground when we need that bird for the afternoon flight to Ottawa."

Ally nodded. "Let me get on the horn with LaGuardia bright and early tomorrow. If we can't solve the issue at the source, then we need to look at the numbers and decide if the route is worth all the trouble."

They were interrupted by the airline manager. "You just had to tell them you own the Admiral!" he challenged.

"That was all KC. I've kept my mouth shut, as agreed."

"Hey!" KC stepped in, arms crossed and tone as menacing as her dark expression. "I spilled the beans. What's the big deal? It's not like I told them we own the airline too."

"That's not the point!" he protested. "I just...I thought you wanted to observe and evaluate the staff before you made any announcements."

"We still do," Ally assured him. "Our restructuring plan is based on them no longer having access to the top brass. That's what this whole transfer period is about."

The manager slumped into one of the stools around the flight planning table. "There's something else. The new kid was towing Sierra Charlie November from the hangar and broke the trailing arm off the nose gear."

"What the..." KC started but stalled, seeing the look on Ally's face. If Ally was mad, that was something.

"Explain why a cabin attendant was towing an aircraft?"

"I told you, our guys get called on to do everything," he answered in a sheepish tone.

"And I told you, 'No more!'" She leaned hard on the table toward him, making sure he understood her completely. "I specifically explained why the jack-of-all-trades-and-master-of-none approach was hurting our bottom line and this just underscores my argument." She stepped back from the table, pacing the small space. Finally, she stopped, asking the most important question. "Damages? And I want to know everything right down to scratches on the paint."

He nodded. "It was PP3. He ordered the kid to tow the Dash-8 out so he could hangar his personal aircraft."

Hangar 1, used solely by Triangle Airlines, was a huge brick monstrosity built during the Second World War, but it was small by the standards of any major airport. The hangar could only accommodate two of the eight DeHavilland Dash-8's they operated. Because of that fact, only aircraft scheduled for maintenance were allowed in the hangar. After all, this was

Canada, and repairing and maintaining an aircraft outside the hangar in winter was no fun, no fun at all. And because of the need for room and conformity to the maintenance schedule, only the aircraft maintenance engineer in charge could order aircraft into or out of the hangar. Personal aircraft were not allowed. Even KC and Ally hangared their helicopters in the Avatar Hangar downfield.

KC interrupted the confrontation, warning the manager, "Don't call him that. He may be an asshole, but drop the PP3 thing."

"Sorry. It's just, well, most of the guys still kowtow to him. They know his grandfather sold the airline, but without a head honcho to take his ego down a notch, well..." He handed KC the damage report and waited for Ally to lower the hammer. For all the world it looked like he expected he'd be fired.

Ally nodded. Turning her attention to her business partner, she asked, "How bad?"

"It's not too bad. Looks like we need to replace everything below the oleo. We have those parts in stock, so we're covered there." She blew out a hot breath, something she always did when she was thinking. When they'd made a play for Triangle Airlines no one, especially themselves, believed they had a chance, but old man Pringle had thought them plucky and fresh—his exact words. And that was all he needed to see. He even underwrote a large portion of their purchase financing. He wanted them to succeed.

To manage their new enterprise, they'd divided their responsibilities. Ally would oversee flight operations, admin, and finance. KC would oversee maintenance, ground operations, and spares. "How much will this cost?" Ally asked.

KC shook her head. "Fifty grand, easy. And that doesn't take in the time the aircraft will be on the ground and out of service." Taking a quick look at the damage report again, she swore under her breath. "They broke the tow bar? How the hell..." KC was trying to clean up her language and had an almost full swear jar to prove how challenging it was.

The manager grimaced. "I don't know, but the connection was completely sheared off, and the bar itself is twisted somehow. I mean you can barely pull it with the mule, and that's without an aircraft attached."

"I'll phone DeHavilland." KC grabbed her phone and moved to the weather station to give Ally room to continue her discussion.

"Ma'am, about PP3, I mean Peter Pringle the Third. I've tried to rein him in but, well, this guy's such an ass, and he doesn't listen to anyone. He's still acting like he owns the airline and it's really hard for everyone to think any different until they see some changes."

Ally nodded, checking her watch. She and KC had asked to keep their identities confidential while they observed and decided what if any changes needed to be made. Four months had been more than enough time for them to learn who was a problem, like Peter Pringle the Third, and who needed their support. She hadn't made her decision about the operations manager just yet, but at least he didn't waste time bringing them gossip and speculation, which was in his favor. "Okay, here's what you are going to do…"

CHAPTER THREE

Connie checked her watch for the umpteenth time. "If she's not here in time, I'll kill her."

"Kiddo relax," Pam offered. "You know Ally. Her head's in the air half the time but once she gets her feet on the ground, she's all in."

"That doesn't even make sense, but I get it." They were alone in the Green Room. The other Primaries, Virginia and Rene, had retired to their rooms to prepare for the evening shoot and Tommy was busy kibitzing with the crew. "Well?"

"I think it's going splendidly. You have a great crew, and the Borderland costumes were a brilliant idea."

Connie snorted. "Have you any idea how hard it was to find Irish kilts in this town? Luckily my production manager is like a bloodhound. That woman can find anything. Speaking of which…" She stood to make introductions as the production manager stormed in.

"A shit storm is about to go down."

"Whoa there." Connie tried to rein her in, but the woman was so agitated it took awhile to calm her.

"Maybe we should talk privately," she suggested, her face tense with serious stress.

"It's okay. Pam's an insider and our legal counsel. What's happened?"

"Virginia Hazelton-Jackson, that's what. Her family found out she's in the show. A team of Jackson family lawyers is camped out in the downtown production office. And her check bounced. They want her off the show. Not only are they threatening to sue us for so many things my head is still spinning, but they've also frozen her trust fund to be sure she knows just how serious they are."

"Holy fuck!" Connie looked more than angry. "Pam?"

"Okay, first things first. What does the loss of her investment do to the production budget?"

Connie was in shock and having a hard time putting the pieces together. "We're fucked," was all she could say.

"Connie, stop! Think! Can you continue without her money?"

"Yes, no, yes, maybe? I'll need you to read the terms of our completion guarantee. But..."

"No buts." Pam ordered, now in her lawyerly element. "One, I need to see your contracts and the completion guarantee. And we better get Virginia down here and see if she can shine some light on this." Turning to the production manager, she asked, "How long before that pack of lawyers descends on us?"

"We've kept our location under wraps. Everyone still thinks we're at Purple Mountain."

"Good. That will buy us some time. Constance Eugenia Coen-Parker! I need to see everything and right now."

"Okay, okay," Connie offered hurriedly as she reached for her radio. "Gary, bring a laptop to the Green Room."

"On my way, Con."

Turning to her production manager, she ordered, "Get Virginia Hazelton-Jackson's ass in here *tout suite*!" The woman bolted from the room, heading for the faculty suites the Primaries were assigned. "Where the fuck is Ally?"

"Calm down and give me your cell. I'll call KC and find out when she left."

* * *

KC had just gotten off the phone with DeHavilland when Connie's number flashed on her cell. "You're in trouble," she sang out before answering. "Hey Connie, how's it hangin"? The look that followed did not inspire confidence. "Whoa there, Pam! Don't kill the messenger or phone call answerer, or whatever," she said, handing the phone to Ally without comment but with big apologetic eyes.

"Look, Pam, tell Connie to relax, I'm...When did this happen?" She listened as her cousin detailed the crisis rocking the production team.

"I don't think you can count on them not learning the shoot location. You may have taken her cell, but not her driver's. I would expect he'll give it up in a heartbeat if threatened with dismissal." She listened while Pam and Connie went back and forth, finally offering, "I'm going to make a suggestion, but Connie may not like it. Why not run the first elimination round tonight, then just announce she's the first eliminated? Yes...I know the legal team's probably making all sorts of threats, but the woman is an adult and signed the contract."

While Pam and Connie debated changing the production schedule and the ethics of eliminating one queen regardless of how the contestants voted, she lowered the phone. "KC, have you got time to fly me out there?"

"Channel One's sending someone over at two to run me through their procedures and shit—oops, stuff, before I fly the drive home traffic report. Why don't you take the Huey?" Ally shook her head like it was a bad idea, but KC insisted. "Dude, the Four-oh-One East is all fucked up with construction. The drive'll be two hours easy. Take the Huey. She's just sitting in the hangar gathering dust. Might as well give her a workout. Besides you might need our big bird if all hell breaks loose."

"I don't know. She costs us twelve hundred an hour to run. That seems like... Yeah Pam, I'm here... Okay. Looks like I'll be flying back. I'll be there in thirty," she promised, ending the call and handing KC back her phone.

"Come on, dude. Let's get the big girl out of the hangar and you on your way."

"What about the problem at LaGuardia and PP3—fuck, I can't believe I called him that."

"You relax and let me handle the hard stuff for once," KC offered. "I'm gonna tow her out and do the walkaround while you grab your gear and file a flight plan. And don't worry about the shi...stuff going on here. It's about time I step up and handle the cra...crew disputes and our problem captain too."

Ally nodded then grabbed a flight planning form. Filling in most of the details by memory, she quickly selected her flight route, calculating the airspeed and flight time, as required by air traffic control. The Bell 205, or Huey as it was commonly known, was their firefighting bird and rarely saw much use in the offseason. This would be her second flight in as many days. It didn't make sense for her to take the big bird but the Jet Ranger was their traffic helicopter and was outfitted with mounted cameras the network could remotely operate, and direct comms and interior cameras for reporting traffic and news live. Besides, the network had paid big bucks to have the station logos painted over the entire machine. Yes, KC was right. If she wanted to get out to Durham fast, she needed to take the big bird. Thankfully, Glendennon Castle had a huge front lawn and had given her permission to land there at any time during the production. They probably weren't thinking she would be flying something this big. Thinking about parking the Huey on the grand lawn, she was equally grateful for KC's insistence that they keep the Bear Paws on the high skids. Designed for use in the snow, the shoes would work just as well at keeping the heavy machine from sinking into the turf.

With her flight plan filed, she trotted down the stairs and out onto the apron to find KC just finishing the walkaround. "She's good to go. Thank Chri... Christmas we fueled her yesterday."

Ally never felt comfortable taking out an aircraft she hadn't inspected herself, but KC was a pro no matter how casual her attitude or her potty mouth. "Thanks, buddy. I owe you."

"Just get your ass in the air and go take care of our girls."

CHAPTER FOUR

The production people had shown Erin and the other women to their rooms. They were staying in what she suspected were first-year dorms with six beds each. She had barely unpacked when the PA returned in a rush and ordered them all back to the ballroom. Being privy to the shooting schedule, she knew something was wrong, but kept her mouth shut. No need to upset the others. Besides, sharing her insider knowledge would cause talk and speculation. Something she didn't need.

Erin, her roomies, and several others trotted down the grand hallway to the ballroom to find Connie standing with the bullhorn alongside one of the camera people who had been following them around all day.

"Welcome ladies! In a moment you will be taken to the dining hall for a light dinner. After that, you will have time to dress for the evening ceremony. Tonight, you will take the playing cards you've been given and cast your votes for your three favorites of our queens, the three you most want to get to know."

"Wait," one woman interrupted. "Don't we get to know them a bit more?"

Connie just smiled and shook her head. "Before you head to dinner, we are going to give you the opportunity to choose your evening wear from the dresses and suits provided by Holt Renfrew for tonight's ceremony. And you don't have to worry about colors, everything is black and super sexy. Are you ready to choose your outfits for this evening?"

Most of the women cheered as they watched a PA pull out two racks stuffed with evening wear. When some of the women started to make a beeline for the new clothes, Connie with her bullhorn ordered them to halt. "Not so fast, ladies. To make this fairer, we have pre-assigned your outfits, but don't stress. If you really hate what we selected for you, we have a second rack with alternatives."

The PA pushed one rack away from the other. "Over on my right is your pre-selected outfit. Take a careful look at what we have for you. These are truly *haute couture* and all from local designers who have provided what they believe will work best for each of you specifically. And yes, if you like them, you get to keep them. The second rack, on my left," she pointed to make sure they understood, "consists of some of the best Holt has to offer. Unfortunately, those we have to return, so please be careful with them. Choose wisely and be prepared to return here to the ballroom in two hours. Any questions?" But the women were much more eager to see what the designers had created just for them. "Okay, on your mark, ready, set, go!"

Erin was almost trampled as the women raced for the racks. Most were hot-fired to see what had been designed just for them while a few headed straight for the alternative rack knowing it would be quickly picked over by those disappointed with the designer stuff. It took some jostling, but she was able to find the hanger with her name attached with a paper tag. Each dress was concealed by dry cleaner paper overlay and women grabbed and ripped off the paper, leaving scraps all over the ballroom floor. As women cheered, laughed, or complained all around her, she looked over the black sheath designer dress made just for her.

It did look to be her size, and it was beautiful, but short, so short. Looking at the women fighting over the alternatives, she sucked in a breath and decided she would stick with the black sheath in her hands. Bare shoulders and a short, short hemline. Did a designer think this would work for her? She'd never worn anything so, so… On the back of the paper name tag was information about the designer. She read it and the attached note. "You have a very athletic figure. I wanted to show off those long legs, slender but strong arms and your square shoulders. With a figure like yours, the dress shouldn't be the focal point; you should be. Wear this with pride. You have nothing to hide and everything a woman (or man) might want. Be proud."

"Be proud," she said under her breath, "more like, be half-naked." Still, the dress was a far distance from the thin or cheap material she so often found when shopping off the rack. *So, this is what it looks like when clothes are made for you.* The dress was of some expensive cloth she couldn't name, and it was lined and formed so well she was sure she wouldn't have to suffer from the creeping hemline characteristic of many cheaper dresses. Deciding it would work and too hungry to fight her way to the alternative rack, she followed those satisfied with their designer creations to the dining hall. Like the lunch they had picked at earlier, a buffet was set up, and a line had formed. She listened to the women gossip about their dresses or suits and the upcoming selection ceremony. Deciding she need to fortify herself for the long night ahead she accepted the beef bourguignon ladled onto her plate, added a large salad to fill things out, and headed for a table. She was tempted to find a place to sit alone and relax, but this was a job, so she joined a new group.

"I'm so excited," one offered, while a second complained about her designer outfit. Most sounded pleased with the specially designed duds while one questioned just who these designers were.

"I can't believe we've got to make our first selection tonight. I mean we hardly got a second with the queens. I'm not sure who I want to vote to keep."

Erin nodded. "I've got a few ideas. What about the rest of you?"

One nodded enthusiastically, and in an animated tone told the others, "I know exactly who I want to get to know. I'm voting for Pam, Virginia, and the pilot girl. I can't remember her name."

"Allyson," Erin offered.

"Yeah her."

Before she could say more, another challenged her. "I thought we could only pick two? Are we picking three, is that how it works?"

"Oh no," the other complained. "I need more time before we go down to just two!"

"No," Erin said, correcting them. "We get to vote for our three favorites now, the ones we most want to get to know. Only one queen goes home tonight, just the one with the least votes."

"Are you sure?" someone asked. "I mean, we hardly had a chance to—"

"Yeah, but we can't spend time with all of them, so kicking one out now makes sense."

"What if we eliminate the one I really like?" another one asked.

Before anyone could answer that, another said, "At least they aren't kicking *us* out. We all have a better chance of making it into the final group."

"How many are in the final group? I mean, I don't understand how we get eliminated."

"It's just like the rose ceremony on *The Bachelorette*," Erin explained. "First we narrow down the queens to just three, then tomorrow we get to spend more time with them, then they get to choose who they like by offering us a rose or something like it."

"What if I get picked by one I don't like?" another asked.

"We can accept their rose or cross over to another woman."

"Holy smokes, nothing like a public rejection!"

"I know, but it means we always have choices right up to the final ceremony. I mean, you're never stuck fighting for a woman who doesn't rock your world. Could you imagine going on a show like *The Bachelorette* and competing for a woman who does nothing for you?"

Erin nodded her agreement. "So, who are you voting for? I mean these women are so different and so interesting."

"I wonder how they were selected. I mean, is it just their money that got them on the show?"

"Wouldn't it be cool if they picked them to match our astrological signs?" one asked. Some agreed, while another laughed at the idea.

"Who are you voting for?" another asked Erin.

"I'm not sure yet," she said, then decided to test the water. "I like Pamela. She seems so together and…"

"I like Rene. Did you see that car? I mean that has to be a million bucks right there. I wonder what her house is like?"

"Are you kidding me?" another argued. "That Virginia is loaded and her family… I mean if you want to join the one percent, she's the one."

"Are you guys wacko or what? Just getting married to money doesn't mean you'll get some of the pie. I'd rather go with someone who's made her fortune and knows what the support of a good woman is worth."

"What about love?" another interjected.

The doe-eyed woman beside Erin squealed with delight. "What about sex! I can't wait to get time alone with Pamela. I just want to rack her bones and make her scream. I bet a woman like that never has time for fun and I'm going to make sure she gets some…"

"When exactly do you think you'll get enough time to make love?"

"Who said make love? I'm talking hot monkey sex. I can't wait to see a tight ass like hers let loose."

Erin stood, grabbing her empty plate and utensils, along with her dress. Most of the women were finished eating and headed for the dorm to get ready for the big night. This, she knew, would be interesting. She also knew the competitive edge was creeping in with most of the contestants. They wanted more time with the queens, that was fair. Some of them, she was now sure, were interested more in the wealth of the queens than the women themselves. A few were stuck on sex. Like there would be time for that kind of shenanigans. At least not until the last night. Which of them were here to find the love of their life, she wasn't sure, but one thing she did know: Pam was a sure-fire finalist. The other spots were still up for grabs and only tonight's vote would tell how the women were leaning.

* * *

Ally had pushed the big helicopter at top speed, guzzling fuel, and clipping along the lake's edge all the way to Glendennon Castle. Approaching the grand front lawn, she was glad to see it empty except for Connie, who stood with what looked like field hockey penalty flags in each hand. She had been taught to signal aircraft as a kid and Ally smiled to see her make an effort. Not wanting to make her feel it wasted, she followed the signals, setting down where ordered. She didn't have a brake on the main rotor of the Huey and would have to follow standard shutdown procedures. Before she could even retard the throttle, Connie made for the left pilot's door and climbed in. She was shouting something, but Ally couldn't hear a thing over the sound of the turbine and the added insulation of her helmet. She managed to reach back to grab one of the courtesy headsets hardwired for the passengers.

With the headset on, Connie's voice came in loud and clear. Too loud. She was yelling.

"Whoa there kiddo, I can hear you. What the hell's wrong now?"

"Just take off!" she ordered.

Never one to split hairs, Ally did just that, pulling up evenly and lifting them off the lawn.

"Keep going," she ordered. "Get me the fuck outta here!"

"Roger." She turned south and took them back out toward the lake, climbing to a safe height. "Where are we going?" she chanced to ask.

"I don't care." She sounded defeated and plainly worn down.

Allyson flew the big bird to the lake then headed east, away from the city and from whatever had upset her talented and agitated young cousin. She didn't pry. Connie would talk when she was ready, and if that wasn't now, then so be it. Not as rushed as she was on the flight from the Island Airport, she cruised nice and easy, heading for the local provincial park, hoping the beach was deserted. This park was one of the least used in the Province. Urban sprawl had long ago made the destination less appealing to campers and this being a weekday added to the good chance it would be empty. Sure enough, as they made their approach, Ally could see only a few folks up on the bluffs and the lower beach was vacant of any life forms. The winds buffeting around the bluff made it a task to get her bird on the ground, especially since she wanted to park with the tail rotor safely pointed toward the lake.

With the Huey finally on the ground, Ally shut down the turbine and sat patiently as the main rotor slowed and finally stopped. With her helmet off, she waited quietly for Connie to talk. It was a ritual that had begun when Connie was just a kid, allowing her young niece to piece together what was on her mind. This time it didn't take long.

"Pam thinks we should halt production."

"Ouch."

"Yeah, I know. I'm so fucked!"

"Okay, back up. What's happened since we talked? Geez, it's only been twenty minutes."

"You were right. The chauffeur spilled and Virginia's gone. If we pull out now, we've wasted half a million, and I'll never get a network to look at me seriously again."

The kid looked so broken it almost killed Allyson. Releasing her safety harness, she pointed to a nearby downed tree. "Come on, let's go have a seat in the sun. I have a feeling we can figure out a workaround."

Connie looked dubious, but agreed with a nod, climbing from the Huey and heading for a huge washed up log that had silvered in the sun.

Constance Eugenia Coen-Parker had always been the tough kid, never crying in front of others even when she broke her arm at hockey or her leg on a family ski vacation. When she began to bawl, Ally was almost beside herself. This had to be bad. Placing a consoling arm around the young woman, she was shocked when Connie threw herself into Ally's arms, her cry that of a wounded animal. Ally held on while she convulsed with heavy sobs.

Finally, Connie began to settle, her tears spent and her eyes practically swollen shut. Luckily, Ally had a stash of tissues in the calf pocket of her flight suit, something she kept on hand for those days when the air pollution made her eyes water in flight. "Here you go. Go ahead and blow your nose. I won't tell anyone you're a snot face."

Connie tried to laugh, but the tears fell again, just a few but enough. It took another ten minutes before she could breathe and talk. Ally didn't push. As far as she was concerned, they had all day. It was after six already, but if they had to sit here all night, they would, whatever it took to make sure she was all right.

Finally, Connie admitted, "I don't know what to do, but if we shut down…"

"You're not shutting down," Ally promised. "Every obstacle is just a challenge in need of a little ingenuity."

Connie snorted, but smiled. "You know, you and Pam are like night and day, but good God, you are both tenacious."

"As are you, kiddo. Now tell me everything that's happened and why Pam wants to halt production. Is it some legal thing she's citing?"

"No, we're not in breach of our contracts but losing Virginia—well, it screws us for the whole concept."

"Can you use what you have of her so far?"

"I don't know. Pam says yes, and even the Jackson legal team conceded the point that Virginia signed a contract. What we have taped we can use, but we can't use her for the ceremony, even if we manipulate the vote and have her eliminated first."

"So…why not just leave her out of the ceremony."

"What? How…"

"Okay, I know I'm not up on all the terms and everything, but isn't tonight's ceremony about the contestants and their viewpoint? I mean you'll film, or tape, or digitize, whatever it's called, all the women contestants as they pick the three Primaries they're interested in?"

"Yeah, but…"

"Yeah, but hear me out. You tape them all as they drop a card from their deck and share their choices with the audience or camera or whatever, right?"

"Yeah, but…"

"So why not shoot the women making their choices or however you were going to film that sequence. Then just use some of the footage you already have when you need to refer to the queens, just pull up some of the shots you already have. Then once the selection is finalized, instead of having all four of us on the stage, just call out the three remaining. You know, like a big reveal. You could start with me, then Rene, then Pam. I expect Pam to be the favorite, so keep her for last. It'll be a shock to some that Virginia didn't make the cut, but so what. It's not like you can spend a whole episode just covering thirty women making their choice. It's like on *Survivor*, when they show who's being voted off. They never show everyone's vote."

"I wasn't going to show all the votes, just edit it later to show off more for the finalist, and just a few of the women who will be going home on the first cull."

"There you go."

"But…"

"No buts."

"But I promised you I'd get you out on the first cut of the queens."

"So, I have to stick around a little longer. Whoopteedo."

"You're not mad? What about your work?"

"I'm not mad, and it turns out I have plenty of time. KC and I weren't planning on making a big announcement about the airline until next month, so that's covered. And as far as the charter side goes…well, to be honest, business sucks. Companies are asking, why pay the big bucks to rent a helicopter and pilot when you can buy a drone for less than what it costs for an hour of helo airtime and shoot all the footage you want. Frankly, the only thing keeping our helicopter business in the air is our traffic reporting contract and the firefighting season and KC's got the traffic handled. As a matter of fact, they love my potty-mouthed business partner and co-pilot so much, they're training her to be an on-air personality."

That made Connie laugh. The resulting snort was more about the congestion all her crying had caused, and it made them both laugh even more. "Oh God, I can see her on the air, 'Yes Dwight, traffic on the Four-oh-One is a complete clusterfuck.'"

They both laughed again. "You should see the swear jar at work. A few more weeks and we'll have enough to pay our fuel bill for the month."

"I don't doubt it," Connie offered amiably. "That woman has a mouth, but God is she funny." Sitting quietly, she took a few deep breaths, seeming to enjoy the fresh air and the late afternoon breeze. Finally, she asked, "You really don't mind sticking it out a little longer?"

"Not at all. Whatever it takes to get you through this. Listen, Connie, I may not say this enough, Pam too, but we are so proud of you. Not many women would have the talent or the gumption to run their own production company at twenty-two. And this deal with the network. I mean it's a big deal, and I'll do whatever I can to help you through. I know Pam's more cautious. That's just the legal beagle in her. She's always been the voice of reason, but don't sweat it. This is reality TV, baby, and we all know there isn't a lot of reality involved."

Connie nodded her agreement. "There's one more thing," she said, stalling before explaining. "How will you feel if you're not eliminated?"

Ally laughed good-heartedly. "Like there's a chance of that."

"Actually, it looks like there is a chance. I've got my spies and not all the ladies are into the super-butch thing. Some are, but most seem only to be interested in Rene's money. I have half a mind to eliminate her second and make sure I have more femmes for next season that truly want to be with someone like her. I know these reality TV setups never work out, but the premise of my show is everyone gets a choice, so there's a greater probability it could work."

Swallowing hard, Allyson admitted, "I'm not exactly in the market for a wife…" At the pained look on Connie's face she revised her objections. "But, if I were to connect with someone special…"

"Yahoo! I knew you could fix this and I know you're ready to settle down. Mom says you've been alone too long and I agree. Pam can get a million women in her bed, but romance—not so much. Oh, could you imagine if you both found Ms. Right? This is so sweet!"

There was no denying Connie's enthusiasm or her renewed spirit. Ally bit her lip, repeating to herself that she had volunteered for this. *These things never work out.*

Popping up from her place on the log, Connie was her old self, even if her face, nose, and eyes were still red. "Come on, Ally, we have to get back. We have a ceremony to shoot."

* * *

Erin listened as the women around her speculated, debated, and drank wine while they waited for the ceremony to start. She still felt self-conscious in the designer outfit. The strapless, short cocktail dress was like wearing nothing but a towel. Each of the dorm rooms featured a full-length mirror over which hung a sign reminding students that their appearance mattered, and like the rest of the women she was bunking with, Erin took time to use it, to make sure she was put together properly. She almost blushed to see how short the dress was, but the designer obviously knew her stuff. It fit like a glove and looked amazing. Far too bold for her taste, but she had to admit she did pull it off.

Erin followed the others down the grand stairs and back to the ballroom. The large French doors that ran the length of the entire west wall were open to the broad stone terrace, and she stepped out to enjoy the last of the perfect summer day. As was her job, she listened to the gossip and the debates over fortune, looks, and a caveat she hadn't considered, the home location of each queen. These women, no matter their motivation, were smart enough to realize they were the ones who would have to relocate if they should be so lucky to connect and be chosen by the queen of their choice. What a concept. They actually had a choice, and it was all they could talk about. Would they like living in Chicago if they were so lucky as to earn Pam's affection? What would it be like to live and travel with a woman like Rene? And they discussed real domestic issues too. Just how many hours a day did these moguls work? Would Rene have time for a wife? Would Pam, for that matter? They all agreed that Virginia's life was far more casual, but did she have to spend time with her family on their yacht, or their vacation compound on Martha's Vineyard? What about the pilot woman? They all seemed to have forgotten Ally's name, but now that they were talking domestic life, they were considering her again and asked interesting questions too.

"I wouldn't mind flying around first class, but I think I'd prefer my wife to be at my side, not up in the cockpit."

"I don't know, I think it's kinda sweet. Still, I'm not sure pilots make that much. I mean, it's not like she's flying for one of the big airlines."

"Does the money matter?" Erin asked. "I mean, they have to be doing pretty well if they were selected for the show."

The woman who quipped about Ally not being an airline pilot fell silent, while another argued, "Pretty well is not the same as multimillionaire. I don't know about you, but I'm not moving to Canada to play housewife if it means actually being a housewife. I want some excitement in my life and Rene's car looks like she understands excitement."

"It could be a lease," another argued. "At least with Virginia you know there's real money there."

"Her family's money," one argued. "What if she's disinherited or something like that?"

Erin listened as they debated money versus career. Moving to the next group she was pleased to hear they were more interested in the substance of the queens than their bank accounts. Before she could decide who they were leaning toward, a PA tapped her on the shoulder. "They need you in the production office."

That turned a few heads, but the PA was smart and explained loudly enough for the curious to hear, "You forgot to sign the release forms."

"Oh sorry," Erin offered, dutifully following the PA out of the ballroom and up to one of the second-floor classrooms, turned unit office. Once inside, she took in the long whiteboard. On it, photos of the four queens were stuck to the top, and all the contestant photos were posted below with everyone's name carefully written under each.

The PA, still dressed in costume, but minus the sword and tunic, asked her to sit, explaining, "Connie needs a word with you, and no, I have no idea what about." Erin had spotted the big Huey landing on the lawn as she was on her way to the ballroom and assumed it was probably Ally or her business partner at the stick. She had stopped for a second to watch the landing. And she'd seen what looked like Connie climb aboard and take off. She hadn't heard it return and imagined Pam had set up this clandestine meeting. When Pam didn't appear, Erin began to wonder what was going on. Was she going home? Maybe Pam had changed her mind and didn't want a spy, or maybe someone had figured out what she was doing and complained. If that were the case, she was sure she couldn't be blamed. She had barely shared a word with anyone, and other than Ally spending their precious two minutes together asking about her, no one had even asked where she was from, much less if she knew Pamela. Still, she squirmed in her seat, feeling like a kid called to the principal's office.

When Erin heard the sound of an approaching helicopter she began to relax, then joined the production manager and the PAs at the classroom window to watch the big helicopter land. It wasn't the one Pam had arrived on that morning. No, this was something different altogether. Painted bright yellow with wide black stripes and a large stenciled "Fire Patrol" painted on the sides it looked more like something you saw in movies, not a private helicopter. Erin had listened to Pam's stories of Ally and her business partner KC helping out during the fire season up north and wondered if they had borrowed it for the show. If so, she couldn't imagine why.

It came down low then hovered its way right up to the front door, settling down on the circular drive. Someone emerged, then scooted out from under the blades. Once clear, Erin knew it was Connie even without the production manager's relieved announcement to her team that the director had returned. The way she said it made it sound like there had been a chance she wouldn't. *Huh.* Once Connie was clear of the helicopter, they watched it lift off again, but it didn't go far; minutes later the big bird settled down on a high spot in the lawn. Almost immediately, the sound of the engine disappeared, but unlike this morning, the rotors seemed to keep spinning on forever. Erin took note that the pilot stayed put until the blades stopped turning. When she finally emerged, Erin was pretty sure it was Ally and it looked like she was taking time to put red covers in key places to anchor the bird.

Connie blew in the door at top speed. She looked a wreck with sunken red eyes, but she had a huge grin on her face. She ordered, "All right! Everyone out. I need the office so get your butts in gear. We've got a big scene to shoot, and I want to start in ten. Now go! Not you," she said to Erin, who was starting to scramble for the door with the others.

Erin waited, her anxiety making her stomach ache. Maybe the beef bourguignon hadn't been such a good idea.

"Relax," Connie ordered with a grin. Once the classroom door was shut and she was sure everyone was well out of hearing range, she pulled out chairs for the two of them. "First off, you're not in trouble. If anything, I am, or I was."

"You look upset."

Connie dabbed her nose self-consciously. It was a characteristic Erin had seen from her older sister Pam many times. "Between you and me, I had a complete breakdown." She paused, not for effect, but as if she were gauging just how much she wanted to share. "Listen, I know you're Pam's assistant and I know she dragged you on the show to have an insider." At Erin's worried look, Connie waved off her concern. "No worries, it's fine by me, actually I get it. If I were in Pammy's boots I would have wanted someone looking out for me too."

Surprised by how much the two sisters were alike Erin began to smile. Even with the years that separated them and Connie's bleached-blond hair, the mannerisms and even the way they approached challenges were almost the same. *Chalk one up for nurture.*

"Here's the thing. We've had some shakeups in the production. I won't give you the whole sob story. Suffice it to say, I'm going to need your insights too."

"Certainly. I mean, whatever I can help with."

"What you can do is give me a read on the women. Who are they gossiping about and just what are they saying?"

Erin blew out a breath. She hadn't screwed up and that was a big relief. "Well, they're kinda disappointed they have to make their first choice so soon, but they kind of expected that. And they're really pleased they even have a choice. I think the format makes a lot of sense and they do too."

Connie was nodding. "What about the queens? Have you gotten a feel for who the contestants like and who they want to cut?"

Erin paused, uncertain how to explain the disconnect she had found.

"Come on, Erin, you can tell me. Pam says you're a straight shooter. I know she counts on you. Please help me out here, it's important."

"I...well, it's just that some of the women seem to have only one interest and it's not about personality, if you know what I mean."

"That could only be money or sex. Which is it?"

Erin grinned. Pam's baby sister was just as forthright as her boss. "For a few, sex seems to be the only thing on their mind. Or maybe that's what they want the others to think. Then there are what Pam would call the gold diggers. They've been debating just how much each woman is worth and what their life would look like on the arm of either Rene or Virginia." When Connie's face looked like it was falling, she jumped back in. "But the real women, the ones looking for love or a partner or wife, whatever, they're talking the most about Pam and Rene. They're also speculating on Allyson. Pam told me she was a placeholder, but some of the women are interested in her. They're not too happy that she lives in Canada, but I bet that will disappear once they get to know her a bit more. *If* they get to know her a bit more."

"And what about Virginia? Are they talking about her?"

"Loads!" she confessed, "but to be honest, it's all about her money or her family's money. I think it's really the gold diggers who have settled on her. The women who appear to be here for the right reasons aren't really interested. They kind of looked at her as too young to get into a serious relationship. The gold diggers are the ones thinking that's a double plus. One even said she couldn't wait to walk her down the aisle then straight to divorce court and some imaginary huge settlement. I kind of feel sorry for her. All they see is a meal ticket."

Connie stood and signaled for Erin to follow. They moved to the whiteboard and Connie asked, "Can you point out the worst of the lot?"

Feeling uneasy, Erin stood looking awkwardly at the photos.

"Hey, Erin, it's okay. I'm not going to toss anyone out. I'm just curious as to who is gunning for Virginia's money and who, if anyone, might actually be intrigued?"

"I don't know…"

"Okay, here's the deal. Virginia's gone. Her family freaked and pulled her out. They actually set a pack of lawyers on us. Thank Christmas for my big sister. She's wrangled them into accepting that Virginia will appear in the first episode, but that's it. We can't even show her image or mention her name after that. Allyson, you know Ally's our cousin, right?" At Erin's nod of confirmation, she explained, "Ally's agreed to stick it out. Pam wasn't sure the women would be into her, but if you're saying some have taken an interest, well, that works for me."

"I'm surprised Pam would discount her cousin so easily."

"Not me. They're best buds, but when it comes to women, Ally's never had much luck. I think it's why she works so hard. Between you and me, this is the best thing that could happen to her. Even if she's eliminated next, it'll be nice to see her spend some time socializing and having fun."

Erin nodded, but didn't know what to say.

"Allrighteeroo. Why don't you head back down and please, please, please, Erin, not one word to the women."

"You have my word. Besides," Erin offered with a smile, now feeling much better, "I know Pam would kick my ass, and I suspect I'd have to answer to Allyson too."

"We're Parkers. Our motto is Loyalty *is* Our Reward." Finally beginning to look like herself, she added, "We might bicker amongst ourselves, but when it comes to family, we always have each other's backs."

"Good to know," Erin said, finally relaxing as she headed toward the production office.

CHAPTER FIVE

Allyson was in her underwear and trying to decide what she was supposed to do with the makeup that had been set out for her when the makeup woman and a PA barged in without knocking. Used to sharing tight quarters during fire season, she didn't shy away, but did curse what was coming. "Please, please don't paste too much of that crap all over my face. It just makes my skin crawl."

"Relax, the director warned us. We have all new hypoallergenic makeup made just for sensitive skin."

Shoulders sinking, Ally knew there was no way out now, and she planted her bottom on a chair as ordered. While the PA fussed with her short curls, as if anything could be done there, the makeup woman went to work.

"Isn't this a bit misleading? I mean, shouldn't these women get a look at the real goods, not some made-up me?"

The makeup woman gave her a swat and ordered her to stop talking while the PA laughed. "Don't worry. If you make it to the final round, they'll all get to see a whole lot more of you."

"What?" she asked, a deer in the headlights, but the makeup woman had clamped her hand on her jaw. "What did I say?"

"Noooo taaaallllkiiiing," Ally pushed out of the clamp on her face.

"Then why are you answering?"

Ally shrugged, and the PA giggled. *So much for being myself.* At least the outfit laid out for her was something she might have chosen. *If I lived in Hollywood!* It was stylish and far too shiny for her, but this was Connie's rodeo, and she had promised to play fair, even if she was cast as the clown charged with separating fallen riders from their bucking broncs. In Ally's mind, her only job was to make the other two broncos look good while she was nice to all those vying for a chance to go their eight seconds on horseback. Except this wasn't a rodeo and Pam, and she supposed Rene too, was in this for love. *Was that even possible?* She had never heard of these reality TV things working out. But maybe, just maybe, with the format and the choices the contestants could make, there was a chance.

It would be nice to see Pam settle down. Goodness knows she had always been the wild one. The last time they spent quality time together had been right here at Glendennon Castle. They had attended the prestigious upper school together, but couldn't have been more different. Pam was always the wild and popular girl, while Ally was the nerd. And while Pam had stayed in the closet until university, she still managed to sleep her way through most of the senior class, and Ally suspected one or two of the faculty as well. Allyson, on the other hand, had suffered for lack of friends, coming out in grade ten and being ostracized for it. Her only saving grace was Pam. Pam had stuck with her through and through. Having Pam's support, plus the fact Ally was the best lacrosse player on campus meant she wasn't completely blackballed, wasn't completely pecked out of the social order. Still not exactly welcome, Ally was tolerated because she was related to the most popular student in school.

With Ally the only out lesbian student, the school had taken some steps to keep other parents from complaining. Ally was moved from the dorm to a private room and bath. It wasn't in the faculty wing but had belonged to the housekeeper who lived in town and never used the space anyway. And, on top of her participating in the computer club, physics club, and playing on the lacrosse team, they set mandatory counseling sessions twice weekly. These weren't to persuade her back into the fold but to help her adjust to her alternative lifestyle. Shy, she suffered through these sessions, while Pam used the opportunity, and Ally's private room, to explore her own "Sapphic fad" as she would call it. It would be years before Pam could admit she had been unfair, letting Ally take the fallout, both at school and at home. By then Ally could only agree it wasn't nice but it was in the past, and what the hell, she got a private room out of the deal and some of the counseling had helped her learn who she was and more about what she wanted from life. Pam had once admitted she envied how together her cousin was by graduation. Ally had come to peace with herself and her orientation early in life. Something Pam would fight for years.

Allyson and Pamela, born just three weeks apart, had mothers who had rebelled against the strong and powerful Parker family, marrying young and getting pregnant before either was ready for motherhood. By the time they delivered, Allyson's mom was heading to divorce court, and Pamela's wasn't far behind. Both returned home to the Parker estate, settled deep in the woods of Highland Creek. As the girls began to grow, and with no sons or grandsons to mentor, their grandfather, a shrewd media mogul who appeared to own a crystal ball, took the girls under his wing and mentored them for business and leadership. And he did something else. Intuitively understanding that with the changes in technology the current world of print media now had an expiration date, he started selling off the newspapers and magazines he controlled, early and at top value. And he instilled the knowledge in the girls that their career and futures were truly in their hands. "The future is going to look much different than it does now," he would say, encouraging them to follow their dreams.

Now, back at Glendennon Castle, Ally had to thank him for being different in his treatment of them. He could have sent them off to some Swiss finishing school, a fate many of their classmates had suffered, but he'd refused, even when their mothers insisted. "No one on the board of General Motors attended a damned finishing school and neither will my grandchildren!" They both knew they were lucky to have him on their side. When Pam applied to and was accepted by Harvard Law, he had backed her and helped pave the way. Ally too was in his debt. Attending the University of Toronto required top marks, and the engineering school, with its anti-female reputation and the impact of its male students' association, the Brute Force Club, had a big say in just who survived. And they made it their business to bully Allyson. So much so, she was on the verge of quitting in her second year. When she finally admitted what was happening at school, he ordered her to stay the course. It wasn't the response she expected, but she respected him and was desperate to earn his respect in return.

It wasn't until the following Christmas break when Pam was home, and the two of them were skiing the immaculately groomed cross-country trails in what Granddad called the back forty, when they spotted surveyors. That night at dinner, he waved off their query, explaining merely that they had too much property to bother with, so he had deeded a portion of the vast eight-thousand-acre estate to the abutting college grounds. It was years before his granddaughters learned the true reason for the severance. He had met with the Chancellor of the University, demanding an end to the Brute Force Club and their shenanigans as a condition of the re-deeding of his property. The very next day, the club, like all the fraternities before them, lost its charter and was banned from association with the university. The cost to secure this agreement was eight hundred acres of virgin forest desperately needed to expand the Scarborough campus. That was just like him. Backroom deals and life-changing agreements happened over drinks, and he never said a word. While not all the sexism in the engineering school ceased immediately, losing their charter spelled the end of the Brute Force Club and their all-male ideology. Ally could only thank him for all he had done. Granddad's only concession to his involvement had been a toast that New Year's Eve: "Change is inevitable. Although change sometimes needs a nudge, on other occasions it requires a great big push along with a good kick in the pants."

* * *

Erin tried not to look like a wilting flower, but the heat of the lights and the growing excitement of the other women was wearing on her. She kept her place in line, with her four oversized playing cards tucked under her arm.

Instead of having just one camera person record the votes of each contestant, the production people had set up two camera stations. The contestants didn't need to speak, so while the small digital video cameras could record audio, it was their job to stand on the mark placed on the floor and silently display the cards of the three queens they were most interested in getting to know. Temporary dividers had been raised to allow them some privacy in their vote, and a handwritten sign was tacked to the wall, outlining when and what they were supposed to do.

When it was her turn, Erin sucked in a breath and took her mark. The sign said she was to say her name clearly, then, with an earnest look, display all four cards before discarding one. With just her three cards left, she was to stand before the camera for a minimum of sixty seconds—two minutes if she could remain still. With shaking hands, she announced her name, as the caption read, "Hi, I'm Erin from Wisconsin." Then she raised the four oversized cards and fanned them out. She then did as Connie had instructed, waiting the requisite sixty seconds discarding Virginia's card, the Queen of Spades. She remained standing for the two minutes, trying to keep the stoic look requested, then exited the mock voting booth to find a PA standing by with large manila envelopes at the ready. They would seal her three cards away for the next vote and hold them to keep the other contestants from learning just who they had chosen.

Erin was still unnerved as she walked to the open bar, helping herself to the champagne one of the uniformed PAs was pouring for them. It wasn't her thing, but she had to admit she felt she'd earned a celebratory glass. This whole undercover gig felt harder than taking statements from victims of crime. Not that she was suffering, but truly, this was starting to feel too real. That, and being pressed into spy duties not just for her boss Pam, but the director too.

Shrugging off her bout of nerves, Erin strolled over to a group of women who had finished voting and stood on the edge of the group to listen to their debate. Would they learn the fate of the queens tonight? Would they know which one was going home? And what about themselves? When did the remaining queens begin paring down their choices? What if the queens they chose were not interested in them? So many questions. She, too, could admit she had a few, but even as an insider Erin knew she would have to wait and see just like the rest. *And this was only day one!*

It took a few hours but finally the voting was over and Connie joined them, exclaiming to the group, "You've done it! You have chosen the queens you like best. Now it's time to learn who has been eliminated and who you will get to know over the next week. Before we film the elimination sequence, I want all of you to be sure you're looking great, and each of you has a glass of champagne in your hands. The PAs are going to move each of you into position for the cameras, but I want you to know what a great job you're doing and how amazing you all look. Tonight, we will introduce the surviving queens and you will have time, as a group, to speak with them. Be warned: there is no one-on-one time tonight. It's just a chance to introduce yourselves again and chat. Tomorrow, we'll begin bright and early, breakfast will be served at seven. Then we'll break into three groups for activities, and you will each have time in the morning and afternoon to spend more time with these amazing women. Tomorrow will be your chance to shine in their eyes because tomorrow evening the remaining queens will vote for the contestants they want to get to know best.

"Now I want to go over the format for tomorrow night's ceremony. Each of the queens will be here in the ballroom, and each will be handing out a symbolic gift. But here's the catch. If a queen offers you their gift, you can accept and take your place in her group or if you have decided you would rather get to know a different queen you can cause an upset by refusing her gift. Here's the thing. If any of the queens choose you, you are in the finals. That's it. Even if you refuse a queen's gift. What you'll do is walk to the queen who has chosen you, but instead of accepting her gift you will bypass her and take your place behind the woman you like best. It doesn't matter how many contestants are already in that group. Being chosen by any of them means you're in. Any questions?" The room exploded with everyone sharing thoughts, concerns, confusion, and questions. Connie took time to answer them all.

Erin could only marvel at the concept and how it would come off on TV. If viewers thought there were twists and turns on *Survivor*, their minds would blow with this. She couldn't imagine what it would be like for one of the queens to select a contestant and have her walk right by to join another queen, but it would make for great TV. Thank goodness, Pam's ego could take any upset that came along. She could only hope it was the same for the other two. Erin instantly worried about Pam's cousin. From all Pam had told her, Ally was very sensitive. How would she take it if none of the women were interested in her? Pam had said most women didn't go for Ally. No, she didn't have a model's stature like Pam did, and maybe she didn't have the same success in her career, but she seemed genuinely nice. She would hate to hurt someone like that. The last thing she wanted was to be one of the ones who walked right past her to join Pam's group. *Oh Ally, I hope you're tougher than you look.*

CHAPTER SIX

Erin tossed and turned all night. She was sharing a dorm room with five other women and two of them she had pegged as gold diggers. She'd named them Twit-One and Twit-Two. Then there was Abby, the nice nurse, Terry, the IT woman and Sue, the glass-half-empty woman who hadn't stopped bitching since they arrived. Between Abby's snoring and the gold diggers whispering all night, sleep was something she would have to go without.

Deciding a stretch and a short walk might help, Erin slipped from her bed, only then realizing Sue and Terry were absent. Maybe Abby's snoring had driven them from bed too. Heading for the long dorm hallway, she paused at the joint bathroom. Even with the door closed, she could hear the two women inside. Deciding it was her job to snoop on their conversation, it only took a second to realize they weren't talking, at least not the kind of conversation two platonic friends should have. Not sure what to do, Erin slunk back to bed, careful not to alert the other women to her wakefulness or her knowledge that they had just broken the number one rule of the competition. No nookie unless it was with their chosen queen. Irritated and upset, she pulled the covers up and begged the gods of sleep and snoring women to let her get some rest. She had no idea what the next day would bring or if she should tell Connie, or Pam for that matter, of her discovery.

* * *

Ally stood beside Pam and Rene at the foot of the Whitby docks, where three sleek sailboats were tied alongside. Together they watched as the contestants were unloaded from the charter bus. They had already been divided into three teams and were decked out in matching T-shirts, one team in blue, one in yellow and the last in mauve. While the PAs sorted them into their groups at the place Connie ordered for the camera, they looked like they were all ready and very excited for a day on the lake.

While the production team prepared for the opening sequence and Tommy Proulx chatted with Connie and reviewed his script, Pam took note of the contestants. "How many are we supposed to have on our teams?"

"Ten each," Ally answered, while Rene double-checked the headcount.

"It looks like we're short a few?"

Ally agreed with her. "And what's with the one wearing the red T?"

"Oh, that's Abby," Rene offered, remembering the woman's name the other two had forgotten. "If I remember correctly, she's a nurse. It looks like the production people are going to utilize her skills with the safety crew."

Pam snorted at the change. "That still leaves us two contestants short. They can't have given up already, could they?"

Before they could guess at the reason for the change, Connie called for everyone's attention. "Let's have your best smiles ladies."

Beside her the assistant director called, "Quiet on the set! Roll sound."

"Speed," the sound tech answered.

"Frame," was the reply from the cameraperson.

And finally Connie called, "Action!"

Tommy Proulx stepped to his mark. Outfitted for a day of luxury yachting, he smiled for the camera. "Welcome back to the *Queen of Hearts*! Today, our three remaining queens will take their teams out for a good old-fashioned regatta. Yes, these wonderful ladies will take to the high seas in a competition to see which team can complete the race course first. The winning team will be whisked into the big city to spend the evening being wined and dined by our three queens while the losers are stuck in port and tasked with scrubbing and polishing these immaculate race vessels supplied by today's host and sponsor, Whitby Yachts."

Moving to his second mark, he gestured to Pam, Rene, and Allyson. "As you can see, our contestants have been divided into teams, but whose team they will be on is still a mystery. Ladies, on the drive to our port of embarkation, you were tasked with choosing your first mate." When he said mate, he added a suggestive hitch to his voice along with a wink. "Will our three first mates please step forward."

Once they had joined him and introduced themselves and the name they had decided on for their team, he held up three flags. "I have in my hand three international maritime signal flags. Each represents a letter of the alphabet, and, you guessed it, each is the first letter of our queen's first name."

When one of the women named as a first mate asked which was which, he shushed her. "Where would be the fun in that?" he laughed. "Now each of you will pick one flag and once, and only once each team has hoisted their flag, will we tell you the actual letter you have chosen and send your queen and captain aboard. Are you ready?"

They looked dubious, but one by one they each chose a flag, then returned to their team holding their choice up high.

Moving to stand with the blue team who had themed themselves the Dolphins, Tommy explained, "Ladies, your first mate has chosen the blue flag with the white square in the center. Any thoughts on which queen you may have chosen as your captain?"

They all offered different guesses, each one adding to Tommy's grin. "Dolphins, this flag represents the letter P. Welcome your captain Pamela!" They hooted and hollered and welcomed Pam to their side. Some offered hugs while one planted a hot wet kiss on her lips.

With the blue team settled, Tommy moved to stand between the mauve and yellow teams. "Well ladies, as you can see the Dolphins have nabbed your gorgeous queen Pamela. Now it's between rock-solid Rene and high-flying Allyson. Are you all ready to learn who your captains will be?"

They cheered, but he didn't give them any hints. Instead, he lined the two teams' first mates on each side of him, first turning to the yellow team. "Now before I announce your queens, let me ask why you picked the flag you have here. And tell me what name you yellow-clad wonders have chosen?"

The first mate and her team snickered, then finally admitted, "We were a little pressed for time to choose, so it was the Yellow Bellies for us."

He pretended to giggle before asking, "And you have chosen the red flag with the yellow cross? Let me guess: it goes with your theme?" They laughed while their first mate blushed.

He turned, saying, "Mauve team, you chose the white and blue flag with the side cut out. Tell our viewers the team name you came up with and the reason you picked this flag?"

The first mate was bolder than the yellow team, announcing with pride, "We are Sappho's Sailors, and we picked the white and blue because, well, there wasn't a purple flag so this was close…and we liked that it wasn't square like the others."

"Do you know how this cutout is referred to?" he asked, holding up the half-white, half-blue clipped flag. "I just learned this morning." At their questioning look, he explained, "It's called a swallow-tailed flag and that, ladies, should tell you who your queen is. Yellow Bellies welcome your queen and captain Rene! Sappho's Sailors, your swallow-tailed flag stands for A, and that means your captain is Allyson! Congratulations."

Both groups cheered as directed. "All right, ladies. It's time to man, or should I say woman, your boats!"

They cheered again and ran to the three sailboats already sporting the matching signal flag hoisted to the top of each main mast while the camera followed their enthusiastic parade.

"Cut!" Connie called with her bullhorn. "Everyone get aboard. We cast off in five minutes!" Turning her attention to Pam, Rene, and Ally, she smiled. "Hope you three are ready for some competition today?" She walked to where they were still standing on their marks and laughed to see their faces.

"Yellow Bellies?" Rene commented, shaking her head.

"It could be worse," Connie said. "On the ride over they came up with some much more colorful names. Trust me, what they originally proposed was far too colorful, even for cable television." As she explained the race course and where they would find the course markers, a PA delivered their captain's T-shirts. These were horizontally striped, a nautical tradition, in the team color with a second chosen specifically to complement each.

Ally groaned, accepting the pink and mauve striped shirt she was handed.

Pam just laughed as she freely doffed her polo, displaying a white bikini top and perfect tan that had all the women cheering from the pier. Rene and Ally, under pressure, did the same but their tank top bathing suits didn't quite draw the same reaction, although there were a few who swooned at Rene's muscular arms. She grinned and waved as she pulled on the red and yellow striped T. At the lack of response for Ally, Pam wrapped her arm around the shoulders of her shorter cousin. "Don't worry Al, you can always woo them with your culinary skills."

Connie laughed so hard she almost choked. "Just please don't actually try and cook for anyone. Our insurance won't cover botulism or kitchen fires!"

Ally gave them both an affectionate push. "That's it, you two. Sappho's Sailors are about to win this race, and we might as well run the crew boat down too!" Rene gave her a high five, and together they headed for their teams and boats.

Ally stepped aboard the forty-foot racing sloop and took in the expectant faces gathered around the aft cockpit. "Hi everyone. I'm Ally and first things first—if you got stuck with me when you were more interested in getting to know my sexy and brilliant cousin Pam, no worries, I'll make it up to you by sharing any dirty little details you like."

That drew a few mouth-drops and a snort. Only two women piped up to say differently, and Ally just grinned. "We're going to have a lot of fun today, so everyone can relax. I have no expectations other than winning." That drew a few hoots and Ally challenged them, "Come on women. You can do better than that. Let's hear it for winning and showing the other queens just how great you all are." There was a much better response, but Ally shook her head. "Clearly, I suck as a cheerleader. So, that's job number one. Which of you will be our cheer captain?" They cajoled and jostled one another until finally a willowy blonde blushingly accepted the job.

"All right. Next, we need to sort out our crew. Which of you are sailboaters or have powerboat experience?"

Four hands flashed up and one woman pronounced with some disdain, "I'm a US Coast Guard-qualified captain. I have years operating sail vessels much larger than this."

"Cool." Ally took her attitude in stride. She had flown with pilots like this. They covered their insecurities with attitude and arrogance. "That makes you co-captain. I'm pretty good with these baby boats so I'll captain, and you can back me up and help with strategy." She moved on to the other three before her bitchy co-captain could say anything in objection. One of the women was from Florida and lived on the intercoastal. She was an avid water skier, so Ally gave her the helm. That would free her to move to wherever she was needed. With so many women having never set foot on a boat before she didn't doubt there would be chaos at every tack. Finally, Ally assigned one of the experienced sailors to man the sail locker and the starboard winch and the other to the mainsail and the port winch.

The five women who had never sailed looked on expectantly. "I'll need two of you up front with the main master, and two with Gail here covering the main mast and the port sheets. And one of you can hang back here and help the co-captain and me with the running lines and the traveler, and don't worry—we'll go over all this stuff again in a sec. First, let's talk safety. On the deck, there are sail harnesses. They are super light, so grab them, and everyone put one on. No exceptions," she said. "Throw me one, please." She showed them how to fit it correctly and how to inflate the hidden personal flotation device.

Once they covered safety, Ally gave them a flash course on sailing, repeatedly drilling in their heads, "And what do we do when the helm calls *Tack*?"

They laughed, and the cheer captain had them chanting, "Tack means duck, Tack means duck, Tack means duck."

She waved them off with a grin. "Oh, I can see this is going to be fun. Okay, let's get underway. I can see the Yellow Bellies are casting off, so let's go!"

Again, the cheer captain had them chanting, while they took to the stations Ally thought they could handle. She cast off the stern line while her sail master took care of the bowline. The woman at the helm cut the first turn out from between the piers too close, dragging the aft quarter against the tire-covered pylon. "No worries, helm. Our fenders caught it. Remember, the rudder is so much farther back than you're used to with your ski boat." Still, the woman at the helm looked upset, or at least embarrassed. Ally stepped to her side, giving her a side hug and a peck on the cheek that had all the others hooting enthusiastically. Ally colored, and that drew more attention. *Note to self: Kill Connie and maybe Pam too!*

They spent most of the morning just having fun, learning how to do their jobs and posing for the cameras on the chase boat, a long rubber-sided rib with a center standing helm station. Connie and the camera crew were situated fore of the helm and had been setting up the boats for several staged shots to be sure she had lots of quality footage to edit instead of depending on what they could catch during the race.

By noon everyone was tired, hungry, and a few needed the attention of Abby the nurse. Many had assumed that because they lived in the southern states, the sun this far north wouldn't be an issue and had gone without sunscreen. Allyson had noticed and asked them to put some on. Later when she realized they hadn't, she was forced to give them a choice: "Put on the sunscreen or get below." One of the refusals came from her co-captain, the woman who believed she knew more than a resident like Ally could. It wasn't their first disagreement since they cast off, but it was the last one, Ally decided, that she would stand for.

They dropped anchor in Frenchmen's Bay to join the other teams for a catered lunch, and with the boats lashed together, women began to move among the different crews and the caterers tied alongside adding to the excitement and chaos.

Ally climbed down into the chase boat and made her way to Connie's side. "Got a sec?"

Connie patted the heavy rubber inflated side of the rib. "Sit and tell me how it's going. I'm afraid I stuck you with most of the troublemakers."

"They're all doing great. Well, all but Colleen." She tipped her head toward her boat and her co-captain, currently standing impatiently while Abby applied a thick cooling coat of aloe to protect her already burned nose. "She's the tall blonde with the sunburn," Ally said quietly.

Connie spotted the woman in question and groaned. Under her breath, she explained her reaction. "That's gold digger number one. What's her problem, other than she's pissed she's not going to get a shot with Virginia, the billionaire heiress?"

"Okay, maybe it's some new thing I'm not up on, but since when does sporty spice go for the ultra femme?"

"Precisely!" Connie grabbed a waterproof case and pulled out a printout, sharing it without hesitation. "She voted for Virginia first and Rene. She dumped you and Pam like hotcakes. And when I posted the boat assignments today she just about freaked. What's she like to sail with?"

"She's a know-it-all. She says she's a USCG-certified captain, but she messes up port and starboard all the time, and she keeps pissing on my teammates if they don't jump to every little correction she calls out and believe me that's all she does."

"Okay, here's what we'll do. I'm going to give Ms. Know-it-all gold digger exactly what she wants. I'll tell her Rene's boat is short on experienced sailors and move her over there. I'll have to move a woman from her boat. Any preference?"

Ally snorted. "Ah, did anyone vote for me?"

Connie checked the voting record sheet. "As a matter of fact, there are two on that boat. Which would you like, Sally or Robin?"

"Why don't you just ask for a volunteer?"

"You sure?" Connie asked.

"Always ask. You know that."

"Okay. You're the boss. Why don't you join your crew for lunch? They're all eyeballing us."

Lunch, for a catered cold buffet, was quite enjoyable. The women relaxed and socialized, moving from the catering boat and back and forth between the three sailboats. As they recovered from their morning workout, sharing stories of their experiences and making predictions on how the afternoon would shape up, they gossiped and joked as they rehydrated and ate to fuel up.

Once lunch was done, and the caterers had cleaned up and cast off, Connie grabbed her bullhorn. "Attention women. You have practiced, and played, eaten and rehydrated. And for a few of you doubters of the power of our northern sun, you received first aid. Now it's time to head back out on the lake and run this race." She pointed to the mouth of the bay. "Tommy is in the second chase boat and waiting to cover the start of the race. The official start line is the port entry marker at the far end of Frenchmen's Bay inlet. And, yes, Tommy has the official timers with him. And they will time you crossing out of the bay and when you reach the finish marker just west of the Port of Whitby. So, here are the rules. Safety comes first. Any crew member spotted without her PFD harness will have her team disqualified. Listen to your captains and watch your heads on that hard tack nearing the end of the course. And if someone on your boat falls overboard, drop your mainsail immediately, and the closest chase boat will pick her up. And if you fall overboard, don't panic. The water isn't cold. Your PFDs will auto inflate, and we have lots of other boats gathering near us to watch the race. So, between the two chase boats, our team boats, plus all the others, no one's going to be in any trouble. Plus, the water temperature is a nice balmy sixty-two, so if you want to swim, we can get to that after we shoot the race. Okay, everyone ready?"

The women offered a variety of cheers, then they cast off, hauling up their anchors and motoring from the bay. They trailed one another single file, navigating the inlet channel back out toward the lake. As they neared open water, Tommy was easy to spot. His camera crew had tied up to the last marker with several curious boaters floating around just clear of the shot. An Auxiliary Canada Coast Guard vessel was aiding a too-large-to-be-out-of-the-channel sailboat from the thick wild reeds along the banks. They had an audience, and it raised the level of excitement as they neared the starting point.

* * *

The first thing that surprised Erin was Ally's apology for needing to move her from Rene's boat to hers. "Connie tells me you used to sail as a kid. I would expect nothing less from Manitowoc woman."

"You remembered?" It seemed strange that Ally would remember her from a two-minute interview when she'd also spoken with twenty-nine other competitors.

"I was honest when I said I like Wisconsin."

The attention and candor caught Erin off guard. She mumbled before asking what she could do.

"How about you stay aft and handle the running lines and traveler. You can cover port and keep watch on our course when you're on the low side. I'll stay to starboard and do the same."

"You trust me?"

Ally gave her the stink eye, but couldn't keep it up, offering a silly grin instead. "You're not a plant here to sabotage our win, are you?"

Blushing, she didn't know what to say, finally admitting, "For Rene? Are you asking…no, of course not… Wait! You're just kidding me, aren't you?"

"Guilty as charged. Forgive me?"

Forgive me? What was with this woman? She shared so many mannerisms and even catch phrases with her cousin, but as far as personalities were concerned, it was as if they were bookends, opposites in the same subject matter. Erin could hear Pam, on the boat farthest from theirs, bossing women around, ordering them to eat, drink, get ready. Allyson was content to encourage and inspire. Erin tripped over her words as she said, "Oh no. I mean yes… I mean there's no need to apologize. I'm having fun."

"That's all I can ask, and that you don't run us into anyone." She was still smiling and looked to be examining Erin closely. She almost balked at the scrutiny, but steadied herself as Ally explained, "Your sunscreen is keeping you from burning, but you might want to grab one of the higher SPFs. I know some women get upset when their freckles start to shine."

"Oh my God. Freckles do not shine, they take over!"

"I like them," Ally said simply, and her smile was as unassuming and sincere as her words.

Turning to a group of women still cleaning up from lunch, Ally asked, "Where's our cheer master? I think it's time to launch Sappho's Sailors and our snazzy boat. Is everyone back aboard and ready to pull up anchor?"

There were a few just making their way back from returning leftovers to the catering boat and collecting flats of half frozen water bottles for their team. Once everyone was accounted for, Ally ordered the engine started and the helm manned, as the sail master used the deck-mounted power switch to winch up the anchor. Once the chain began clacking onto the deck and the crew wrestled the remaining rode into the well and strapped down the anchor in its mount, Ally had them moving and led the other boats down the wide green channel and toward the starting point at the last marker. "We have to wait for the flag before we can haul up the sails. Be ready on the main sheet. Sail master, ready with the Genoa?"

"Ready, Cap, but I think we should rig the spinnaker too. It looks like we'll be downwind for the last leg."

Allyson considered her suggestion. It would take time for an inexperienced crew to swap their Genny for the clumsy rig, but if they could get it done without too much chaos, it could make a difference. "Okay. Rig it but be sure it's not going to get in the way for the first leg. I don't want anyone falling down or overboard because we have too much gear on deck."

"We can rig it and stash it at the ready," she promised.

Ally agreed. "Good work. All right cheer master!" She chided herself for not remembering the woman's name. "We're nearing the first camera placement and the starting point. It's time to let 'em know who we are!"

The cheerful blonde didn't hesitate, and within seconds everyone in the bay, the channel, and probably south of the 401, knew they were there. They cheered and chanted "Sappho's Sailors." When they realized the boat trailing them in the channel was making more noise, they upped their game, shouting out a chant they had created during lunch and matched it to a standard protest song melody.

Erin noticed Ally was quiet, her attention on the channel markers and the boat ahead. She was bobbing up and down, but she never once added her voice. Maybe she wanted there to be no mistake when they finally heard her give them commands. Nearing the final marker, Erin, like Ally in front of her, could see Tommy in the chase boat, with timer in hand and the camera focused on him for their approach. It looked to be a great opening shot. She knew Connie would have other fixed cameras mounted in the area, but kept her focus on her captain and the approaching marker. She watched as Ally explained something to Mary, the contestant manning the big nautical steering wheel. Ally's lips were moving and almost touching Mary's ear. Erin wanted to turn away from the intimate gesture, but steadied herself, believing she should listen to any and all direction from her captain.

Moving in close, she could hear what Ally was saying to her: "The wind looks to be more from the forward quarter this close to shore. We can use it to confuse the others. Once we pass the marker, put hard to starboard then steer for southeast."

"How long? I mean if the off shore winds are from the west?"

"Until the second you feel the southern tip easing off. Don't worry. I won't be far." Turning to Erin, Ally smiled at her. "Oh, good you heard my strategy for making use of the inshore winds."

Erin balanced herself with a foot in the cockpit well and her knee on the port side bench. She was ready for anything.

Ally gave her a thumbs-up then turned forward again, making sure to catch the eye of the woman she'd put in charge of the right side of the boat and named sail master. The women with her were excited and chanted their song. She gave her the signal confirming they were seconds out and received a thumbs-up in return. On the left side, the women charged with keeping the winch humming and manning the mainsail were chanting too. It took a painful few seconds to get their leader's attention, but when Ally did, she was happy to see she understood her signal and had her mates at the ready.

A bowrider was tied to the last marker and was filled with volunteers from the local sailing club. They looked more like a boatload of senior day sailors than timekeepers, but that was their job. Ally watched the gent in the bow seat raise his flag. As soon as he let it fall, she would know their bow was over the start line. This wasn't how most regattas were run, but it was necessary to make sure the cameras and the host could capture each of the teams as they began the race. A gray-headed beauty in the stern of the timer's boat was flashing a flag at her, warning her to stop her engine. They wanted her to cross the line without any motorized assistance.

Reaching around the woman at the helm, Ally switched off the engine and gave the woman a thumbs-up. Seconds later, the commodore raised the start flag along with the alpha or A signal, then brought them down at once. Ally and her team were free to raise the sails and take to the course.

"Haul! Haul! Haul!" This was the signal they had all agreed on. Without hesitation, the team on the mainsail were working together as the sail began its journey up the mast. Up front, the sail master had the Genoa hung and run. As the helm pulled tight to the southeast, a few of the women did turn to look at the helm and Ally. Erin watched as she gave them the same salute she had bestowed on the sailing club commodore, before she added that quirky grin she was coming to understand was Ally's way of saying don't ask, just have fun. It was interesting to see just how much that meant to her. Ally liked to take care of all the details. And she looked to be prepared. Pam was like that too. Always be prepared—except in her world, Erin was the one handling all the details to make sure Pam was in top form. Ally, it seemed, was happy to do the grunt work. Maybe she had an assistant somewhere too, busily picking up the slack?

"Secure those lines!" Ally called to the starboard team.

Looking forward on the high line or her side, Erin could see the starboard party had the Genny up and tight but had left the sheets for the half-rigged spinnaker on the deck along with the mooring lines. When they didn't seem to understand Ally's order, Erin offered, "Let me get them squared away."

Her reward was a smile and an almost silent, "Sorry."

Ally stood with a leg braced in the cockpit well and her other knee resting on the starboard bench, much as Erin had been doing on the opposite side. She had a perfect view of the starboard deck and some of the port from below the boom. She couldn't help but watch as Erin made her way along the steeply pitched lower deck, all the way to the bow. She was grabbing the mooring line, demonstrating how to gather and tie it to the deck rail. Ally couldn't hear what was being said, but she did see Erin pointing out other problems and watched as the bow team worked to make them right. "Good work, Erin," Ally said, whispering her appreciation to the wind.

On the port side the team handling the big mainsail was squared away. The sheets were even and the mainsail tight as a drum, their running lines all safely secured. And they were all sitting on the deck, bare feet dangling over the edge. They had left the crank inserted in the winch instead of removing it and stashing it in the special hold designed for its storage. Ally always did the same on short day sails and especially when racing. She would have to say something nice to the woman she'd put in charge on the port side. She knew her stuff and had no problem leading her team.

Back on the starboard side, things were getting done, but there looked to be a clash of wills, with Erin refereeing some dispute. Ally was about to go forward herself to straighten it out when she felt the wind fall off on their current heading. The woman at the helm felt it too, but looked to her first.

"Set your course to one-eight-zero. Head south! You've got it!" Why could she not remember their names? She watched the woman manning the overly large stainless steel wheel. She spun the wheel a few turns left, watching the compass spin. She must have spent some time learning to read a compass in movement. While the bow swung left toward the south, the movement caused the compass to spin in the other direction. You had to understand procession, to be able to calculate the reciprocal properly. Most day sailors just looked for where they thought they wanted to go, aimed for it, then checked once the compass had settled to see if they were on track. The helmswoman knew her stuff and swung the wheel and the rudder to midships at the exact reciprocal heading. When the compass swung back, they were on a perfect southern course and right on her planned track line for the first turn. By Ally's calculation, it would take them twenty minutes to finish this leg. Connie had designed the course so that they would pass, temporarily so, into American waters. Making this officially a truly two-nation race.

Erin was back at Ally's side. She tipped her head aft. "Looks like Rene's boat had some troubles getting started. That's Pam's boat behind us."

Ally tried not to stiffen at Erin's tone when she said Pam's name. Of course, Erin would be interested in Pam. Everyone was. Even Connie admitted she hadn't realized just how much effect Pam still had on women. Of all of them in the competition, she knew two had been sent home for fooling around together, and Connie had quipped without thinking that Pam had been either everyone's first or second choice. Excluding the gold diggers, there wasn't a woman, except the two already sent home, who'd voted just for Rene and Virginia. Ally wasn't surprised at all but wondered if having insider knowledge was wise. Guessing she was not the favorite was one thing. Knowing it was a whole other bandwagon. Seeing Erin's open affection was a gut punch, a small one but it still hurt. In a way, this was almost as bad as high school. At least this time she had Connie feeding her info. And it wasn't like she expected to win. That would be Pam. She could see her on one knee asking the perfect woman for her hand. Maybe that was Erin's dream too?

She turned to look aft and could see Rene finally had her sails up. She had a lot of water to cover, but she seemed to have picked up on the wind change close to shore and turned to get abeam of the quartering headwind. Pam, on the other hand, had set a hard course for south right from the get-go. That was just like her. Headwinds be damned. She always steered straight for her goal and never considered altering her course. It might be the only advantage Pam ever left her. "She's not taking advantage of the inshore winds. We might be able to use that on our downwind run."

"What about the next leg?" Erin asked. "If we're not careful, we could end up in irons."

It was a smart observation, and Ally smiled. "That's why we're going to overshoot the first marker. Hopefully, Pam and Rene will think we screwed up and they'll turn inside us and head straight for the next leg. If they keep the most direct route, they'll be bobbing like ducks while we cut back from a lower compass point. We won't have the wind abeam, but we can make a quartering wind work."

Erin agreed with her captain, as did the woman at the helm who was listening. Erin moved away to kneel on the port aft bench.

Ally had a good line of sight, and the deck pitch wasn't too excessive. She wasn't going to push these women too much. After all, this was supposed to be fun. Climbing from the cockpit, Ally made her way along the port side, taking time to chat with each of the women manning the mainsail and boom. Just because this was some weird group date didn't mean she should ignore anyone or spend time with just a few. If she were serious about this competition and imagined herself a real contender, she would be happy to let the women come to her, but the stakes were high for Connie and in a way, Pam too. Pam wanted a wife and Connie needed a commercial hit. If Ally spent some time trying to be charming, it would please Connie. If she got to know a little about each of the women she would be prepared when Pam came to her to discuss her choice. Or would it be choices? With Pam, she always kept her options and mind open.

It took thirty minutes to make her rounds of the boat. When she returned, she found her helmswoman and her co-captain Erin in a deep conversation. She felt a little like she was interrupting, but what the hell, this was her boat and wasn't this queen business supposed to be all about her? "Sorry to interrupt…"

"We were just talking about you," her helmswoman said. "Don't worry, it was all good. You do realize you're the only one of the queens who's interested in the details of each woman? I was just saying how nice it was that you even asked simple things like where we're from."

A little embarrassed, Ally was tempted to make a joke or slough it off, but such nice words deserved a comment. "Please forgive me, but I don't always remember everything I'm told. Will you be upset if I have to ask a second time?"

This she asked of the woman at the helm. The smile she received told her the jig was up. "I wondered if you would ask or just get one of the PAs to tell you. My name is Mary, and I'm from—"

"No, don't tell me. You're the University researcher from Portland?"

The woman's smile radiated more than forgiveness. *Okay. Maybe one or two might like me after all. Hmm.* A little embarrassed, Ally turned away from the helm, trying to look like she had other business needing her attention. She hesitated when she realized Erin had been listening to the flirting going on and maybe knew just how uncomfortable it made her. *As if a beautiful, smart woman would be looking at me like I'm a prospect.*

Probably she's thinking, how did I get stuck spending the day with such an awkward nerdy-girl? "All hands. Ready for the turn to port! Prepare to tack!"

"Tack means duck!" they all called back as they had practiced that morning, and had their heads down and eyes on the mainsail.

"Tack! Hard to port. Helm set heading zero-seven-zero!" They swung around one-hundred and ten degrees and began the hard fight to harness the wind coming in just twenty points off their nose. While their ground speed slowed appreciably, Ally's strategy to extend the first leg had worked like a charm. She felt a hand on her shoulder and turned to Erin's questioning eyes. She could fall into eyes like that, live there even, but right now she was sure her interest was about winning, not her.

"Rene's boat is in irons like you predicted. It worked!" Erin's excitement had finally returned.

"Pam's still doing okay, but judging by the flutter in her sails she'll be forced to tack a few times before the next marker."

"That's good. That's good!"

Ally couldn't help but return that gorgeous vote of confidence. It felt nice to believe Erin was on her side, even if her heart or interest lay elsewhere. Checking the course chart, and their time, it was easy to calculate their four-knot speed through this short leg designed to do just what it had done. She was surprised Pam had fallen for it. Of the two of them, she had always considered Pam the better sailor.

The year before they started boarding school, their grandfather had purchased an authentic Chinese junk. It was easy to prove it was authentic, as he got it from a family selling their catch on the weirs of the Yangtze River. He'd had the best chandlery in Hong Kong refit and kit her out, including adding a brand new set of blood-red sails. He paid a commercial transitioning crew to sail her west to the isthmus of Central America, through the Panama Canal, east to the Atlantic, north to the Gulf of Saint Lawrence and on to display for the grand opening of Ontario Place. The girls had grown up underfoot as he learned, but not well, to sail the extravagant barge.

Pam had always been the one to take the helm and from Ally's position, take command. It was her grandfather who changed her understanding of the situation when he much later explained it was his strategy to keep an eye on her. Ally was the one he trusted to be in the right spot and do the right things. He counted on it, and that knowledge had done plenty to ease her battered ego where her perfect cousin was concerned. Pam would always be the brilliant attorney and the beautiful woman. Ally at least could win a race.

"Okay, crew! Be ready to tack. We're going to go a little long on this leg. Sail master! Be ready to run out the spinnaker!" she ordered, turning to catch Erin putting more sunscreen on her face. "Aww. I liked the freckles."

Erin gave her a look that said she didn't believe a word of it. Behind them, they could hear Pam bellowing at her crew to move faster. As predicted, she had them tacking back and forth like an angry zig-zagging shark, her mainsail battened tighter than plastic wrap across the mouth of a bowl. "They're catching up!"

Ally calmed her, explaining, "They can't actually catch us on this leg. What we need to do now is make sure we don't give up our advantage when we drop our Genoa and run out the spinnaker."

Looking determined, Erin was nodding vigorously. She pointed to the course marker. "We're there."

Checking the marker and the women on her crew, she waved for them to hold their places. "Two more minutes! Be ready to tack hard! Sail master, are you ready with the spinnaker?"

"Ready, captain!" she hollered back.

Ally wasn't one hundred percent confident they were, but she wouldn't undermine the woman she put in charge. Turning back to Erin, she warned, "We might have to run forward and grab the sheets. If so, I'll go to port just in case they need help with the spinnaker pole. Can you handle starboard?"

"Sure," Erin said, sounding pleased to have an actual job to do. "Do I run it through the Fairlead block?"

"No, use the turning block," she started to say, then realized there were no turning blocks on the aft transom, just cleats.

Erin, looking back, must have understood her confusion and immediately opened an aft storage cover. She pulled out two blocks attached to short shock cords. "I spotted these earlier. Will they do?"

Checking her watch, Ally nodded. "You just saved the day." She reached out, taking only one of the blocks and attaching it to the aft cleat, watching to be sure Erin did the same. "Ready?" When she nodded, they switched places. Erin reached for the rail, and Ally called to the crew, "TACK!"

"Tack means duck!" the crew called back.

"Hard to port. Helm, make your heading two-seven-zero. Bow, raise the spinnaker!" All around them, women rushed to make the changes necessary to get the forty-foot sailboat moving in virtually the opposite direction. The boat swung wide and the luft loosened to capture as much of the tailwind as the design could amass. She called out to the women on the mainsail, letting them know she was proud and pleased. Up front, the bow crew wasn't doing as well. She'd had a feeling this would be harder than it looked but couldn't blame them for trying. Nodding to Erin, she placed a hand on the helmswoman's shoulder. "Keep her pointed right at the Whitby Harbour Mark—"

Bang!

The helmswoman fell into her arms while Erin, who was just climbing from the cockpit, was saved from falling overboard by the woman placed in charge of the mainsail. Lucky for Erin, she was kneeling at the traveler and tying off the running lines when Pam's boat ran into them.

Righting her clingy helmswoman, Ally turned, checking her crew before turning on Pam and company. Before she could issue a single expletive, Pam's boat, which had turned too late not to hit them, scraped ahead, its bowsprit snagging their spinnaker and dragging it with them. Mad as a hatter, Ally tore down the port side of her boat, managing to grab the tail of the now submerged spinnaker. The women working the bow, as confused and riled as the rest, caught on quickly, jumping to action, and worked with Ally to retrieve their soaked secret weapon.

One of the women had the spinnaker pole in her hand. "It's bent now. Can we still use it?"

Looking at the pole, Ally knew it was too short for a spinnaker, even an asymmetrical one like this. "No. But it's okay. That's not it. It must be a reaching pole or something like that. Where's the spinnaker pole, ladies? This isn't it. What we're looking for should be about three inches thick and longer than the boom."

"Got it!" Erin had made it forward. The pole had been unnoticeable, simply lashed to the deck with all sorts of other equipment they didn't need or recognize. She had it freed in seconds, handing the end that attached to the mast to Ally. She had it connected and hoisted into place in a second. It took all of them a good three to four minutes to haul up the wet spinnaker. By then, Pam had a good lead on them, but she was playing it safe or didn't know they had a spinnaker on board. Behind them, Rene was gathering some steam after fluttering her way through the second leg. Her team had been slower getting going, but they were smart and learning fast. That or just copying Ally's strategy. They were struggling to raise their spinnaker too but had a great advantage. Their brightly colored billowing foresail was dry and light. Ally couldn't guess how much weight the water added to the sail much less if or how it would affect the performance characteristics. She couldn't help but smile to realize this was a great debate topic to share with KC.

"That's an interesting smile," her helmswoman suggested as Ally climbed back into the aft cockpit. "I wouldn't mind getting a little of that."

"If it's debate with a good friend on aerodynamics, then you're in luck."

The woman shook her head in disbelief then offered Ally an unsolicited and very wet kiss.

Allyson froze on the spot. She was not used to being the object of open desire for one woman much less a whole group. She blushed when she realized Erin was back and looking at her with the oddest, almost disappointed look. Ally mumbled under her breath, then, not knowing what else to do, obfuscated, calling, "Cheer master! The Yellow Bellies are on our heels and those boat-ramming clodhoppers are up ahead. Let them know we're gaining on them and we plan to win!"

To her relief, the cheer master sprang to her feet, more than enjoying the attention. She was really into it and led their team to cheer their hearts out. While they chanted, Ally took the opportunity to escape the overexcited helmswoman and her thorny co-captain. Moving from woman to woman she took her time, making sure each one was having fun and getting some attention from her. She was sitting with the women manning the bow when her boat eased up beside Pam in the lead.

"Nice work hitting us back there!" Pam called out.

"What? You monster! Admit it, Sappho's Sailors have what it takes to win, and we're gonna beat you!"

Pam just laughed as they eased by, pointing past Ally's shoulder.

She turned expecting to see one of her crew standing behind her. What she found was Rene's boat off her port side. She had rigged her spinnaker perfectly, but instead of using the asymmetrical rig, she had found and understood how to use a fully symmetrical rig with double spinnaker poles. Rene's boat looked like a water beetle with its two big wings floating out front and dragging them forward at a better pace than they would muster with the smaller and very wet rig. She'd been so fixated on catching and beating Pam that she had forgotten all about Rene.

"Come on Sappho's Sailors! We are not going to take this sitting down! Well, some of us will," she joked with the women around her as she got to her feet and began working her way aft, "Time to lace her up nice and tight. Let's stretch some knots out of these sails!"

Immediately, the crewwomen who knew what they were doing went to work capturing every ounce of wind they could harness and trimming their heading for the best angle to capture that wind. And they sang. They might not win, but they would finish and finish knowing they had done their best. It may not make for great TV viewing, but she wasn't actually here to find a wife, so viewers would have to settle for living vicariously through Pam or Rene. She herself would play out her role for the rest of the week. The contestants would have their say, she'd be out, and Rene and Pam could fight for the affections of the remaining contestants.

Stopping to check the traveler and the main boom were out as far as the rigging would allow, she was scolding herself when she rejoined Erin and the helmswoman. *What the hell is her name and why can't I remember anyone but Erin?*

The woman at the helm offered immediately, "Oh, what happened? Where did that secret smile go? I bet I can turn that frown upside down." And she suggestively slid her arm around Ally's waist.

Ally pulled out of her arms with as much neutrality as she could muster. She hated assumptions. That, and public displays of affection. She didn't have a problem with a couple walking hand in hand, any couple for that matter. Nor would she begrudge any blissful pair the odd spontaneous kiss of joy or even passion—but making out, or just putting it on for others to watch, made her skin crawl. "No worries. Listen, keep your eye on the heading and tell me the minute you feel the winds shift like they did when we when left port. It should be subtle, but you'll know," she reassured the helmswoman as she moved to increase the distance between them.

The woman smiled as if some secret promise had been made between them, then turned her attention back to steering the big sailboat through the last leg of the race course.

Letting out a breath of relief, Ally was pleased to find Erin at her side as they passed the finish line in second place to Rene. She offered her hand to her co-captain with a warm and appreciative smile. "We did it, Erin."

In return, Erin's eyes offered that warmth she was starting to enjoy. "Not first but a very respectable close second. And the best part, we left the others in our wake!"

CHAPTER SEVEN

Ally slid into one of the wingback chairs in the faculty lounge, turned queens' lounge, where the production meetings would take place. Beside her, Rene groaned. "I don't know which was harder work, trying to follow your strategy or keep from killing my co-captain."

"Yikes. Sorry about that," Ally said, admitting, "I was kind of hoping Pam would get stuck with Ms. Bossy-Boots."

"Me too. Still, we did leave old Pamela in the dust—or should I say lake?"

"Nice talk!" Pam offered, defending herself as she joined them to learn what they had planned for the evening.

Ally was hoping for some solitude and had a feeling Rene was leaning that way too. Pam, however, had already showered and changed and looked for all the world like a woman refreshed from a day at leisurely play. Rene and Ally mentioned the voices of unused muscles having their say regarding the day's activities. Both queens were in the lounge looking for Tylenol and sympathy. The Tylenol was on its way, the sympathy not so much.

Connie walked in with Tommy and Sandy, the lead videographer. She tossed the Tylenol to Ally, ordering her to share before taking a seat at the head of the faculty meeting table. Ally wasn't surprised when Pam immediately took the chair at the other end of the table. The videographer sat on one side closest to Connie with Tommy settling in beside her. That left Rene and Allyson a seat on each side of Pam. Neither looked to care as Ally poured water from the icy glass jug, then poured a second glass for Rene. The woman from the crew, along with Connie and Tommy, carried in super tall Tim Horton travel mugs but Pam, already dressed for the evening, had an almost full wineglass in hand.

Connie hemmed and hawed, reviewing notes on her tablet. "Shoot delivered some fantastic footage. Ally, that crash is going to cost us, insurance wise, but it'll help ramp up the competitiveness between you three."

"Ally? More like Pam." Rene said, teasing a response.

"That's right, Constance," Pam said, "I take all the credit for creating a scene of competitive discord. Besides, Ally got in my way. What else could I do?"

Connie just shook her head with both Tommy and the videographer stifling their amusement. "Save it for Granddad. And yes, Pam, you can pay the deductible for the damages because I know you, and I know you hit Ally's boat on purpose and yes, it does work for us, so you are, as you always are, off the hook. 'Nuff said. Now it's time to talk and sort out the details for the rose ceremony. Only it's not called that. Instead of giving each woman a rose, you will each have six silk scarves…"

"Silk?" Pam questioned. Her brows shot up.

"Silk-like scarves," Connie corrected. "Now here's how the scene will play out. Tommy will bring you out one at a time to the first camera and your first mark. He will ask you a few questions then he will direct you to your second mark. We'll practice this but basically you will each line up by the table, at center stage. On it will be three stacks of scarves, six each, in your colors. Red for Pam, gold for Rene, and Ally you're pulling in the blue. Once you're all in place and the cameras are moved, you will each, one at a time, name the six women you want to continue."

"Wait," Rene protested. "What if someone picks a woman I'm interested in? I mean, or what if the one I pick is more interested in someone else? Oh, this is worse than dating."

"Oh, please," Pam quipped, "you love this. I saw your shipmates at the finish line. I swear they looked at you like you're some tall yummy candy bar."

"Oh, I am." Rene puffed with delight, then shared a fist bump with Ally who was enjoying both Pam's loss of the race and her discomfort in competing with the tall, dark and handsome Rene.

Connie waved her hand. "Yeah, yeah. You two blockheads make me want to scream. Pam may have lost the race, but she made for some spectacular reality TV. Although that make-out scene may be too hot and heavy even for our network."

Ally and Rene shared a look. They had both been perfect gentlewomen. Evidently, that did not make for good TV. "Sorry there, boss," Ally offered. "We'll try and misbehave for the rest of the week. Promise."

Connie brushed their apology aside, her face earnest. "I hate to ask, but I'm going to need to know who you will each call up, and I need you to each accept I may have to make a few changes. If for nothing else than to make some great television."

Around the table it was clear none of them was expecting this. Rene, braver than the others began, "I was thinking…"

"No. No!" Connie said, interrupting just in time. "I'm going to have each of you, one by one, go with me into the production office and show me which of the six you are interested in. Then we'll come back here and talk about how the ceremony will go. Everyone okay with that?"

They all agreed, but Pam wanted to go first. Connie caved, but promised Ally and Rene the order they gave their choices to her would not affect what would happen during the scene. There were no arguments and Ally watched Connie lead her big sis from the room.

"You two look tired," Tommy offered.

"I certainly am," Rene admitted. "I forgot how much work sailing can be, especially with an untrained crew."

"There," he said. "That's the kind of remark I'll need when I interview each of you. Rene, you know I'm going to bring up the America's Cup..."

"*You captained in the America's Cup?*" Ally spit out.

Rene hung her head, but only slightly. "I was on the crew for all of six months. It doesn't count."

"Doesn't count?" Ally teased. "And you decided to borrow my strategy?"

Now Rene was laughing, as were Tommy and the videographer, clearly in on the joke. "When I received my oh-so-helpful, *not*, co-captain, she didn't waste a second giving up your whole strategy including what you thought Pam would do. I decided you had the inside track on Pam and your strategy to run a spinnaker on the downwind leg made perfect sense. So, I decided to follow it. When I read through the list of sails and equipment available, the symmetrical spinnaker was the only advantage I had."

"There was a list of equipment?" Ally asked. "Why am I the last to hear these things?"

"Like you needed it," Tommy offered, clearly intending to soothe her with his playfulness. "Besides, you beat Pam and boy-oh-boy, you should have seen her face when you scooted on by." He mimed fanning himself. "Oh my, it was absolutely diabolical."

"It certainly made for some great TV," the lead videographer added. "That and the kissing contest. Phew. That was hot, hot, hot!"

"Kissing contest?" Rene started to ask.

Just then, Connie returned and pointed to Rene. "You're next, girlie. Let's get it on!" As everyone snickered, Connie had to replay the conversation before she said, "Oh shit. Sorry, Rene. Not what I meant, sorry."

Rene laughed, offering, "No worries," as she followed their director.

Alone with the host and videographer, Ally made polite conversation. "How did the rest of the shoot go? Did you guys get the footage?"

Sandy smiled, explaining the electronic format they used and how they stored and retrieved the footage and matched it with the dozen or more wireless microphone packs posted in key places and on key people, like the queens. Ally had forgotten she'd been wearing one all day. Pam too, so even if the crew or one of the remote videorecorders missed Pam's kissing contest, the sound engineer didn't and probably would have clued the chase boat into the activity going on. "What a day!" Ally commiserated. "You guys must be the most tired. I can't imagine what will go into shooting tonight's ceremony."

Sandy agreed they were being pushed, but claimed she didn't mind. "We have every angle covered for tonight. Two of the PAs and the assistant director spent all day getting the scene set up and fixing all the camera places. I'll basically be shooting the scene from behind an editing table as if we're shooting this live. Connie wants realism, and I plan to make that happen."

Ally couldn't help but hear something else. Was this woman interested in her young cousin? She seemed more personally determined than someone simply driven by professional perfection. She had to remind herself that Connie was an adult and could choose her companionship even if she thought Sandy was too old for her. Deciding to butt out, she turned her attention to the conversation flowing between her and Tommy. Yes, the production was going well, very well, if you could believe these two.

Connie was finally back. "Your turn, slugger."

"Slugger?" Ally questioned. "Have you been drinking?"

"Of course not," she said, leading Ally from the lounge and down the hall to the production office. "It's all that sun. I think I've got a bit of heat exhaustion. And no. You are not to say a word to Pam. You know what she'll do. Anyway, I'm okay. The set medic gave me some Tylenol and got me to drink one of those electrolyte drinks. I feel like I could walk to the moon right now."

Ally looked her over with concern, finally admitting, "To the moon and back. I thought going to one hundred percent oxygen was a fast way to put yourself back in the game. I'm gonna have to tell KC about this."

"That KC. She still burnin' the candle at both ends?"

Standing in front of the candidate board, Ally admitted, "You know KC. Never happy unless she's sharing the love."

Connie laughed, taking the time to finally cross out the two contestants sent home for fooling around. "Everyone else is open."

Ally shook her head. "You mean after Pam and Rene have their pick."

"No," Connie corrected her. "This is going to be fair. Well, as fair as I can make it. Each one of you gets to pick once. So, it'll be Pam, then Rene, then you, then it's back to Pam. You each pick up a scarf, then pause for effect. Then you announce the name of the woman you would like to spend more time with. Now here is where we give the audience the upper hand. While you can see the other queens and all the contestants, the audience will also see who each contestant voted for."

It took her a minute, but finally, Ally nodded. "So, basically Pam calls out a woman's name and the camera zooms in on that woman, then you show her and the cards or votes she made the other day?" Connie nodded. Thinking of some of the women she had met, Ally had to ask, "What if I name a woman who didn't vote for me?"

"I'm hoping you will. What will happen is the audience at home automatically knows there's some divided loyalty. They know which queen the woman is really interested in, but they also debate her motivations 'cause they get to see what she's up to by her reaction. See, you call a name, and that woman can do one of three things: She can join you. She can choose to step past you and choose another queen. Or she can say no, she's not interested and pass."

"Pass?"

"Yes. If it's early in the naming and a woman is set on spending all her time with just one queen, she can pass in hopes that queen will call her before all the scarves are taken. If she isn't called again, she's out."

"And what if someone does get called up? Does she just spend time with that one queen? I mean, they're still at the place where they should be interested in more than one of us. Although, now that I say it, it doesn't sound so great."

Connie grabbed her arm, giving it an affectionate squeeze. "Don't worry. Yes, there's going to be a few upsets this evening but all and all, nothing the three of you can't handle."

Ally nodded. "Okay, I'm trusting you on this. Now, you might as well tell me, because I haven't got a clue, who do you want me to name?"

Connie gave her the slyest look before wrapping her arms around her. "I love you, cuz. I don't know why I forget how easy you are to deal with." She moved to the opposite side of the room, retrieving a notebook. "Are you sure there isn't anyone you might be interested in?"

Ally shook her head. "I can't even remember their names yet, much less decide if any are wife material. Shit Connie, I don't think I even know what wife material is."

"You sure?"

Walking to the board, she pointed to the woman who had helmed their boat. "Not that one. Too forward for me. And not that one," she added, pointing to the bossy sailor both she and Rene had butted heads with. She was about to wave the others off when she recognized a certain redhead. "I kind of like her. Erin?"

"Erin?" Connie looked surprised, then concerned. She checked her notes and looked to be counting numbers when Ally waved her off. "It's okay. I think she's got a thing for Pam."

Connie snapped, "What makes you say that?"

"Whoa there! I get it. I'm not supposed to know stuff, but you can't hide when a woman reacts to another woman's name."

Connie nodded slowly. "You know what? Let's put her on your list and see what happens."

Ally groaned. *Great. Here we go. Prom all over again.*

CHAPTER EIGHT

Erin stood looking at the reflection of herself wearing the latest black designer dress. This one had been created by a different student designer. She'd gotten a lot of compliments and kept telling herself it wasn't as skimpy as she imagined. All she had to do was get Pam through this next stage of the competition, then on Friday, when they made their final vote for the queen they wanted to be with, she would follow whichever queen Pam advised her to vote for, and she would be out. She would head home or take advantage of Pam's generous offer and hang out either here or at the virtually empty Parker family estate and enjoy a week of doing nothing by the pool. Ah, that sounded exactly like what she would need after another week of this.

Erin followed the other twenty-seven women, some in designer dresses, a few in suits, and all in black. She could only wonder what that meant for how the queens would be dressed. If Pam had a say, she would wear red. That woman loved to be the fire all the world craved. She expected something flashy from Rene, too, but more her sporty style, like racing leathers.

Ally was a conundrum. Would she wear a dress or suit? What color would she choose? Nothing bright or ungainly. *Everything about her is subtle.*

It took an hour of shuffling and changing lights and moving this way and that, before the production assistant delivered the queens and the filming of the entry sequence began. Connie had explained that they wanted to do this as if they were shooting live. If they were going to sell this to an audience, recording their reactions, their every move was necessary. "Be your authentic selves," Connie said. To which Erin thought, *If I wanted to be authentic, I would be sitting on my parents' back deck, drinking beer and wearing my old cutoffs and whatever T-shirt I had bummed around in all day.*

"Action!"

First up was Ally, and Erin had to admit she was looking particularly attractive in the tailored charcoal suit and matching pumps. It was easy to compare her to some of the power lawyers in her office. They could do with a lesson from Ally on wearing masculine clothing and still looking like a woman. She realized, belatedly, that she hadn't been listening to the interview and forced herself to quiet her babbling brain. At this point in the interview, it sounded like Tommy was trying to elicit some anger from Ally over Pam ramming her sailboat and trying to win the race. To her credit, Ally just laughed.

"When it comes to her and me and competing, I always expect something unexpected from Pamela. It's why she's so good at her job."

"Come on," Tommy encouraged. "You must have been a little upset. After all, her cheating cost your team the win."

Ally laughed openly, then answered with a reassuring smile. "I did read the rules, and I have to tell you there wasn't a single word written on ramming your competitors, so kudos to Pam for being creative. Plus, my hat's off to Rene for grabbing the opportunity and turning it into a win. All and all it was a hell of a day and I wouldn't change a thing."

Standing behind Erin, Ms. Helmswoman, inappropriate groper of her captain, whispered to the woman beside her,

"That's me she's talking about. She wouldn't change a thing about me." It was all Erin could do not to snort. She had seen Ally's face and her eyes. There was nothing about that advance that had been enjoyed by their captain.

Ally was moved to her second mark and Rene was next in the interview spot.

"Welcome, Rene," Tommy said with his trademark horn rims halfway down his nose. "How was your second week as the Queen of Clubs?"

Erin was confused by that question. They had only been filming for two days, but for the audience, this portion of the filming would be part of the second or third episode. She was right about Rene wearing leathers, but the white leather suit wasn't what she expected. The woman did look good. Okay, not her type, but Rene would melt the hearts of all the KD fans in the crowd. When Rene moved to her second mark, she felt herself holding her breath waiting for Pam. She didn't disappoint, strolling out like the belle of the ball in the most alluring red dress. Behind her, she heard the helmswoman's cohort say, "This is the one I've been waiting for."

"Are you kidding?" the helmswoman replied under her breath. "I'm going for the short one. I think I've got a better shot with her. Everyone is going for Rene's money or Pamela for…well, look at her. That's something we all want to get with."

Wrong! No way do I want to get with Pam. Yuk. I mean…she is smart, and she is beautiful, and she is…my boss…yuk!

Tommy took his second mark, announcing the stakes to the camera. "Tonight, ten of our wonderful contestants are going home. Our queens will each choose six of the contestants they want to get to know better, but unlike other shows, we have a little twist. As the *Queen of Hearts* is all about choice, both for our queens and our contestants, we are going to share with our viewers at home just how each woman voted when it came to her interest in our queens. But that's not all we're going to do. Tonight, when a queen names a woman she wants to present with her silk scarf, the woman can accept it from the queen who invites her up, or…yes, we have a very big *or*…

"Tonight, when a woman is named, she has three choices: join the queen calling her name and accept the silk scarf she presents, pass on the invitation and hope to be selected by another, *or*...or bypass the queen who named her and join the queen she wants most to get to know. Yes, folks! Forget about the one who brought you. Now, just a little warning to our women vying for the heart of a queen. If you should decide to join a different queen than the one who selects you, you will join her group, but you will not receive the scarf of your selected queen. That means that while you will go into this second round of the competition with a disadvantage, you will proceed at the side of your favorite queen. Is everyone ready?"

Erin wasn't. And the choice to accept or walk on by irked her. Who would do that? At least she knew Pam would select her. That was the agreement. She would hang around until, as Pam described it, the next cull of the dating pool. She wasn't surprised to see Pam pick first, and her first choice was no shocker. She picked the prettiest woman in the group. That was just like Pam, thinking with her vagina again. Erin could only hope some of her other choices were about more than sex. As much as Pam thought that was all she wanted, she needed a partner. Someone willing to take a backseat to her career and be happy to take care of all the little things. In a way, she could imagine Pam's wife dropping by the office with lunch. They would enjoy it over her desk while they discussed Pam's work or their social obligations for the week.

She had no idea what Rene or Ally would need. They both seemed so independent. And they both had business partners who could jump into the fray to pick up the slack here and there. Not like Pam. Right now, without Erin, the woman would be lost.

Pam was down to her fifth choice. She grinned before she picked up her second-to-last red silk scarf. "Sandra."

Behind her the helmswoman's friend squealed her delight, trying desperately to pull herself together as she tried not to run to Pam's side. Pamela, all formal and debonair, draped the scarf around her shoulders ever so slowly, before giving her a warm, welcoming hug.

Erin was starting her feel her anxiety rise. Nothing like leaving her to the bitter end. She watched Rene and Ally make their fifth choices. There were some subtle differences, but she was too wound up to try and make sense of it right now. She held her breath as Pam picked up her last scarf. She was playing this to the hilt. Looking to the cameras as if this last name was going to be one of the most difficult choices of her life. "Summer."

Erin almost choked. *What the fuck?* This was all Pam's idea, and here she was leaving her on the slab like the other losers standing with her. She was so bound up in her confusion she almost didn't hear Allyson call her name. She looked up to see the woman watching her. There was something in her eyes. Was she trying to explain something? Pam hadn't been able to meet with her privately before the ceremony. Maybe this was all planned. So far, no one had passed on an invitation, nor had they walked past the inviter to join another queen. That must be it. Connie must have planned this with Ally and Pam. Not wanting to hurt Ally's feelings, but sure this was part of the script, Erin sucked in a deep breath and walked toward the place Ally was standing. For a split second, she questioned what she was doing. Just in case, she avoided Ally's eyes. Even if this were scripted, it would still be hard to just walk by Ally. *Poor Ally. Of course, she gets this job. What a good sport.*

The room erupted as Erin nodded her head in Ally's general direction, then walked right past her to join Pamela. Pam grinned and gave her a big hug. From there the cameras followed the action of the ten women now eliminated, and of course, as the five contestants named by Ally gathered around her, looking to offer sympathy or who knows what. As far as Erin was concerned, she didn't mind the role she was playing, but would have appreciated a heads-up. Still, she didn't quite understand why she couldn't bring herself to look at Ally. She didn't know what she expected to see. Maybe Connie had directed her to act angry or maybe sad. Either would upset her. At least she could content herself with the fact it wasn't true. If she understood what Pam had insinuated, Ally was set next for elimination, and that would be the end of her part.

* * *

Ally escaped, first chance she could, to the lounge and a waiting bottle of premium booze and some good old-fashioned privacy to lick her wounds. No wonder Connie was so surprised earlier when she mentioned Erin's name. She must have known the woman was for Pam and Pam alone. *Shit!*

She grabbed her drink and walked to the other side of the room to a set of wingback chairs in front of the windows. They faced the grand lawn, and the landscape lighting had been left on all night as a security measure with her Huey still parked there. She was just contemplating her second sip when the door flew open, and Rene marched in. She was alone, thank goodness, and stopped to pour a drink. She sampled it right on the spot, something that reminded Ally of her grandfather, then strolled over doffing her jacket and flopping down to roll up the sleeves of her purple paisley shirt.

"That was harsh, man. You okay?"

"Yeah." She appreciated Rene's sensitivities. Something she knew her cousin lacked. "I had a feeling it would go down like that. Still…"

"Yeah, still." Rene sipped more of her drink, finally offering, "Let's talk business instead of this… this. How about you tell me what your reservation system is facing, and I'll run a few solutions by you?"

That was the first thing anyone had said to make Ally feel better. She thought she and Erin had made a connection. Yes, she could see she had it bad for Pam too, but she'd bet Erin would see through Pam, especially when Pam didn't pick her. Frankly, Ally had wanted to pick Erin first, but Connie had ruled that out. She assumed it was a strategy thing, wanting Erin to know Pam wasn't going to call her. It was hardly the first time a woman had chosen Pam over her. But for some reason, knowing Pam had used up her six choices and hadn't picked Erin, and Erin still went to her… *Who does that?*

Rene lifted her glass. "I hear your pain, buddy. Here's to good booze and better women. May we one day lift the one to toast the other."

"Hear, hear."

CHAPTER NINE

Ally woke with the hangover of the century. She hadn't tied one on, she never did. With zero tolerance, two doubles of the premium booze was all it took to knock her off her feet.

"Wake up, you lazy bugger!" Pam called with joy, stepping up on the bed and jumping up and down.

That was all it took. Ally rolled out of bed, wrestling with the bed linen as she did so. Face planted in the carpet, her boxer-covered ass in the air, she swore at her cousin, "You are so lucky I can't lift my head…"

"Yeah, yeah. You would kill me, right?" Pam laughed. "You never change," she said, climbing down from the bed and flopping down to sit on the edge. "Poor baby. Does your hair hurt too?"

Ally rolled over, slowly sitting up and kicking the blankets away. "To what do I owe the pleasure? And yes, the pleasure is all yours."

Laughing at their old joke, Pam kicked her feet out from the high bed, toeing her high heels against Ally's bare feet. "You're not mad, are you? I mean about last night?"

She shook her head. "My ego took a bruising, but it's what I expected, so no, I'm not mad." Watching her cousin carefully, she noted dryly, "But that's not why you're here. Go on, Pammy. Spit it out. What do you want now?"

"Only if you're sure you're okay?"

"Are you kidding?" Ally tried to toss the bed linen at her as she crawled to her feet. She stood for some moments, letting her body find its equilibrium. "Look, I promised you and Connie I was in for whatever you two cooked up. So, I'm good. What do you need?"

Pam offered her most charming smile. "Ally…"

"Oh boy. You do remember that doesn't work on me? Now spit it out. I hear the shower calling my name. That and some serious breakfast, like steak and eggs."

"Uh, you might want to go easy on the breakfast if you're going to be flying."

"Flying? Ooooh!" Ally grimaced to no effect. If Pam wanted her to fly them somewhere, then Pam would get her to fly them somewhere. "Fine. What time and where?"

Pam was on her feet. "Perfect. I'll tell Connie it's on. You're going to be flying me, and my group, for a tour of Niagara Falls them drop us off on the roof of Casino Niagara."

"You do know, in the executive configuration, I can only take five passengers and one person up front. Where are you going to put your other two contestants much less the production crew?"

"Don't worry. I've already got everything organized. The production crew packed up and left an hour ago and I called KC to talk about the seating issue, and she told me she could stop in and drop off the utility seating after her morning traffic report."

Trapped, Ally just nodded. "I take it you have your return trip all scheduled too?"

"No worries there. Connie's laid on two limousines for the trip back. Most of the women will ride in one and two she chooses will go with me. And they will film everything. They're down in the yard right now, adding cameras to your chopper. Now chop, chop. We want to take off in an hour and twenty minutes," she explained, heading for the door. "You still want that big breakfast?"

Ally groaned. She was feeling a little light-headed from the tornado that was Pamela Parker. "Ask catering if they can rustle up toast and poached eggs."

Standing in the vacuum left by Pam, she grumbled to herself, *No problem Connie, whatever you need, Connie. Sure Connie, I'm here for you, Connie. Yes, Connie. You can count on me, Connie. Oh, I'm an idiot! See, this is what I get for buying her that stupid videocamera when she was nine.*

Dear Goddess of the Universe, I think I hate me today! Please protect all those smarter than me. Goodness knows that must be ninety-nine percent of the world right now!

* * *

It didn't take long to get them all strapped into the big helicopter. Erin was one of the lucky ones, given a headset. The director wanted them to fly with the doors open and low out over the lake. Another helicopter had landed, and it was parked on the grand driveway with its tail out over the lawn. The way it sat hadn't prevented the limousines taking Rene and her group to Mosport for a day of race-car-driver training. It was surprising to learn the smaller helicopter could take four passengers. Right now, it was being rigged with a large camera under the nose, and PAs were securing monitors and other equipment in the rear passenger area.

Belted into the door seat of the other helicopter, the big one, Erin watched as Ally addressed her passengers, explaining what to expect during the flight and what to do if they were feeling sick. She was ordering hair be tied back and giving the women who didn't score headsets hearing protectors that looked very much like the headset she held in her hand. Ally, she noted, never shied from her as she explained the safety rules and what they needed to do in case of emergencies. This was one flight safety briefing where the passengers did listen. And it was different having the pilot stand at the door and deliver it. Everything about this was different.

Up front, Pam made herself at home in the left-hand seat. Erin, a little confused, thinking the captain always sat on the left, noted that the other pilot at the smaller helicopter, KC, whom she had just learned was Ally's business partner, was loading the assistant director in the left seat of her helicopter too. *Maybe that's how it's done.* Erin watched KC with interest. She was a striking woman even in the unattractive flight suit she sported, a match of the one Ally wore. Watching KC flirt with both contestants and crew, Erin couldn't help but wonder if there was anything between KC and Ally. *Were they lovers? Had they been?* The lesbian community was notoriously collective.

Over the noise-canceling headphones, Erin could hear the hum of the engine start. It took longer than she expected, but finally the big main blades began to move, slowly building momentum. It was interesting. The tip of the main rotors were painted bright yellow, making it easier to pick out the arc of the blades. She watched as the arc climbed from lower than she thought safe up to a nice level. It was like a Frisbee spinning high overhead.

Over the intercom, she listened as Ally and KC, all business, repeated their flight strategy and the KC woman doled out orders. "Call sign for the duo portion of our flight is Film Flight One. Sierra Echo Zulu, you are Film Flight Suez, and Gulf Tango Bravo will act as Film Flight Lead. In flight, you will also hear from the unit director. Her designation is Film Flight Director. Follow my lead. Our flight window is three hundred feet to five hundred on the shoreline and from the deck to five hundred once we're five hundred feet out. Suez, you lift off first… Belay that order. Film Flight Suez, stand by while Film Flight Lead takes position for the first shot."

"Understood, Film Flight Lead. Suez standing by and ready for takeoff."

Erin listened as another voice explained what she wanted from Ally as they sat watching KC's Bell Long Ranger hover, then climb into place for the opening shot. Once she looked to be in a fixed position, the camera attached under the nose moved through a series of positions, finally looking like it had zeroed in on them. Over the intercom, Pam's voice rang out. "Here we go, women. Let the fun begin!"

"Suez, Flight Lead, climb straight to thirty feet ground radar, then pass us at ninety degrees. And don't go far in case we need to do it again."

She listened as Ally's voice came back, "Suez climbing to thirty indicated."

The big helicopter felt a bit like an old bear lumbering to life. First one side lifted off then the other, but the back of the skid seemed to drag as if it were slightly arthritic. In the air, she behaved much more smoothly, climbing to the requested height and slowly turning to pass in front of the smaller machine operated by KC with the film crew.

Erin held her breath, secretly worried she would be one of the women Ally had prepared to feel a little disoriented or even nauseated. Instead, it took a second to realize she was feeling the exact opposite—this felt truly freeing! While either the director or KC ordered them to fly this way or that, she was overwhelmed by the rush of the experience. Yes, she acknowledged to no one but herself, the rush was probably adrenaline or maybe even pheromones, but even so it was fucking awesome!

Flying along the edge of the lake, ripping over empty beaches and startling bluffs, Erin enjoyed the morning sun on her face and the fresh air while protected from the slipstream even with the huge side doors open. For a moment she understood why her brother and his friends would spend weekend after weekend in the basement watching *Apocalypse Now* and a host of other similar movies. It wasn't a guy thing; it was a better than chocolate thing. *Now that's something!*

Before she realized, they were setting down on the roof of Casino Niagara. A film crew was on the roof along with what looked like hotel security and management. Yep, everyone wanted their fifteen minutes of fame. Ally had turned the big machine's feet before setting down so the cameras would capture Pam and the women exiting from the left side. With her flight helmet on, no one would even know it was Ally doing the flying. Erin wanted to say something to her over the intercom, but she couldn't think of a damn thing. Maybe it was knowing KC and the camera crew were circling the landing pad, listening in as they recorded what they called B roll.

When the last passenger, Erin herself, didn't immediately climb out, Ally looked back to be sure she wasn't trying to exit on the side furthest from the camera and away from the reception group. Erin scooted forward, wanting to catch her eye. The moment she did, Ally's face seemed to brighten. "Hey you," she said quietly over the intercom, "looks like you have to follow the pack and pretend a casino is fun." Erin's throat felt constricted like someone or thing was preventing her from speaking. It was worse than one of those dreams where you know you're about to be killed and can't scream to save your life. Ally, her eyes clear with concern, like she understood, told her, "Not my idea of fun either but… this is what we signed up for. Why don't you go ahead, hang, have fun, and enjoy all the freebies they've got going? I would try the prime rib. It's to die for and then when they drag you down on the casino floor, how about you try twenty bucks in the big machine for me?"

Erin nodded. Then pulled off the headset as Ally mimed for her to do, and hung it where indicated.

Pam was waiting clear of the helicopter along with the hotel staff. She had that grin on her face she got when she thought she knew the other lawyer's strategy. Plus, she had that irritating raised eyebrow too. *What does she know? I'm just trying to be nice to make up for having to snub the woman yesterday!*

* * *

Ally set her helicopter down, snug in the parking lane for Avatat aircraft awaiting fuel. KC had landed just minutes ahead of her and had already pulled her main blades clear and attached the safety line. It wasn't a difficult place to land unless the seaplanes were out of the hangar. They were tall enough that KC or Ally needed to land on the far side of the apron to be sure their blades remained clear. Other than a few private Cessnas and a Beech Baron, the apron was relatively clear this morning. Good. She wasn't in the mood to deal with an over-full apron or cantankerous fuelers who didn't like to drive the three hundred yards to the auxiliary parking area. She couldn't help but feel a bit cantankerous herself. For the amount they spent on fuel every month, they should have gold-plated parking spots. Not this bullshit of having to take whatever spot was left.

Ally reminded herself that would change, along with a whole lot of other junk, once they formally announced their takeover of Triangle Airlines. Triangle had been named for the Golden Triangle, a flight route dubbed "Made of Gold" by the one-time Crown Corporation, Air Canada. The route, Toronto, Ottawa, Montreal, was the one true moneymaker in the country from year to year, season to season, but no airline before Triangle had been able to compete against Air Canada and make it profitable. Triangle was close, but it too was hemorrhaging cash, unable to compete against the goliath. Both KC and Ally knew the history of the route and could name all the airlines which had fallen at the feet of the endless deep pockets of Air Canada. But they had a plan, one that old Mr. Pringle agreed had a real shot at success. They both agreed the golden triangle still had lots of gold to offer everyone, but competing with a competitor with deeper pockets was always a losing proposition.

"What's your strategy?" Pringle had asked during their one and only meeting.

"Simple. If we can't compete on their fare-scale, we don't." His brows raised skeptically, but she didn't back down. "Triangle has one and only one advantage. Location and equipment. We can go places a Boeing 737, which is what AC operates on this route, can't go. So, passengers can go to Pearson or Trudeau or now Kennedy, spend two hours jumping through security hoops and waiting in line after line or they can make a faster trip to a muni like Billy Bishop Airport. Spend ten minutes going through the exact same security measures, then walk fifty feet and board our sleek and modern turbo-props. Our dash-eights can operate at the same speed as any aircraft flying the same routes and they're the same size and have the same passenger configuration as the regional jets."

"So, you're saying what? Triangle is better?"

"No sir, just more civilized. Why spend an hour driving to Pearson? Pay a limo or pay for parking, then spend ninety minutes clearing security, only to have to wait in line for a ten-dollar cup of Tim Horton's coffee only to guzzle it down at a crowded gate so you can board an overfull aircraft? If it's for the loyalty points, are they worth that much effort? What if we could offer a loyalty alternative, and sell civilized? First, there is always an up-and-coming airline intent on competing with Air Canada. We've seen a lot come and go. Ward Air figured out the don't compete to compete thing but way too late to make it work. Canada 2000 never got it and Canadian Airlines was run by a bunch of ex-American Airlines guys who didn't have a clue what it means to operate aircraft in a country as rugged and stretched out as this. Now the new guys, they're running with this 'We are owners too' campaign. You know, where a flight attendant chases a business class passenger around the globe to return his forgotten credit card? A little sexist for me, but the one where the male flight attendant follows a family to return a lost stuffed bear did better. The point they are building on is that while AC may offer loyalty points, they offer loyalty. And it's working for the new guys and I think we can make the same ideology pay for us, the idea being that we are loyal to our passengers above all else."

"Did you know, back in the day, Pan Am would have the fight attendants memorize the passenger list to be sure they could offer personalized service?"

"Yes sir, I do. I know the volume is too great to ask something like that, but the technology has changed too. There is no reason why in-flight crews can't call on that information, especially with our frequent flyers."

"Hmm..." He looked to be in deep thought, finally admitting, "We tried something like that. The cost to bring it from the table to fruition proved to be prohibitive."

"I suspect so. Even a few years ago, the cost to develop systems that could connect or communicate would have been a no-go. Today, we can have an app—meaning, a mobile program inflight crews could access on their cell phones that would use the closed gate file as the application upload which would automatically search the loyalty database for the records of checked-in passengers. This would take seconds and happen seamlessly when the boarding closed, as soon as the station attendant submits the closed aircraft loading report. On the aircraft, the purser would get the passenger loading report, but the app would organize it, so she would know who the loyalty passengers were and where they're seated, and she would have access to a list of each returning passenger's preferences. Next, we'll replace Air Commissary with something more enticing."

"Not many choices for commissary out there," he said, looking more amused than skeptical. "Especially if you need them to drive down from Pearson every day."

KC just shook her head, grinning as Ally explained, "Mr. Pringle, why bother trying to beg some overpriced commissary company to do us the favor of stopping by every other day when we can give our passengers exactly what they want? They want Tim Horton's or Starbucks, and they would much prefer a freshly baked cheese croissant or giant cranberry muffin. And before you ask, yes, we have approached them, and because of our location, they don't see a problem. As a matter of fact, if we give Tim Horton's the contract they are willing to place a kiosk-style servery in the check-in lounge and bake all our orders fresh on the spot. We're just waiting on word from the Harbor Commission to tell us if it would violate the contract they have with the restaurant downfield."

That had been five months ago, and now Ally and KC were excited to announce the change of ownership next month, as was old man Pringle. Ally dropped her helmet on the nav table and pulled out a chair from the other desk, plopping herself down.

"Holy crap on a cracker, Bat Girl!" KC teased, "Who pissed in your porridge?"

"How much will that cost you?" Ally asked, pointing her head toward the swear jar.

"I've already hit my limit for the week. I tell ya, that kid of yours is making me work my butt off."

"Connie is hardly a kid and certainly not mine, but I hear ya. I'll have a word when I get back."

"You most certainly will not!" KC ordered before her grin gave away the game. "I can't help it. Those women are hot, hot, hot. So are the crew. Did you check out the assistant director Connie had supervising the air shoot? Where was Connie? Oh yeah, I asked her out."

KC was always like that. All over the board with her conversation. Usually, Ally could follow. Hell, most of the time she was way ahead of where KC's brain was going but not so much today. "You asked out Connie? Are you…"

"Hell no. I asked out the assistant director. Her name is Kip, or Dip, or something like that. You can find out exactly what, right? Anyway, I asked her out and she's all excited. Cool huh? Oops, I shouldn't be bragging when you're licking your wounds. Sorry."

"What are you talking about?"

"The ceremony last night. Kip, or Skip, or whatever, said you got the brush past and by your last choice, or was she your first choice? I don't know what your strategy was but…holy fuck! You like her! And she gave you the cold shoulder for old perfect Pammy. Yikes."

"That's not what happened."

KC gave her a stare that would do any tween proud.

"Okay, it was like that, but I think it may have been planned. I'm not sure. Maybe I'm making it up in my head."

"Was she with Pam's group today? I mean, how did she act? Was she all huffy-puffy with you or weirded out? Most chicks would just pretend you weren't there. I mean that's what I would expect from one of those stuck-up gold diggers."

Ally knew KC was just trying to help in her special way. "They're not all gold diggers. At least I didn't think so. Anyway, I don't know how I'm supposed to pick up on a woman's interest when you only get to spend a few minutes with them at any time."

"A few minutes? Bring 'em in here, and I'll have them all sussed in ten seconds flat."

"Yeah, yeah, speed dater. I bow to your superior skills with women. I, on the other hand, continue to be a slow learner."

KC pulled out another chair, taking a seat with uncharacteristic humility. "You've got a good heart, partner. If the bitches can't see that, they don't deserve you. Fuck it. Let Pam take the show and propose to one of them. You know she'll never make that walk down the aisle. It's not in her."

"She thinks it is. She has Connie convinced she'll meet the right woman, fall deeply in love, and walk her down the aisle. She even signed a contract giving Connie's production company first option at televising the wedding."

"Our Pammy agreed to get married on TV? What's next? Maybe she wants to run for governor, mayor, judge or dogcatcher. I know they all need to get elected down there. Could this whole push for the perfect-looking relationship be more about her ambition than some sudden need to find companionship?"

It was the first thing anyone said that made sense. "Pam has a luncheon booked on Friday at RMI. She's tight-lipped, but she did ask me if it would be better to book you to fly her in or take a limo. She was dead insistent that she not be a minute late or too early either."

KC stood, and moving to the board, grabbed a clipboard and tossed it to Ally. "Here you go. A one-way charter, one passenger only, from Glendennon Castle to the Island airport. She actually asked if I could get permission to use the landing pad next door to RMI. Can you believe it?"

"Next door to the Royal Military Institute?" Discounting the hospital landing pads on that stretch of University Avenue, it took Ally to second to sort out what that left. "You mean the US Consulate?"

Laughing at the gall of her partner's cousin, KC rehung the charter clipboard back in place and returned to her seat. "If she's trying to make a big impression by taking lunch at an institute as elite as the Empire Club, then she must be meeting some heavy hitters. Can she practice law here?"

"Sure. Pam must have taken the bar in three different states and two provinces."

KC snorted. "I'm surprised she didn't write the Quebec bar too. That has to be the all-time challenge."

"You'd think, but they practice French civil law, not what the rest of us have derived from English common law. Besides, her French sucks worse than mine."

"Finally! Something you have over her. Let's build a list of all the things you're better at…"

"KC! Eyes on the prize, girl. Let's figure out what she's up to first."

"I think it's simple. Pam's ready to move up, and in Chicago she's already a senior partner with a large firm. Unless she runs for Justice, or a judgeship, whatever they call it, it looks like Pam's finally hit a ceiling she can't break through. But if she comes home, especially if she's looking all settled and such, she could take the top post with any firm, start her own, or if she's got the right connections—and I'm sure your grandpa does if she doesn't—why not move straight to the bench? There's no election stuff to worry about, and some would look at her as untainted by her past cases or relationship to attorneys in her courtroom."

Ally was so bowled over by her logic she was left without comment. She took a minute to work her own ideas through KC's well-spun good sense, finding she couldn't argue with or add to a single point. "My aunt and uncle just announced their retirement and they bought a condo up here. They said they wanted to spend more time with Connie. With them leaving Chicago…"

"Pam's all alone, so she either wants a wife to keep her warm on those cold Lake Michigan nights or a job up here that's as good or better than what she has there—that would make sense."

"I don't know, KC. It would be really hard to find anything better, especially better paying up here. She didn't pick Chicago just because her parents were there. Pam is serious about the money."

"Show me the money...Show me the money!"

Ally groaned. "Come on, I'm serious here, Cuba junior."

"I know, and so am I, but you're forgetting a big thing here. Pam doesn't need the money. She's got what she's earned from her practice, she's got her trust fund, and isn't Gramps going to hand you each a great big piece of the family fortune next year?" When Ally concurred, KC pushed on, adding, "All that's left for Pam is about how she's perceived. Being named to the provincial or federal bench, or whatever you call it, or chairing a Royal Commission, that would be a feather she can't get down south."

"I can't fight your logic."

"But you're still not talking. Why won't you tell me about it?"

"It's not you. It's this whole thing. How the hell do I tell if someone is interested in me?"

"Oh, dude. You got it all backward. All you have to do is decide which ones you like. Do you like any of them?"

"The woman helming my sailboat yesterday put the moves on me."

"There you go. And what did you think of her?" Ally's face looked like she had just sampled the worst vegetable in the world. "Okay. That's good. Strike her off the list. Let's go through the women still competing for you. Anyone in the group who interests you?"

Pursing her lips, Ally contemplated her choices. "There's a woman from Virginia who seems nice."

"Nice? Holy scooter-booters, Al. You're not shopping for nice. You should be looking for hot, smart, like-minded, monkey sex-capable women, not—"

"Monkey sex? That's *your* fall-back position."

"What's wrong with having a woman knock your socks off in bed and refute your hypothesis? All I mean is, you're the complete package. Why aren't you demanding the same or at least someone who gets what a prize you are? I know Pam likes to make like she's the only one worth looking at, but that's her ego talking. Really, Al. You have no excuse for playin' the wallflower."

Ally knew her face looked a little pissy but KC was right. She had bought into her cousin's story that she was second best. Maybe, compared to Pam, she didn't turn many heads. Who would? But that didn't mean she couldn't stand on her own. She was a damn fine pilot, an accomplishment in itself, and she and KC ran a tight and profitable ship. They weren't making millions, but they were making money, which was a lot more than most people in aviation could say. "What would you do?"

"Me? Hmm... I would start by laying down a little KC charm on the ladies, then I'd be myself and see just who could have fun with me. Remember this, Ally. You're the prize at the end of the rainbow. Let them work a bit. As for the one that got away, well I'd be nice, but I sure would let her see just how much fun I was having without her."

"You are a devious woman," Ally said, but she was smiling again. "Okay. I'm going to head out. You want the Huey?"

"Naw. I told that PA to load all their stuff in her. I've got the 206 rigged perfectly for the traffic report."

"They're still here? I thought they got off at Casino Niagara."

"Naw," KC offered, grabbing a Company Flight Plan form and completing it for Allyson. "You're stuck flying them back. I told them to wait in the lounge while Buddy got their stuff loaded."

Ally knew she was speaking of the new ground attendant, the same one who had sheared the nose gear off one of their Dash 8's. "You trust him?"

KC nodded, handing the form to Ally to check and sign. "He's smart, knows his way around the Cessnas. He just needs a little training, and I've been working on that."

"Wow. Nice. Listen, thanks so much. You didn't have to take up all the slack. I want you to know I appreciate it."

"Well, I'll appreciate it when you do me the favor of walking some nice girl down the aisle. That and puttin' a good word in for me with the first assistant director. How about it?"

Ally just smiled at her friend. "You, buddy, are brilliant and relentless. Yes, I'll gab you up all the way back."

"Hey, not too much talk! Don't wanna to scare her off too fast. Besides," KC added, playing the goof and leaning her head on Ally's shoulder, "you forgot to mention my eyes."

CHAPTER TEN

When Erin awoke, she couldn't remember how much champagne she had polished off. The whole group had taken to the casino and the level of service as if they were born to it. Some speculated on whether the day-to-day life of Pamela would be as exciting, much less flamboyant. They had enjoyed a VIP tour, dinner in the private dining room, and access to the VIP lounge after the show where the talent was enjoying themselves, and spent time discussing TV and reality TV and all that is showbiz. Pam had lost interest in not being the center of attention and pulled the group back onto the gaming floor.

The earlier private class on all that is gaming, led by a senior floor boss, had interested Erin and gave her the confidence to do more than just play the slots. She was careful and cautious, but she tried roulette before settling on blackjack. She spent time watching the poker tables, but they looked to be mostly occupied by unsocialized males, so blackjack got her attention. She had been playing the five-dollar table for hours when Pam found her. "Come on kiddo. Time to head back."

"Really? I thought you would have gone all night."

"The bar is closed. No point in playing if you can't enjoy a cocktail too. Besides, the limos are here. And I'm anxious to learn what Charlotte and Denise think of me. They'll be riding in the second limo with you."

"If they're ones you're interested in, why aren't they riding with you?"

"Intrigue, and Connie's best intentions. Look, here they come now. Give me a little peck on the cheek."

Instead, Erin offered a hug, whispering, "In your dreams, playgirl. In your dreams." Then remembering Ally's request to drop a lucky coin in the big prize slot machine by the front doors, she said, "I just need to make a quick stop. I'll meet you all at the limo."

Pam just gave her a look, advising, "Best make that pit stop now. The drive back takes a good two hours, at least."

Erin promised not to take too long. A couple of hours didn't sound like a long time for someone used to Chicago traffic, but it was two in the morning. Plus, it hadn't taken that long to get there, and that was with them being filmed flying back and forth at certain spots along the lake plus enjoying an aerial tour of the falls!

Erin could see most of the other women walking with Pam when she detoured to the giant slot machine. The sign above it promised a total jackpot of five million dollars. She was feeding the machine her handful of silver and gold bear coins when she realized Pam and the group were gathering behind her and knew the camera crew wouldn't be far. *Might as well play it up.* Instead of pressing the spin button, she reached up high and pulled down the huge arm. Behind her, the women cheered and called their encouragement, including Pam who she secretly worried would be pissed. Not expecting any results, she was momentarily confused when a brief ring sounded.

Pam stepped up, wrapping an arm around Erin, "You just won your money back plus twenty. So you won something, right?"

"It was a bet for someone else," was all she could stammer. Pam only smiled.

Back at Glendennon Castle, coming half awake from a too-brief sleep, Erin spied the time on the bedside clock: just after ten a.m. Today they had the morning to relax. Looking across the room, she could see one of her roommates was sunburned by yesterday's racing activities with Rene at the Mosport Track. The other two, including Denise from Pam's list of desirable women, were probably down at the pool. Yes, this place had two pools! Once the castle's conservatory, the pool area featured several sets of French doors which opened to the south-facing side of the grand terrace, and from their dorm room Erin could see several women sunbathing and making full use of the amenities and serving staff hired just for the shoot.

Connie, she decided was smart, very smart. During Erin's ten minutes alone time with Pam yesterday, she'd learned more about the plans for the rest of the shoot. She now knew they were headed north tomorrow for some outdoorsy adventure. *Lesbians do love their time in nature.* Today though, they had this time to recover and have fun. Cut off from the electronic world, a few would be suffering withdrawal from their phones by now, she was sure. It was smart for Connie to pull all electronics including cell phones. It created a bubble for them to consider exactly how and what they were feeling. *Like, what the hell am I feeling? I don't know what to say. "Hey, I'm still the woman who snubbed you and chose your cousin." Why would she still be so nice to me?*

It took her an hour to get showered and coifed and somewhat presentable. After some breakfast, Tylenol, and sunshine, she'd be fine, she decided.

Reaching the dining hall, Erin was relieved to see catering was still hard at work, taking equal care of the queens, contestants, and crew. Rene was at a table by the window with two women from her group and one of the camera people. They looked to be retelling details of their day at the racetrack, using coffee cups and cutlery to illustrate the excitement. Most of the women from Pam's group were absent while others from both Ally's and Rene's groups lounged just outside, soaking up the sun.

She poured herself coffee and loaded a plate with the basics, then stopped. She didn't want to eat with anyone, but worried how it would look. So she joined a table with a single open seat. One of her roommates and two other women were eating and talking. They all welcomed her, including Mary, the woman who had been so forward with Ally during the regatta.

Today would be much easier. She knew there was some sort of sports thing scheduled for after lunch. Rene and Ally had been trading jibes, and both were scheduled for camera time this morning, separately and together. Erin had no idea what Pam was up to, but seeing that all the women in her group were present, she decided this afternoon's event must include them too.

Tonight, each of the queens would go on a one-on-one date with a contestant chosen by Connie, and it was the talk of her table. Erin sat back and let the conversation flow around her. She'd pegged Mary as a social climber from day one and nothing she said now changed her mind. Thankfully, she was on Rene's team and her problem. Denise, sitting across from her, was on Pam's team and even if she didn't know it, had the clear inside track. It was the woman next to Denise, the one from Allyson's team, who was starting to worry her. "You're quiet this morning," she said to the willowy blonde she remembered had been cheer captain.

Her Florida accent, usually so mellow, sounded crass as she explained, "I think I made the wrong choice. I can't believe the fun you all are having! You know what we all got to do while you were racin' cars and winnin' at the casino? We drove. That's right, we drove, didn't even get to fly like you all did. We drove to some farm upstate a ways and you know what? They took us to some old barn. When we got out of that old bus I was expecting a good old trail ride but oh no! We ain't trailin' no horses. We're gonna learn how to ride all English and prissy. We didn't even get outta the barnyard, had us doing all that horse whispering circles and such. Then, and can you believe this, they had us muck out the stalls and rub down the horses! Between your ear and the good Lord, yep, they made me clean up after a horse like I'm some bl...working type person."

Erin watched the other women to see their reaction. Even Mary looked to be a little troubled, but it was Denise who took the reins. "I bet yesterday was more about learning whether you like some of the activities of our queens. Remember the profiles we each received? I read that both Pam and Allyson were avid equestrians. It makes sense they offered that experience. What did Allyson do during the outing?"

"Oh, she was right in the middle of the whole mucking experience, and she taught the class too, showing off and all."

"Imagine," Mary quipped, "the ice queen actually getting dirty!"

"That's hardly fair," Denise argued. "Besides, she was up at the crack of dawn both yesterday and today, servicing her helicopter and getting ready to ferry the rest of us wherever."

"Sounds like you like her more than me. How's about we switch up now and save us the trouble of changing our vote later?"

Denise just smiled. "I'm happy where I am."

* * *

"You need *what*?" If Ally were ever going to lose it with Connie completely, this request would be it.

"I know it's short notice, and I know it's a big ask, but I ran it by KC and..." That was the wrong thing to say.

"KC? You ran it by KC? Why don't you just get KC down here to take my place? And while you're at it explain just how she will fly Traffic One twice a day and then pull an aircraft from the line without fucking up our schedule, and then fly us to Petawawa?"

"Ally, please..."

"No, Connie. No! This is... Have you any idea what it costs to operate a Dash-8?"

Ally was pacing and thinking. Connie knew she had to sell her situation now, or Ally's answer would stay no. "The bus company we chartered just went on strike. We can't get coaches or school buses. Nothing. I found a company operating out of Gatineau willing to take a charter in Ontario, but they can only handle the return trip. I'm down to renting thirty cars and getting the crew and contestants to drive themselves, and we would have to drive back. There isn't a car rental company in the country that will even consider a one-way rental to nowheresville. Have you any idea how much it would cost to rent thirty SUVs?"

Ally sank back down in her chair. The evidence of Connie's efforts to find a solution was scattered all over the office. Connie stood across from her, hands on hips, her tool belt or whatever they called it hung low on one hip as if her two-way radio were a holstered six-shooter. It was easy to picture her the sheriff of this town, even if she was wearing Tilley's shorts and a faded and worn *Lost Girl* T-shirt.

"Shit… What did KC say—and don't think you can make an end-run around me every time you want something, young lady. KC and I are going to have a serious—"

Connie's body slammed her full force. "Thank you, Ally. Thank you. I knew you would come through for us."

"For you, kiddo. I'm doing this for you, and you are going to pay the fuel bill. Is that understood?"

"Hey, whatever. It has to be better than the cost to rent a fleet of vehicles."

Ally checked the time on her watch. "What, you must have been up at the crack of dawn to get KC on the phone before her morning traffic report." It wasn't a question. "Let's see if we can get her on the phone now and find out what she came up with for you. And yes, I see your look. And I promise to hear out whatever crazy balancing act she's devised. First, though, I need another cup of tea, and you need to straighten out this mess in here before my OCD kicks in but good."

* * *

Erin was just returning her breakfast plates to the servery when she and Denise spotted Ally on her way into brunch. She looked like she'd been up for a while, judging by the grease stains on her bare arms and her old sleeveless T-shirt. She was wearing the flight suit, but the top half had been rolled down and tied around her waist.

"She seems so focused, so fierce, but solitary," Denise offered, adding quietly, "I thought it was brave when you passed on her. I'm not sure I would fare well in a relationship with such a strong woman."

"You don't think Pam is strong?"

"Strong-willed, yes. Strong in purpose yes. Capable of a lifelong commitment, that I'm not so sure." Erin realized she must have given Denise a look when she added, "Don't get me wrong. Of these three women, Pam does it for me. She is amazing, but she's also smooth. Sometimes I worry she's just a tad *too* smooth."

"You think she'd cheat on you?"

"Umm, that's not it. I think it's my admiration I'm questioning. I watched her yesterday and last night. I love how she can instantly put herself in the moment. What I had to fight was how well she could do it with anyone. I guess there's a little green monster inside me telling me I'm no more important or noticed than anyone else."

"You looked like you were okay with everything last night. It looked like you've played the part of the patient partner before."

"Maybe that's the thing. I don't mind playing number two to a career. I know most women would, but I have my own work that keeps me busy, so the long hours are not an issue. I guess it was watching Pam last night that got me thinking about how different we all are. I mean, look at her…" She tipped her head to Ally, who was at the craft table stirring honey into her takeout cup and talking with one of the PAs. "She gives everyone the same attention. No judgment, no condescension. Pam too is like that except she's not. Don't you find she can be a bit full of herself?"

Erin sighed. Yes, Pam was always full of herself. It was how she coped. Ally, she was guessing, became the intense grounded adult much as Denise had been last night. Maybe that was why she liked Denise for Pam. Maybe what Pam had lost after high school with her cousin right here at Glendennon Castle, was Ally's solidity and her ability to keep her grounded. And maybe Ally just needed someone to lift her higher than her aircraft could.

CHAPTER ELEVEN

The afternoon had been more fun than Erin thought possible. While Pam was still nowhere to be seen, the rest of the women had been gathered in the backfield. There had been all kinds of speculation when they were sent to don athletic gear and when a PA knocked on their dorm room with a bag of team shirts. Each was customized with their names on the back. Most of the women were betting they were headed for the softball field while a few speculated on soccer. Erin half-expected it to be lacrosse, knowing that was Ally's sport while she had been a student here. What she forgot to consider was Rene's background. If Connie had decided on the sport, she must have chosen based on what both Ally and Rene were willing to play.

The contestants had taken to the field to learn they would be playing field hockey and they had already been divided into teams. Following the colors used for the regatta, Rene's team was in the red with gold numbers and Ally's team in mauve and white. Erin wasn't surprised to find herself on Rene's team. She was more impressed to see Connie had divided them regardless of which queen they supported. There was a fair mix on each team.

Rene as their captain had been fun, but driven to win. A little too driven by Erin's account. Still, the afternoon delivered a great game and some much-appreciated sun. A few of the women spent more time on the bench than others, but that had been their request when the game got a little rough. When things heated up, Ally called timeout, taking Rene aside and telling her who knew what. She returned to their side, and the game resumed, but the extreme competitive edge softened slightly. It made Erin think kindly of Allyson. She must have been concerned for injuries and a loss of sportsmanship.

After the game and the socializing, they learned their evening schedule. Erin had to rush to be ready in time to join Pam and their group for dinner at a local French restaurant. While Glendennon Castle had once stood alone with nothing but miles of Lake Ontario's rugged north shore as its witness, today Toronto's suburban sprawl had eaten up all the lands surrounding what was now an exclusive girls' boarding school. It was hard to imagine how remote this place must have once been, much like a Scottish castle high above the moors. Erin did know of huge estates almost as big as this scattered along the coast of Lake Michigan but French restaurants, not so much. Even in what might be considered the suburbs of Chicago, she couldn't think of a place where such high-end establishments were found. And Pam had told her the entire region surrounding Glendennon Castle was uniformly working class, a result of the local auto industry. Yet the restaurant was very French and was amazing. She'd been expecting French Canadian and imagined she would get her first chance to try poutine, whatever that was. But the place was a true French bistro, the chef born and trained in Nice, France.

Erin enjoyed dinner with Pam, Charlotte, and Zara, another one of Pam's wannabes. Too bad Zara hadn't made Pam's list. Now, back in the ballroom, Erin was feeling over-full and decidedly not interested in the salsa dancing class Pam was leading. That was all right, too, as Pam and the others had taken no notice of her. Instead she stood, wineglass in hand, enjoying the cool evening breeze. The music wasn't so loud as to disturb the group outside. She didn't know where Rene's group had disappeared to, but Ally was on the lawn just off the patio. She had a bunch of telescopes set up and was moving between each one, helping different women find certain stars or maybe star systems. She hadn't realized she was walking toward them until Ally turned and smiled, asking her to join in.

Not wanting to be rude, Erin agreed to check out the viewfinder of the closest telescope. It was a stout fat thing, and Ally stood to its side holding some sort of controller attached with a long coiled cord. She was patient, and never touched Erin, just showed her what to look at. Erin had made an unofficial study of Allyson Parker and knew she was the kind of woman who touched when she talked. But she wasn't making a pass or being condescending with her touch. It was just her thing to shake hands, or grasp a shoulder, or take an elbow to turn someone around. The fact that she didn't so much as breathe on her said she was treading softly, determined not to make Erin feel uneasy.

"I can't see anything."

Ally checked the controller in her hand. "These school telescopes might need calibrating. Can I have a quick look?"

That caught Erin by surprise. Who asks to see their own telescope? She stepped back to allow Ally to do whatever needed to be done. All around her the other women were joking about what they could see and trading comments and coordinates as they made their comparisons. With Pam's group, the women were on edge as if every second with Pam was total competition. Ally's group was laid-back and more concerned with enjoying themselves.

"There we go. Give that a try. It's the center star in Orion's Belt."

While Erin looked, she heard Ally check in with the others. They asked a few questions, made a few jokes, and were once again just as pleased to do their own thing.

She jumped when she heard Ally beside her, asking, "Is that better?"

Trying to cover her nervousness, she pretended she wasn't impressed with the colors and details of the star system she was seeing in full splendor for the first time in her life. She remembered the one trip she made with her grandmother years ago, a birthday trip to Chicago. It was then, as a mature, newly turned eight-year-old, that she decided Chicago was the place she would live when she was all grown up. The trip included a visit to the planetarium. The awe she remembered was just as deeply felt now as it was then. "It's okay."

"Okay?" Ally teased. "Clearly you haven't felt the earth move."

Erin was shocked by her forwardness. She was stuck somewhere between wanting to call her out and needing to slap her face when the effect of her words hit Allyson.

"Oh no. No, no. Oh, I'm so sorry Erin. That's not… I mean, I wasn't… I… It… Oh frack, I suck."

Buoyed by the level of self-flagellation, Erin asked, "What were you trying to say?"

"I… Why don't I show you something?" At Erin's raised brows, she added, "You can count on me to be a perfect gentlewoman. Can I show you something interesting?"

Aware of how much she already knew Ally would be good to her word, Erin forced herself to relax. Yes, she knew she could trust her. She would have known that just by the stories Pam had shared over the five years she worked for her. Erin nodded her consent, still stiff and trying not to look it. For some reason, she was always nervous around this woman. She told herself it was just worry over the prospect that Ally may discover she was Pam's spy and not a contestant.

"I want you to take this," she said, offering her an empty cardboard tube.

Erin looked at it carefully, then decided Ally was screwing with her. "What…"

"I know. Its just cardboard, right? Not a telescope, but it's perfect for this. Here's what you do. Close one eye and see if you can make out the tree line out past the sports field."

Erin frowned. "It's pitch black, how am I going to see the field?"

"You're not," Ally explained with the same patience she had shown on the sailboat. "I want you to focus on the black outline of the trees first."

She waited while Erin skeptically raised the tube. "I can't see…"

"Will you stop fussing and listen to my directions?" she asked with amusement.

Erin could just make out Ally's face in the light from the ballroom. The music in the background was more mellow than earlier, and she knew Pam would waste no time getting a woman in her arms. In a way, she envied how casual she could be. At least Ally seemed to understand her boundaries and respected them. That was nice. She was nice. But if Ally was trying to convey some crazy lesson, she was failing to understand it. "Okay, let me try again." She closed one eye and raised the cardboard tube to the other. She found the line of trees. It wasn't so hard with the highway buzzing below it. "Okay, got it."

"All right. Now, slowly, very slowly, I want you to raise the tube up so the bottom is still on the trees and the top of the circle is filled with stars."

"If I can barely see the trees, what do you expect…"

"Hold tight there," Ally suggested softly.

Within seconds vertigo hit her full force. She felt herself falling and took Ally, who was trying to stop her fall, down with her. In a total panic, she wrestled to get off Ally and away from this mess.

"Easy there, kicking bird." Ally was laughing and playful, as she rolled Erin over and free of their embrace. "Wasn't that amazing!" she offered, pleased with the effect of her little trick.

Still on the ground beside her, Erin was not in a hurry to get up. "You tricked me, but I must admit, it was sweet! How did you do it? I mean what the hell?"

Ally rolled onto her side, resting her head on her hand. The light from the ballroom provided just enough illumination that Erin could see her eyes.

"How did you do that?" Erin asked again, wanting to restore the equilibrium between them.

"What you experienced was the effect of our Earth in motion. You see, we can't feel it while we're here on the planet. And we normally can't see it even when we take to the stars, but if you focus on something fixed on the horizon, especially with just one eye, then suddenly you see the stars spinning by. Your eye tells your inner ear you're moving really fast, and your body reacts." At Erin's poker face, Ally added with a weak plea, "I was planning on bracing you so you wouldn't fall, I'm so sorry."

Erin believed her. And realized she was having fun. Fun with her boss's cousin. She wasn't a contestant and didn't want to be. So why did she want Allyson Parker to take her right here and now, and why the hell did the woman have to have such expressive eyes? Ally offered her hand to help Erin to her feet. Looking around, Erin wondered how it was no one had commented on their behavior, she realized the others had drifted off to join Pam and her group.

Getting to her feet, Erin kept hold of Ally's hand to help her up. "Can you show me again? I won't fall again, will I?"

"Your brain will be ready this time, so don't expect the same effect, but I promise, I am here if you get dizzy."

That smile she offered so freely was more than reassuring, more than the "I'm the nice one" shtick she offered everyone else. Yes, Erin was sure Ally was feeling the same thing she was. Somewhere in the back of her mind, she knew Ally would not be the instigator. Not here. Not that she was shy or anything. She just knew Ally was a woman who played by the rules. Erin raised the tube again. Ally helped her aim it at the horizon then work up slowly. The vertigo lasted less than a second, but for a moment she experienced the same thrill, that feeling when you realize the earth beneath your feet is moving. "How fast are we going?" she asked with excitement.

"At the equator, it's about a thousand miles per hour. When you're this far north, it's slower, about seven hundred and fifty miles per hour, but that changes according to the season with our planetary wobble."

"Wobble?" Erin asked, knowing what she meant, but unable to look away from Ally's eyes.

"Yes, we wobble. Of course, that speed doesn't take into consideration how fast we're moving around the sun. The seven-fifty is just our rotational speed."

A PA called to them, breaking the moment, ordering everyone to the ballroom. Erin ached to say something, anything. Instead, she turned to the terrace and the French doors. Almost across the patio, she realized Ally wasn't walking with her.

Don't look back. Don't look back. Don't look back.

She stopped at the open doors and looked back. Ally was standing by her telescopes, hands in her pockets. Ally had been watching Erin walk away.

Ducking in through the open doors, she walked with a conscious effort to join the gathering group. Neither Rene nor Pam was there, and now she understood why. Connie was making her way to them. She had her ever-present tablet in hand and smiled to see them all gathered.

"Is everybody having a good time?" As the cameras were rolling all the women were enthusiastic, the answer an overwhelming yes. Even Erin felt like everything was copacetic in her world, joining in with the excitement.

"Settle down, settle down. I've got news and a packing list, because tomorrow we are boarding a flight and heading to parts unknown for a remarkable adventure. Are you ready to know where we're going, or do you want the packing list first?" Connie was teasing them and as expected, a few women called for the list while all the others hollered to know where they were going. "All right, women! So, you all want to know where we're going? Let's see if anyone can guess from the packing instructions."

One of the ever-present PAs began passing out photocopied lists to each of them. Those first to grab them were speculating wildly. Erin, not as thrilled as the rest, noted another PA making her way into the ballroom. She was pulling a furniture cart stacked with boxes. She placed one of the boxes, the top one which was already open, on the floor next to her director.

"What, still no good guesses?" Connie pushed. "Oh, you guys suck. I know Rene and Ally would have had it just by the weight limit. Okay…" She shook her head, placing her tablet on the floor and pulling a knapsack from the box. "Each of you gets one of these amazing packs from our sponsor." She reached back into the box and pulled out a few more items. "You'll also get one of these and…"

"Oh my God, they're going to make us skydive!" one woman shouted, whether in panic or glee it was hard for Erin to tell as all manner of chaos broke out. She watched as Connie gave one of her PAs a look. She was still outfitted as a referee, the role she had played during their afternoon challenge. Her shrilling whistle halted the arguments, and Connie raised the helmet in her hands. "Ladies, really? We haven't got that kind of insurance, and besides, it's not that kind of show. We are, however, filming in Canada, and that offers a few things we might not find in other locales…"

"Rafting!" another woman called. "Are we going white-water rafting?"

Connie groaned over the lucky guess, but nodded. "Yes, you are all going rafting down the Ottawa River. Yes, everyone is going. Yes, there will be safety training. Yes, certified instructors will lead each rafting party, and yes, you will all get to stay in a group with your chosen queen. Any questions?"

There weren't. There were always women who wanted to be heard and had something to say, but no one had any real questions. One woman did ask what would happen if she refused to take part. Connie's answer was swift and unyielding. "Anyone who wants out is welcome to quit. If you fail to board the aircraft tomorrow, consider yourself eliminated and on your way home. Any other questions?"

There were none. The prospect of immediate elimination settled them completely. The PAs began handing out their new sporting gear and helping women fit their helmets and packs.

Erin convinced herself she just wanted to be helpful and took the opportunity to look for Ally. To her disappointment, Ally was gone and all the telescopes with her. She would have to wait until tomorrow. Maybe this was a good thing. Time and distance would fix this. She turned her attention back to fitting her gear and trading jibes with Denise. Tomorrow they were going white-water rafting. Erin had no idea where the Ottawa River was, but assumed it was somewhere near Ottawa. which didn't help her much. Erin could point to Toronto and Vancouver on a map, but not Ottawa. She'd heard the name, recognized it as Canada's capital, but other than that, she didn't have a clue.

CHAPTER TWELVE

Erin was lucky enough to snag a ride on one of the helicopters, the smaller one operated by KC. Like their outing to Niagara the other day, the rear of the craft was packed, jammed with camerapeople and their monitors and who knows what. With the assistant director on the ground at their destination and preparing for their arrival, the front seat next to the pilot was empty, and KC insisted there had to be another person up front for something she kept calling the "weight and balance." Erin was that other person.

Strapped in, she wasn't surprised by the offer of a headset. Learning that only she and KC would be on the intercom did surprise her.

"You know why you got stuck flying with me?" KC asked her.

"I…no."

"Ally promised me you wouldn't puke. Please tell me she's right. Have you any idea how hard it is to get upchuck out of a machine like this? You know what a helicopter is? Thirty-thousand parts moving in opposition to one another."

"I was okay in Ally's helicopter." Even to her ears, her answer sounded lame. "I mean, I didn't have any trouble as a passenger in the other helicopter your company operates."

"Whoa, Nelly. I wasn't barking for recognition, but now that you mention it, it's nice to be known as the other party on the hook for all this gratis flying."

KC had just finished what Erin now recognized as the start-up sequence. She listened and watched as first the roar of the engine began to grow, then just like on the big machine, the blades slowly started moving. She couldn't help but grin. This flying thing was infectious. Some of the other women had sworn they would never step foot in anything smaller than a 737 after their one flight experience. Erin, in contrast, was seriously contemplating signing up for flying lessons once she was home again.

"You like this?" KC challenged. "What's your name again?"

"Erin."

KC was grinning as she worked through a list of checks printed on a laminated sheet. She began singing, "Erin's got the flying bug. Erin's got the flying bug…" As Erin's face reddened, KC stopped, offering with kindness, "No wonder Ally suggested you get the left seat. We don't let just anyone ride up front you know."

"Pam was up front with Ally."

KC just laughed before pressing some button that made the intercom sound all hollow. "Hey, I've decided our call signs should be Hornet and Big Bird."

Over the headphone speakers, Allyson's voice rang in crystal clear. *Really? You just can't go with the basics, can you?*

"Ah now Ally, baby, where would be the fun in that?"

There was a long silence followed by the sound of KC laughing on the intercom. "She's busy, but she'll take it like a big girl," she told Erin.

"Do you always torment her this way?" Erin didn't know where that question came from or why the sudden overwhelming need to defend Ally.

Still, KC wouldn't be provoked. Laughing harder, KC took a minute to settle down. She threw a switch on the instrument panel and called, "You guys back there ready to go? The other machine is signaling they're ready."

"*Yeah, we're rolling. Anytime,*" was the answer.

"Cool. Now we can't hear you on that com channel so if you need anything, just reach up here and tap one of us on the shoulder. It'll take a sec to change frequencies, but once I do, I'll hear whatever it is you need to say. Understood?" They gave their answer and KC pressed one button, and the hollower sound of the radio greeted their ears. "Big Bird, Hornet. Cameras are rolling and at the ready. You are clear to hover."

The Huey, with its rear doors open again, lumbered into the air. looking far more majestic once she was off the ground. She was a big machine, and Erin was overwhelmed by how massive yet tranquil she looked, the convergence somehow truly appealing.

"Like I said. Thirty thousand parts moving in opposition to one another. Pretty cool eh?"

"Yes. Yes, it is."

"*Hornet. Big Bird, light on the skids.*"

KC began slowly pulling the center console stick up, answering the radio call at the same time, "Hornet light on the skids. Big Bird set course for Yankee Oscar Oscar. We'll follow and maneuver around you at the film crew's direction."

"*Big Bird, heading set for Yankee Oscar Oscar direct. Will you land before me or after?*"

"I'll stay in the air for this rotation. Just fly it like I'm not even here."

"*Don't tempt me! Big Bird is climbing out.*"

Erin watched the big Huey climb majestically up from the castle grounds. She was so intent on studying the transition, she hadn't realized they were climbing out too. "Oh!"

"Easy there, Erin. Eyes in the air, not on the ground and you'll be fine."

"I'm okay—I guess I'm just susceptible to surprises."

KC made another radio call. This time to some faceless, unknown controller somewhere in the ether. Then she switched the intercom over to check with the camera crew. "I can keep us beside them or do some this side and transition over or under to get you a shot from the other side, whatever you want. Tell me now, because we'll be on the ground at Oshawa in all of four minutes."

"We'll stay here, but we want you to stay high as they unload the girls."

"Girls?" KC teased the crewman, one of the few actual men on the crew. "I didn't know you had girls on the Big Bird. Please tell me it's the Girls National Soccer team? I've always wanted their autographs!"

"Sorry, ma'am. I meant the women."

"Ah, why didn't you just say that. Now I'm all bummed!"

Beside KC, Erin was shaking her head. This woman was certainly outspoken and full of fun. Unlike her quieter more intense business partner, KC felt no compulsion to play nice. She wasn't sure how that would play in business. Still, it was fun to listen to her tease the crew in the back. She wasn't kidding when she said they would be at the airport in four minutes. She could already make out the airfield. As expected, several vans and official airport vehicles crowded what looked like the vacant side of the field.

"This used to be a Commonwealth Air Training Base during the war."

"I'm sorry," Erin said. "I don't know what that means."

"Oh, it's pretty simple. Although, don't ask Ally, she'll chew your ear off for hours with a history lesson. Anyway, we are part of the British Commonwealth. It's basically what's left of the British Empire. So, back in the war days, England needed a safe place to train pilots from all over the world, this was one of those places. Unfortunately, the local town council had no idea the gold mine they were sitting on and tore down most of the base." KC maneuvered them over the south side of the field, giving the camera crew lots of time and some perfect angles to capture the unloading of Ally's passengers. "You up for another rotation? she asked, giving Erin a serious look. "I mean, if you're not I can land, but we have to pick up the other two groups. Up to you."

Ahead of them, she could see Ally's helicopter was free of passengers and already hovering and waiting for permission to leave. "Yes. I mean I want to keep flying. Can I?"

"Are you kidding? Let's have some fun. Shall we?" When Erin gave a vigorous nod, KC transmitted. "Big Bird, Hornet. You are clear to depart. Follow me out."

"Hornet, Big Bird. I'm on your six."

"All right! Let's have some fun. Follow me and see if you can keep up."

"Affirmative."

Beside her, KC pulled the center stick up fast and pushed the stick between her knees forward at the same time. A second later, Erin almost screamed, reaching above her head for something to hold as she stared at the fast-approaching ground. In her head, her brain decided they were about to crash before she could recognize the motion that carried them forward was also pulling them up at the same time. Moments later the nose returned to a somewhat normal angle and she sucked in a breath. She didn't want KC to know how scared she was but the laugh from the woman said she couldn't be fooled. "You did that on purpose!"

"Sure did. Want to give it a try?"

"Try what? To kill us? No thanks, you...you crazy woman!"

KC was still laughing as she pointed to the guys in the back. They had ignored her call to put on their safety belts and were pulling themselves off the floor. There was a good load of cussing going on back there too, that no amount of noise canceling technology could mask. "Come on Erin. Don't be mad," KC coaxed her with her irreverent grin.

"You do know you're certifiable?"

"Does that mean you don't want to take a turn at the controls?"

The damn woman was still grinning. "Fine. How hard can it be?"

"Right on, right on, sugar bear. Now get your feet up on the pedals. Some folks would call these rudder pedals, but I am here to correct them. These things control the tail rotor. Just rest your feet on them, and I'll show you. Press this one in, and the tail rotor speeds up and turns us this way. Press the other, and it slows down, and the corkscrew effect of the main rotors twists us in the opposite direction. Okay, you give it a try."

Erin did and immediately grinned to see she was making the helicopter face away from the direction they were moving. "We're facing more away, but we're still going in the same direction."

"Smart observation." Under her feet, she could feel KC turn the nose back in alignment. "Helicopters are truly different than airplanes. Okay. Put your right hand on the stick. Yep, that one between your legs. I know, only guys would design a machine where a guy has to check to be sure he has the cyclic in his hand and not something else. Go ahead and move it a bit. How's it feel?"

"A little disgusting now that you've got me thinking about men and their other stick."

That comment made KC roar. "You have no idea," she lamented. "Okay, put your left hand on the collective. That's it, that one on your left. Now hold the cyclic steady, yeah, that center one and pull, slowly, pull the collective up a bit."

She did so and was shocked a moment later to realize they were climbing. "Oh my God we're going up! I thought you had to pull the cycl—stick thing back to climb up?"

"Cyclic," KC offered gently. "As I said, it's a completely different way to fly." She stopped Erin's climb and set her up for the approach to Glendennon Castle. "Okay. Can you see the school grounds?"

She looked around and realized, belatedly, that pretty much everywhere she could see was a part of the Castle grounds. There was no missing the place. "Got it."

"Great. Now keep your eyes on the front driveway. That's where Ally will land and where we're going to film. Now just follow me through on the controls. It'll give you a feel for how she behaves."

"She?"

"Of course. You don't think something this complicated could be male, do you?"

There was a fierceness in KC's voice that made her proud. Below her feet, she could see the mounted camera through the clear Plexiglas panel. It was turning, and it took a moment for her to register that the guys in the back were filming Ally's approach and landing ahead of them. They made a few passes overhead, finally hovering several hundred feet from where the Huey had landed. Allyson did not shut down her engine, hovering closer to where the next group of women were waiting before setting her skids down. Two PAs wearing fluorescent safety vests escorted the women below the spinning rotor and into the open helicopter. "That must be Pam," Erin noted, watching as a tall, leggy woman opened the pilot's door and climbed in front with ease.

"Don't tell me you're a fan?"

"What?" The question confused her.

"A fan of good old Pam's." KC's tone was so neutral, it was hard to imagine what she was thinking.

"I... Yes, I'm in her group. Is that a problem?"

KC just grinned at her response. "Hardly. I love old Pammy. But I'm curious to hear what you see in her?"

"I..."

"Hornet, Big Bird is light in the skids."

"Big Bird, you're all clear. Hornet is on your seven at one hundred feet. We'll copy your ascent and hold your nine o'clock."

"Big Bird, Wilco."

Before Erin could decide what it was she wanted to ask KC about her boss, the camera guy in the back tapped her shoulder. She pulled one side of her earphones away from her ear. "KC," Erin said, relaying the message, "the crew guys want to know if you can get Ally to let Pam try and fly like you just did with me and he wants to get more in front of them so they can shoot down and through the cockpit windows."

KC punched the intercom switch and connected to the guys in the back. "Look, guys, I can ask, but Ally's pretty tight with the rules. Can you wait till we get her passengers on the ground before she hands control of a two-million-dollar bird to old Hotlips there?" Before they could mount an argument, KC reset the intercom for just them, then hit the transmit button. "Hey, Big Bird. The kids want to shoot from twelve o'clock high, and they want to know if you'll let the cuz take the controls?"

"Hornet. Hold your course. Big Bird is transitioning to your six low. And that's a negative on request two."

"Aw, come on. Tell you what. Give Hotlips two minutes of dual, and I'll stop assigning you lame ass call signs."

There was no immediate response and Erin could see they were approaching the airport fast. "What's Ally like to work with?" she asked. She wasn't sure where the question came from. She was supposed to be interested in Pam, but here she was, sitting with Ally's business partner. Who would know her better? Pam, who had shared her youth, or KC, who shared her vocation?

"Ally?" KC sounded confused by the question.

"Hornet, Big Bird. Transitioning from your six to your three. Inbound for the landing. Advise cleared."

"Big Bird, Hornet. You are cleared. Did you let Pam have a go?"

"I did. So you owe me."

KC just laughed, then reported their progress to the tower, and followed Ally in the Huey as she climbed out again and headed back to the school for their last group. As they began to climb, she encouraged Erin to follow her on the controls again. It wasn't until Erin's hands and feet were engaged that she bothered to answer the question. "Ally's my best friend, harshest critic, the keeper of my secrets, and the one and only reason we've been as successful as we are. She might be a stickler for the rules, but she's a friggin' genius when it comes to making our ideas work. Plus, it doesn't hurt that her name will get us in any door. Christ knows we would never have pulled off the airline deal without her being a Parker."

Erin didn't know what any of that meant and made a note to ask Pam when they had a few minutes to talk.

"I'll tell you something else. Not all the queens are the marrying kind. Trust me on this. If you want my two cents, it's Ally all the way. She's the real deal."

"But not for you?" Erin asked.

KC erupted with laughter. "Oh God could you see it! We would kill each other inside a week. No, no, no. We are two lesbians who will never see eye to eye on the relationship level. Besides, I don't defecate where I make my money. And good old Ally has the vision. You ever hear the joke, 'How do you make a small fortune in aviation?'" She paused to look at her, before delivering the punch line. "'Start with a big one.' She's the reason we have work when just about everyone else in the industry is slowly bleeding to death. Maybe Pam's like that too. We'll have to see how she does on the bench."

Again, Erin wasn't sure what KC was telling her, but decided to file it away for now.

"Hornet, Big Bird is light on the skids."

"Set your course Big Bird. We'll work around you."

Erin stood with Pam and most of the other women, watching their aircraft taxi to the south side of the field where they were gathered around the production vans. Their baggage was already unloaded and set in a neat row along with an interesting array of production equipment and the luggage of the crew. Someone had pointed out a commuter plane when it landed, but she didn't think it was for them until it turned in their direction. As they and the parked helicopters were the only things on the south side, there was no refuting this was their ride. Some women complained, but most mused that if they could survive the helicopter ride they could handle something as small as a regional jet.

Ally had parked the Huey, over near the only building on their side, and she and KC looked to be battening it down to face any weather condition. Red flags hung from places she suspected were crucial, and the main rotor blades were draped in red safety covers and tied to the tail section and the ground. The smaller helicopter, the one KC was flying and flew daily for traffic reporting, sat beside the Huey. Members of the production team were busy stripping their monitors from the back cabin, and the camera once attached to the belly gimble had been detached and now sat on the tarmac waiting to be retrieved. Erin decided that meant the helicopters would not be joining them on this outing. She still wasn't sure where they were going and was slightly relieved to hear everyone else was as geographically ignorant as her.

Standing with the group made it easy to tune out and look around. But her eyes never seemed to travel far from where Ally was working. Like the other day, Ally had pulled the top of her flight suit down and tied it around her waist. Ally was so different than Pam. Yes, she was shorter, noticeably so. Yes, she wasn't the sharp dresser that Pam was, nor did she possess the razor-sharp mouth her boss had. But watching her work was relaxing. She was enjoying the basics and taking care in her work. Work which she assumed many pilots would view as beneath them. Ally wasn't just doing her grunt work; she was having fun and taking care. Erin found herself thinking about going over there and helping. She wanted to be part of the fun, and she wanted to be closer to her.

"You're staring!" Pam teased, but her tone conveyed disapproval—or was it time, in Pam's mind, that could be better spent? "Let's go for a little walk."

It wasn't a suggestion, and Erin let Pam pull her along by the elbow. "So where are we going?" Erin asked her.

"Who cares? Probably some boring old lodge out in Mosquitoville somewhere! Forget the location," she said, leading Erin quietly away from the others. "Tell me about... you know. Tell me everything they're saying about me."

Erin sighed internally. Yep, Pam wanted to talk and guess what? She wanted to talk about Pam. Why was she not surprised? "Who first? Charlotte or Denise?"

CHAPTER THIRTEEN

Relief was all that Ally felt as she and their guide pulled their raft onto the humongous granite outcropping which would serve for their midday beachhead. Except it was already closer to dinnertime than lunch. They had started out late, very late, when the outfitter realized they needed more than just the three rafts for the group. They also needed two for the camera crews and at least two more for all their camping equipment. While they could supply the rafts, they were seriously short on certified personnel, especially for the camera boats. No one had explained to the outfitter that the production crew would be too busy doing their jobs of recording the program to paddle their own rafts. Finally, arrangements were made to have all their gear driven into the bush and delivered to their campsite.

The two indigenous female cooks got stuck with that job. First, they would drive a treacherous logging road to where the tour would stop for lunch, set up and prepare the midday meal for almost fifty including contestants, crew, and the huge team of guides. Once the tour was off again, they would clean up, pack up, and head to the campsite and start all over.

Ally could see that they had the site well ordered. They were set up under the treeline canopy; their still overladen truck sat squeezed in between the trees. She couldn't spot anything even slightly resembling a road or even a path. She had to hand it to those ladies, both elderly in her eyes, for managing so much. Watching them already serving their bush-cooked hot meal to the horde of hungry and somewhat cranky guests, she marveled at their resilience even as they fielded ridiculous requests and joked and worked to make everyone feel welcome.

Waiting until everyone had their plates full, Ally was truly last in line. When one of the ladies spotted her, she immediately apologized. The fish was all gone as were the Indian tacos. "There isn't much of anything left, but we can make you some sandwiches or…"

"How about that corn soup? Can I split that with you two?"

The ladies just smiled at her, their soft round faces alight as their eyes danced with comprehension. "You like corn soup?"

"I love it, but I don't know a single soul who can make it."

They nodded, accepting the compliment. While one served out the largest bowl of soup she'd ever had, the other dropped fresh dough into the jerry-rigged fryer. Ally admired the ingenuity and hard work of these indigenous women. Their bannock fryer was nothing but the lid of a gas barbecue, removed and flipped to sit on the burners. Before the one woman had her soup ready the other was delivering her very fresh and still piping hot frybread.

Ally thanked them with the only native word she knew for thanks, not sure which people these women were from, or even if she was saying it right, "Miig-wech."

They giggled like schoolgirls before returning to their cleanup work without another glance at her.

It was their way, and Ally respected that. Carrying her soup and frybread, she looked for a place to sit. Everyone was engaged in conversation and having fun. She headed for the granite beach, stretching out there and resting for the first time since the break of dawn. The day had begun when Connie woke her up with the latest disaster and dragged her to the production office even before she could shower.

The bus drivers had gone on a wildcat strike, and that meant they needed her to borrow a Dash-8 and crew from her company. She'd already agreed to that, and she and KC had managed to make it work, but only because it was the weekend and Triangle Air was primarily a work week commuter line. On weekends, other than the scheduled route to New York, all the Ottawa and Montreal runs were cut in half, reducing the number of planes and crew required on the line. So that was settled.

This morning's shakeup had begun when Connie called the local public transit line, which she had booked just yesterday to get everyone to the Island Airport for their departure. As of midnight, the local bus drivers had walked out too, and even Connie, with all her finagling and contacts, couldn't come up with an answer.

"You know this is my Hail Mary pass? Come on Ally," she begged.

"Geez kiddo. You're pulling out all the stops. Is it that bad?"

"Sorry Al, but nothing's moving. I was even considering just putting everyone on the Go Train, but with local transit out we would have to walk or shuttle everyone in the production vans and hope the cops don't spot us. Then I checked, and the subway is shut down for maintenance along Bloor from Young to Spadina."

"So even if you managed to drag everyone onto the train, they would have to walk from Union to what, Queens Quay? Let me guess: that's okay if you're not carrying a ton of gear but... Oh, for frig sakes! Is this all because you don't want your contestants to see the underbelly of Toronto? So people are living in the underpasses. So what? They're homeless, not dangerous or anything. Hell, most of them tuck their belongings away and tidy up down there. You have to admit a teenager's bedroom is far scarier...but you're still worried?" She sighed, trying to think without any caffeine in her system. When a PA appeared with a hot cup of tea, she gulped it down, burning her tongue in the process. Setting the cup down, she picked up the phone. "Morning, buddy. Please tell me you've got eight hours from bottle to throttle?"

When she hung up, Connie was at her side, eyes wide and expectant. You would swear it was her first Christmas.

"KC's on her way here. Between her with the Long Ranger and me with the Huey, we'll taxi everyone to Oshawa airport. It's just ten kilometer from here and big enough to accommodate a Dash-8. Our crew was supposed to be ready to load at the Island at seven a.m. KC's calling them and asking they go wheels up at seven. That should put them on the ground here by seven-ten, fifteen, at the latest. We can probably make up most of the lost time in the air, so we should have everyone on the ground at Petawawa by eight thirty, as planned. It'll depend on how much time they waste loading."

Connie, utterly relieved, had rushed into her arms, gushing her thanks.

"Yeah, yeah. Just remember that when the Emmys come calling and you have to decide who gets to sit at your table."

* * *

After the big lunch, the last thing Erin wanted to do was get back in the raft. The scenery was breathtaking, the sun was warm, and the breeze was working to keep the bugs away. Why leave? But this wasn't her show, and she didn't have a voice. Getting into the raft with the other women and Pam, she felt out of sorts or maybe out of sync with their revelry and excitement. Deciding to just go with the flow, she smiled when appropriate, sang when the others sang, and mostly just watched the living river and the banks of the boreal forest flowing past her. There had been some excitement. After the last run of rapids, they all seemed to crash from the adrenaline rush at the same time, their quiet paddling the only sounds to be heard for a time. How Erin cherished that silence.

"Heads up, ladies," the guide warned them. "Time for our last run of the day. It's not as challenging as the last, but definitely the longest. Is everyone set?" Not satisfied with the few hoots and hollers he received, he led the cheers himself, adding a few local sayings he had taught them.

By the time they reached the first of the rocky outcroppings that made the Ottawa so challenging, they were hyped and ready. While he steered them hard left the water pushed them right then turned them to slide down the first rapid backward. They turned again and turned once more, again rushing backward around the rocky outcroppings which looked to be everywhere. This part of the river didn't descend like the other rapids they had traversed with success, but the section seemed to go on and on. Tired and not paying attention, Erin missed a call to hang on as their raft swung around, then kicked up over an outcropping, slipping over it like a bucking bronc. Only this bronc had a hell of an after-kick. While the front and middle of the raft fell to earth, the stern kicked high almost dumping the rear passengers in the front. When it slammed down, it was still on the rock. Their guide had his hands full controlling the raft, directing his passengers and keeping himself in the raft. Erin, sitting beside him, wasn't as lucky. Her back and head snapped rearward so fast her head was underwater while her legs were still in the raft. She could hear yelling and imagined she felt hands on her. Then nothing. Instinctively she knew she was underwater, but her fear of smashing her head against a rock battled her instinct to find air. Sure enough, the moment her head broke water, it was to crash headfirst into the next section of granite blocking the path of the water.

* * *

For this leg of the trip, Ally found herself at the stern of their raft and last in line after Rene, Pam, and the two camera boats. That was fine by her. It gave her the chance to observe the other four rafts as they entered the rapids and learn what she could from their successes—or in this case, failure. Pam's raft was in trouble. It had scooted around the first obstacle with ease, but was somehow out of position to take on the second. From her viewpoint, it looked like they were trying to blow right over a series of visible and invisible rocks that made this part of the river so treacherous. Then someone was overboard.

She couldn't tell who, just that it was one of their group as their helmets were a different color than those of the outfitters. Ally watched as first one, then the other crew boat tried to make it over to grab the woman in the water. They were moving too fast to get close. Behind them, Rene's raft made attempts, but nothing close.

As they neared, her pilot's precision eye quickly calculated the speed of the river and their progress compared to those ahead of her and she knew they would fail too. Operating on pure instinct, she pushed herself over the edge of the raft, keeping her head above water, her eyes open, and one hand still clinging to the raft's safety line. She was close, so close, and managed to grab a limb, an arm of the woman floating facedown, clearly unconscious. Her plan was to pull her in, then perform mouth-to-mouth, but they weren't on some quiet run or near the shoreline. Still hanging on to the unconscious woman and the raft, she was struck hard by a passing rock and almost lost the victim she was intent on rescuing.

Instantly the river tried to pull the woman in one direction and her and the raft in the other. Even with several hands clamped onto her arm, the force was too great, and she knew the drowning woman would soon be pulled away from her and the last raft. Making a choice, she consciously let go of the safety line, clamping on with two hands to keep hold of the woman.

She had her, but the raft, and hands desperate to keep a hold on her, separated. As the raft flashed past, the guide yelled that a rescue party would be back for them. Then they were out of hearing range. She could see worried looks and mouths shouting, but the roar of the river did everything it could to separate them first in sound, then distance, and finally, they were gone.

Fighting the river, she clung to the woman. She knew the best defense was to keep her feet ahead of her and concentrate on keeping her head above water and her eyes open and focused on what lay ahead. With the dead weight in her arms and the river intent on separating them, it took everything she had to hang on. Twisting and rolling, she could barely keep her own head above water much less the woman she was struggling to hold. And as for turning to keep her feet ahead to protect herself, there wasn't a chance with her load uneven and dragging her this way and that. Her only course was to hang on tight, taking the blows as they came and praying she could stay conscious long enough to get them to shore. Hit after hit, she knew she'd be badly bruised. Bruises heal, broken bones too, so she fought with every inch of her being to keep her head above water. If she were knocked unconscious or worse, neither she nor the woman in her arms would survive and knowing that made her fight even harder.

She didn't know how long it had been, but finally, Ally was pushed more than swam into what she would have called a tide pool. They weren't clear of the rapids, but in a section relatively calmer than the rest. It would take some work to get to shore from here, but first, this woman urgently needed her help. She wrestled with the limp body, only realizing who it was when she had maneuvered her into a position to perform mouth-to-mouth.

"Erin—no!"

She blew, counted, and observed, watching for Erin to take a breath, then she did it again. Ally was starting to panic, unsure she could revive her under these conditions. Her position was tenuous at best. She couldn't be sure she wasn't over-flexing the windpipe and there was zero chance of performing CPR under these conditions of no solid ground. Was Erin even getting the oxygen she was repeatedly forcing into her lungs?

Try after try after try…then Erin began to cough. She coughed and battled wildly making it even harder for Ally to keep hold. "You're okay, Erin! You're okay! I've got you! Don't fight me!" she screamed over the roar of the rushing, breaking water. "You're okay Erin! I've got you."

Ally wasn't sure if her words were reaching her or if she was just too tired to fight, but the wild struggle stopped only to be replaced by collapse and a rush of tears. "No, no, no. No crying, baby. I'm here, and everything's going to be fine!"

Erin looked confused, trying to find her bearings.

"You got pulled from your raft. Me too. And we're okay, it's just we need to get to shore, and I need to get you warmed. Will you trust me?"

Erin nodded, but the tears were still flowing strong. Her own emotions were running high too, and she hadn't been knocked unconscious and almost drowned. "No worries, honey, okay? We'll pick an easy route, and I promise, no matter what happens, I'm here, and I'm not letting you go." That seemed to calm Erin more than the prospect of trying to get from the relative calm they had found past the wash of moving water all around.

From where they were, the north bank was closest but the route most treacherous. Ally gambled on the longer course hoping it was as steady as she hoped. "Erin honey, listen to me. I need you to get on my back, kind of like a turtle, and you've got to hang on tight! If I lose my footing, we need to go feet first down the river until we hit another shallow area."

That caused a rise in tears, but Erin, for all her trials, nodded, allowing Ally to turn and wrap Erin's arms around her neck. "Legs too," Ally suggested. "Erin, you need to wrap your legs around me too." She had one hand on the rock face in front of them, and the other tucked around the two arms pulling against her neck. She didn't want to tell Erin to loosen her grip, but she was slowly being strangled.

"Okay Erin, keep your head up. Whatever happens, you need to protect yourself first. You hear me? Try to keep your eyes open, then you'll know when it's safe to breathe and when to hold your breath."

Digging her booted feet deep into the sediment that was the river bottom, Ally pushed her back against the tide and began her trek toward the shore. She lost her footing here and there, but always regained control; then one slip cast them back in the full current. They ripped downstream at an alarming rate, but this time Erin hung on, and she was able to keep her feet forward for the most part. They tore past rocky outcroppings, but Ally was unable to get a handhold anywhere. She came close once, but all she managed to do was get them turned around, with

Erin's back taking the blows. She grabbed and grabbed with her hands and kicked and dragged her feet until they were turned feet first again. Erin for her part never let go. Finally, she was able to get a handhold on an overhead branch of a fallen jack pine. The branches on the bottom side were ripped away, and the trunk was slippery with the water and moss buildup. Still, Ally was determined. Plus she could feel Erin's hold slipping. Whatever her condition, they needed to be out of the water and out now.

Hanging onto the water-smoothed trunk with both hands and digging her fingers into soft spots on the upper side of the log, she managed to drag them to the rocky edge of the river and pull first their upper bodies and eventually their legs out from the wild current.

Exhausted, they lay on the rough rocky bank, clinging to one another. Erin cried like a baby, then began muttering her apologies.

"Hey now," Ally soothed. "Nothing to be sorry for. The river has her own idea about how things get done around here and to be fair," she said, through her exhaustion, "I was watching your boat, and your raft master screwed up. I think he was trying to give the cameras a better show and almost launched you guys into orbit. At least that's how it looked from where I was sitting."

"It was my fault. I wasn't paying enough attention."

Ally, still holding her, smiled. "How could you. I mean, have you looked around at this place? Have you ever seen anything so, I don't know, rugged doesn't sound right, maybe…"

"Unspoiled?"

"Yes, unspoiled. You just don't come across that…" Erin was shaking in her arms. "You're cold, aren't you?" Erin looked embarrassed, but finally nodded. Ally's greater concern was for shock.

Ally didn't need to check her watch to know it was almost after eight. Even with the long summer days, here under the deep boreal canopy it would be dark soon. How long until the rescue party made it to them? Would they radio for rescuers? If so, the best she could imagine would be three to five hours.

If the foot party didn't find them tonight, air search and rescue would be out at first light unless one of the camera teams and their four guides on board decided to backtrack and find them first. Still, with the speed of the river and the lack of landfall places suitable for a raft, she imagined they would be a good few kilometer downriver or more. How long would it take an experienced crew to hike the dense forest back to where they fell in? Remembering she had grabbed a tourist map from the lodge as they were preparing to get underway, she sat up, gently letting go of her grip on Erin, and pulled the soaked trifold paper from her pocket. Lucky for them it was resin coated, which kept the ink from running or fading. Ally laid it out carefully. It didn't have a scale marker or any standard map markings, but it depicted the route and their stopping points.

"You think you know where we are?" Erin asked.

She was too exhausted to sit and that too worried Ally. She showed her the water-logged page that threatened to separate at every fold or crease. "This is our lunch place, here at this mark. I can't imagine we're much farther than here," she pointed, "at least when we fell out. What do you think?"

"It just looks like a bunch of squiggly lines. What does it mean if we're here? Can we walk to camp?"

"No, the bush is way too hard to navigate, especially at night. We'd be lost before we were a thousand yards from here. It's always better to stay put. I don't imagine it will take them more than two or three hours to find us." Tears began to well again in Erin's eyes. "Hey now, no more tears. I've got a plan. First step. We get a fire going. How does that sound?"

"Like heaven."

Ally grinned. "Then one heaven coming right up."

CHAPTER FOURTEEN

"Are you kidding me! We can't just sit here. We have to go back—"

"Pam, stop! Just stop and listen," Connie begged. "They have procedures for this."

They had cleared the rapids and had come alongside the camera raft holding their director Connie, and the three rafts carrying contestants. The fifth raft, the second one holding a camera crew, held their distance recording everything.

Trying to defuse the tension, the expedition leader, sitting aft in Rene's raft, explained, "We have choices to make. One, we can stop here, and everyone waits as we send guides back to find them and bring them to us. The problem with that is simple—a kilometer is a lot of distance to cover in the bush, and we're already three hours behind, which means it's going to be pitch black within the hour. Getting the rest of you down the river in the dark is dangerous and just plain stupid."

Pam took offense with the "stupid" comment and had to be shut down by Connie again. "For God's sake, Pam. Just listen!"

The guide seemed to realize that presenting options was not the best course of action and said decisively, "This is what's going to happen. All of you will proceed down the river to the base camp where you will report our situation to the women running the camp. They know what to do. While they're doing their part, the rest of you will set up your tents and settle in for the night."

Pam couldn't help but interrupt again. Ally and Erin were her closest friends in the world. "If you think we're going to play happy little camper while—"

"Lady, you haven't got a choice! We're out in the middle of the bush. You can't exactly call for an Uber or anything else for that matter. And it's nightfall. And whether you understand that or not, it changes everything. Even if we called Trenton right this second for search and rescue, there is no place to put a chopper down. The best they could do is drop them a radio and survival kit and hike in tomorrow morning. Stop!" he ordered, seeing Pam ready to pounce. "We are going to send one raft back." He pointed to the camera raft circling their impromptu armada. "I will take three of those guys and emergency gear and hike back to find them. By the time you have your camp set up, we'll have found them, and you'll know their condition. If all goes well, we'll all catch up with you at the base camp tomorrow."

"I'm sending the camera crew with you," Connie said with firmness.

"Look, I get that this is a big show and all but—"

"They have floodlights," Connie added, signaling her crew who immediately hit all the lights. The pool of rafts lit up brighter than the ice for a hockey playoff game.

"Okay, we could use that, but pick two guys who can keep up." This he said looking directly at the rather robust woman handling the camera rig in Connie's boat.

That pushed her over the edge. "Listen fuckface! Were all stressed! Insulting my people is not in the best interest of our situation. And for your information, Sandy here can bench press three-fifty, so stuff your—"

This time it was Pam's turn to talk down her sister. "Enough. My friends are in trouble. Take whoever you want, just figure out who that is and get going. Please."

He nodded. Then signaled to the raft circling them. "Jimmy, switch with me. Then get these ladies downriver and settled in. I'll call you as soon as we have word." The young man he called Jimmy gave orders to his fellow guides paddling the raft and they moved quickly alongside their leader. It took only seconds for the experienced men to switch places and then they were off. They would paddle hard as far as they could upriver. Then they would land guides on each side and begin the trek on foot to find the missing women.

Jimmy was much more careful with his charges. "I'm so sorry folks. But I don't want anyone to worry. It's nice and warm tonight, so even if your friends don't remember any of the survival stuff we covered this morning, they'll be fine."

"Ally's a pilot," Rene offered. "She'll know what to do."

Nodding, Jimmy looked relieved to have positive news. "Oh, they'll be fine then. Hell, by the time the guys get there, she'll probably have a summer cottage built and a big mouth bass smokin' over the fire."

It wasn't a great line, but it was enough to dissipate the extreme anxiety they were collectively feeling. "You're right," Pam added with authority. "As teens, we would camp with our grandfather on these alpine expeditions. You know, a week cross-country skiing somewhere. Ally was always so resourceful. Every time we stopped to camp, she'd serve up all sorts of things she would collect along the way, from berries to dead leaves and stuff she'd boil into some remarkable teas. And nothing scared her, well nothing but our grandfather's campfire tales."

Between Jimmy's authority and Pam's personal experience, the others began to relax. They weren't back to their earlier level of fun and camaraderie and couldn't be, but they were better, enough so to tend to their own needs. "Okay, ladies. I gotta say, you are the toughest group we've ever had go through here. It's nice. If you were all guys, the fists would be flyin' and most of you would be in the water by now, so this is cool. We ready to get goin'?"

Now in agreement, and with Pam and Connie calmed, they put their paddles back in the water and worked to finish the last five kilometers of the first-day course.

* * *

The last thing Erin wanted was for Ally to stop holding her, soothing her, but she was cold and it was getting dark. Ally had tried twice to extricate herself to build a fire, but she seemed unready to let Erin go either. Now, realizing just how fast the dark was creeping in, she knew she was too cold to help and that Ally would have a hell of a time finding firewood in the dark. "I'm…I'm still cold, but I'm okay. I want to help, but I don't know what to do."

"Can you manage a few minutes alone? I won't go far, I promise."

"Yes, okay," was all she could say. Slowly she let her cold, stiff arms and hands fall from Ally's warm body. As Ally moved away, struggling to get to her feet, it occurred to her that Ally might be as cold and sore as she was.

Sitting up, she wrapped her arms around her soaking sweatshirt, then decided it was probably better if she got the wet thing off. Ally was right. The air wasn't all that cold. It just felt so after spending so much time in the water. If they were camping as she used to with her family, she would have found a sunny spot and let nature dry her off. From where she was sitting, she could see the last rays of daylight on the trees on the other side of the river while their side was already plunged in deep shadow. Both her fingers and Ally's had been too numb to unfasten her helmet chinstrap. So, with nothing to do while Ally gathered wood, she fussed with the snap, willing her numb and shaking fingers to do her bidding. It took work and determination to make it happen, but minutes later she was able to toss the thing away. Rubbing her head and trying to finger-comb her tangled hair, she did know the helmet had probably saved her life. That and Ally. Ally had not been long on specifics in telling her what happened, but Erin had a good idea she was unconscious when

Ally found her. She could remember the shock of being revived and the stinging burn her closed throat felt as she struggled to gulp in air.

Ally had been there. She had calmed her racing thoughts and comforted her aching body. Ally. Of all the people who could have gone in after her, it had to be her. And now they were alone and maybe for the night, and she couldn't think of what to do or say. How could she be so tongue-tied and nervous now? Unwilling to confront that question, she forced herself to concentrate on their situation. Ally had said the first task was a fire and she was right. While she was hunting in the dark for firewood, the least she herself could do was prepare a fire pit. At lunch she had noticed the long pit dug in the sandy silt and ringed with granite rocks the size of her head. At this spot, there was no shoreline of any kind. There was fast-moving water, then you were in the woods, with zero transition. With no idea where to light a fire, much less how, she focused on gathering rocks to build a firewall. She couldn't manage any of the larger rocks but accumulated a rather large pile of fist-sized specimens. It was hard to do with her hands still raw from the cold water and her trip down the river, but it had to be easier than Ally's job.

Hearing the sounds of something breaking through the nearby brush gave Erin visions of a bear finding her, but Ally stumbled through, almost falling on her. "You can't see a thing in there. Remind me, if either of us has to pee, to stick to the shoreline."

"Can't you hear the river and follow it back?"

"Naw. The sound is dampened the second you're more than twenty feet inside the treeline, and it's ubiquitous. You hear it coming from every direction." She dumped her bundle of small broken branches on the ground beside the rocks and began looking for a place for the fire.

When she finally decided, Erin had to ask. "That's right on top of that old fallen tree we crawled along. Aren't you worried it will catch too?"

"I'm hoping it will, but it's really wet, and even the punky parts are soaked. Still, if it catches, it gives rescuers a better chance of spotting us from the water and the air. Even if they hike in, which they probably will, it'll be easier to spot than the kind of fire we would light if we were camping here."

"Oh. What I wouldn't do for a little camping gear. Even just a change of clothes."

Ally smiled, nodding to the discarded sweatshirt. "I know. Me too." Looking at the pile of rocks, she asked, "Did you get them from the water or dig them up?"

"I just grabbed the ones I could reach from here. Sorry, I didn't want to put my hands back in that water."

"Hey, don't be sorry. You did perfect. Stones from the water can have moisture in them. If we put them in the fire, they might explode."

"Explode?" That confused Erin. "And why are we putting them in the fire? I mean, I thought we needed them to go around, you know for safety."

Ally stopped what she was doing, giving Erin her full attention. "We don't need a safety ring as much as we need warmth. We'll build a fire, and these rocks will get warmed in it. They hold the heat for a long time, so once they're hot we can bury them under the soil, down just far enough for some padding. The heat will rise from the rocks and help keep us warm all night."

"You think we'll be here all night?"

"Maybe, maybe not. All I know is a rescue boat can't get up this river, and a helicopter can't land here. That leaves having a search and rescue team winch us out or waiting until morning for the search party to show up. Either way, we might as well get comfortable."

Erin was just about to ask how she was going to light a fire when she pulled out a waterproof lighter and a folding knife from her cargo pocket. "I always carry these," she explained. "Part of our helo safety equipment."

With the knife, she started dragging the blade at a ninety-degree angle along a piece of dead wood. In seconds she had a large pile of shavings. These she arranged between the stump and trunk of the fallen tree. With the lighter, it burned easily, and Erin watched with interest as Ally began feeding small sticks then larger ones until she could add a few of the larger branches she had dragged back.

"That won't last long, but at least I'll be able to find my way back now. Will you be okay if I go grab more firewood? We're going to need a lot more than that to last the night."

"Can I help?"

Ally looked her over carefully. "You can keep this fire going for me. How's that? Take your time and always leave room for the air to reach the fire. Here, look. Try adding branches by piling them on like lodge poles."

Erin watched her add firewood in a pyramid shape, up and above the fire. They looked unaffected by the flames then one by one they caught, the flames dancing up the dry wood faster than she'd imagined. "Oh! Okay, I can do that," she reassured Ally, who still looked reluctant to leave. "I should come with you."

"Most certainly not. Not with a possible head injury. I'm just… You'll be okay, right?"

"Yes Ally, I'll be all right, and I'll keep the fire going. Promise."

That garnered a big smile, and Ally was off without another word. That was something she admired about Allyson. Unlike Pam or even chatty-Cathy Connie, she was a woman of few words. Not that she didn't like to talk. She was as talented a conversationalist as was Pam, but Pam's focus was, well, on Pam. With Ally it was different. They shared the same family upbringing and most of the education, but Ally was all about inclusion, and she genuinely liked to hear about others, their struggles, and their triumphs. And she was first to call bullshit and to suggest others reconsider their viewpoints from several perspectives, but not in the confrontational way Pam banked on in court. Ally was interested in people believing in themselves. She worked hard and truly thought it was the work, the effort, that set someone apart from those unwilling to contribute.

Deciding the fire needed attention, Erin tried adding wood the way Ally had only to have those sticks fall. It was harder than it looked. Determined to get this right and have a solid blaze going by the time she returned, she tried again, rescuing a few of her branches and leaning them together. This time they stuck, and she watched in fascination as the flames climbed and the embers began to build. She carefully piled some of her rocks around the edges. She wasn't sure if they needed to be in the fire or just close. If they needed to be in it, she decided she needed to build a bigger base of coals first and added more firewood. Ally was right. It looked like the old wet log wouldn't burn, or at least not until it was thoroughly dried out. Until then, she'd concentrate on building her coals and adding her rocks around the edge. Even if it didn't help, the work was keeping her spirits up and the heat was a salve for her soul.

Erin heard Ally long before she could make her out in the all-consuming dark. She tried to keep her attention on the fire, but it was hard to concentrate when she couldn't see anything around her except for the treeline on the opposite bank of the river. And Ally was right—it was hard to hear above the sound of the river. It was pervasive yet hushed somehow, like the trees themselves worked to diminish its force.

"You're back." To her ears, she sounded unsure, maybe even scared. Ally, for all her abilities, never made her feel stupid or unprepared.

"You're right to worry. Twenty feet in and I couldn't see the fire. It would be so easy to get disoriented. From now on I'll forage along the river bank. The deadfall may be wetter, but I'll have a better chance of finding my way back."

"Were you scared?" The question surprised her. Until this moment, Erin had convinced herself Ally was invincible and completely in her element.

"Yeah, a bit. My hearing sucks, so it's impossible for me to tell the direction of the river in the dark. The deeper you go, the harder it is even to see your hands much less where you're putting your feet."

Erin watched as Ally added more wood to the fire, finally asking, "You must have a lot of survival training. I mean, you have all the stuff we needed on you…"

Ally's grin stalled her thoughts. "I carry a lot of junk in my flight suit. Belt cutter," she said, holding up the folding knife and showing her the angled inboard cutting edge that reminded her of the little cutter her mother used to open the corner of plastic bagged milk. "Weatherproof lighter. There's more I usually have and could have used if I hadn't let Connie rush me to get out of my flight suit. I do have a little pack of basics." She pulled out and zippered open a wallet-sized case. "I have fishing lines and hooks."

"Ooh, can we string the fishing line and see if we get lucky?" The enthusiasm she felt renewed her hope.

"We sure can. You want to pick out one of those long sticks to tie one end to?"

While Ally tied the line to the hook set in paper, she looked to be in deep thought. "We need to think about what we can use for a sinker. In water this fast, a hook and line will just bob on the surface. You don't happen to have any toonies on you?"

Erin was confused by the question. "Connie collected all our electronics."

That made her grin. "Sorry, I mean those Canadian two-dollar coins."

She did, but it took some trying to get it free of her wet pocket. "It's from the twenty I won for you. I meant to give them to you today." She handed it to her, curious to see how she would use it.

"You did good." Ally grinned at her, then explained, "What I'm about to do is technically a federal offense, so I'm swearing you to secrecy. Understood?"

She offered a Girl Scout salute, promising not to divulge a word. Ally carefully laid the center section over a low spot on a rock, placed her heavy blade against the polar bear in the center gold section and used another rock to pound on the knife. It took a few tries but finally, the inner coin separated from the outer silver ring and instantly she had a weight and spinner all in one. She handed the gold-colored bear back to her. "A souvenir of our adventure," Ally said, hunting in the thin, rich loam for a squishy worm and then hooking it on. "Okay, I think that's the best we can do. You mind being pole keeper? Oh, that sounded wrong."

Erin was all smiles. "You know, you're quite ingenious?" She chuckled. "Yes, I'll guard the fishing pole," she said, carefully stuffing the polar bear inner coin back in her wet pocket and taking hold of the stick to which the line was now tied. "What else have you got in there?"

"Hmm, let's see, Band-Aids, antibiotic cream, bug juice…"

"Would that work for mosquitoes?"

"Yeah!" she said, and Erin was immediately hopeful for some relief. "I'm sorry. I don't get bit much, so I don't notice." Ally opened the soft plastic vial, squeezing the clear liquid in her hands. "Just say where."

"Oh um…My face and arms."

Ally rubbed mosquito repellant on her arms then the back of her neck, carefully covering her face with just the gentlest of gestures with the tips of her fingers.

"I could have done that."

"This is military-grade stuff. You don't want it in your eyes. Which is easy to do if you get it on your fingers."

She watched as Ally washed her hands in the cold river water. "What else have you got in there?"

"A signal mirror, which is useless until we have sunlight, and a mini compass which I've found to be accurate within one hundred and eighty degrees. Not sure why I haven't tossed the thing."

"Oh, so not much help for us."

"We don't need it," Ally reassured her. "Rescuers will be here long before we have to think about walking out alone. I just wish I'd thought to grab my flashlight too. That would have made life easier. Oh, look. I forgot I have the solar blanket. It's not much, but it should help keep your back warm while the fire takes care of the rest."

"I…" *What if I want you to take care of the rest?* "What about you? Can't we share?"

Ally smiled again. It was warm and unpresumptuous. "Would it be okay if I got in behind you and cuddled in? We can share body heat, and I can wrap the blanket thing around us both."

She nodded, not trusting her voice and sitting rigid as Ally maneuvered around to sit with her legs on each side of Erin. She slid in close, gently gesturing for Erin to get comfortable.

They were quiet for some time before Ally admitted, "KC once dragged me on a week-long survival course. I wanted to kick her ass for signing us up, but she was right as usual. It was something we needed." When Erin didn't say anything, Ally asked, "You all right?"

"Just looking at the stars. Even with the fire and the trees, I can see, like, a million. I've never seen so many stars and so clearly."

They sat cuddled up, the fire keeping them warm and the stars looking down at them. Nothing in the moment felt more important to Erin than just sitting here, in the dark woods, with Ally. She reached for Ally's hands which were resting respectfully at her side and pulled her arms around her. The immediate response was Ally pulling her even closer. Holding her, comforting her. She felt protected, and something more. "I don't know how you feel about me. I mean, there are so many women…"

"Are there? I hadn't noticed." She didn't sound flippant or ironic. She sounded sincere, finally stating softly, "I thought you were into Pam?"

"I…no. I mean she's nice. I do like her, just not…"

"It's okay. I know women see me differently than my cousin. They always have. I guess it's my shyness that gets the best of me. Pam, on the other hand, has always been the outspoken go-getter. Like Harvard. She decided at the tender age of eleven that she would study law at Harvard then move to Chicago."

"I thought she moved there to be closer to her mom and stepdad?"

"More like the other way around. My grandfather is a persuasive man, and he worried about her being alone, so he opened an investment office there and persuaded Uncle David to set up a shop to monitor the Chicago commodities and options exchanges. It's a made-up job but it suits him and my aunt just fine."

"I had no idea."

"How could you? It's not something Pam would share on a first date."

For a moment Erin almost panicked, remembering Pam and Connie's warning not to tell anyone she was Pam's spy. Surely that couldn't include Ally? Except telling her didn't feel right either. What would she think? Would she decide Erin wasn't really into this thing and give up on her? *Was* she in this thing? She certainly never intended to be part of the whole game, just an unofficial observer. That's what she had told herself, and what Pam had repeatedly said on the flight to Toronto. *In or out?* She couldn't say.

"You okay? I didn't mean to give you a hard time. Whatever you feel for Pam or anyone else is, well, they're your feelings, and you should honor them."

That didn't make Erin feel any better. Still trying to decide what to say, she needed to sit up, turn around and say it face-to-face. Turning, she caught the firelight dancing in Ally's eyes and something more. Desire? When was the last time a woman looked at her like this? She'd been feeling it too. Was it just the situation or was it the woman? It was so hard to tell, yet here she was, in the arms of a caring and gentle woman. Circumstances aside, she had never felt better.

"THERE THEY ARE!"

They both jumped at the triumphant shout of the search party.

"Holy cow, you guys are a sight for sore eyes," said Sandy, the woman carrying the camera pack, then she flipped on the floods. "How are you both?"

The moment gone, they submitted to medical checks by the field medic. Most concerning to the medic was Erin's possible head trauma. Pleased to see her alert and responsive, he ordered the other guides to make camp, then pulled out his satellite phone, calling the base camp and the lodge to let everyone know they had been found and were injury free, except for some bruising, and in good spirits. "The director wants to speak with Allyson," he said, holding out the phone.

Ally took the phone. "Ally here...Yes, Connie, we're fine... She did hit her head, but she hasn't shown any symptoms of concussion...Yes, I have been paying attention...Let me ask her." She turned to Erin, asking gently. "Connie's willing to call in a helicopter to take you out tonight. It's up to you."

"I thought you said they couldn't land here."

"They can't," the medic said. "We'd set off flares, and they would lower a basket on the winch line. We'd strap you in, and they'd pull you up. It's easy. Nothing to worry about and we shouldn't fool around. If you have any symptoms, tell me now. It'll be safer to get you out."

"Where would they take Ally and me?"

"Just you. They'll only winch out injured parties. Allyson here can walk out tomorrow morning with us. Right?"

Ally nodded, adding for Erin's sake, "It is safe. If you're feeling any symptoms, I would rather err on the side of caution."

"I'm fine. I told you that. No nausea, no headache, nothing."

Both the medic and Ally looked chastised, then Ally reported to Connie, "She's in fighting form. I think that means she wants to stay. Is that a problem?" She listened intently, finally answering, "Got it. Okay, put her on." Turning back to Erin she said without emotion, "Pam wants to talk to you."

Erin could only wonder if Ally felt betrayed, considering their conversation. Ally stood, joining the others just feet away, leaving Erin to feel cold and alone. "I'm here Pam, and I'm fine." Of all the times for her boss to make a fuss. *Damn it!*

CHAPTER FIFTEEN

It didn't take Ally and the guys long to set up the survival shelters. The biggest challenge was finding three somewhat level spots big enough for the lightweight two-person tents. While they were working on setting up camp, the camerawoman sat with Erin by the fire and interviewed her on all that had happened. Ally could only wonder what was being said.

The guys teased her while they worked. "Woulda thought you'd built a shelter by now."

"And a shopping mall," another joked.

"Naw," the third chimed in. "I was betting on an escape vessel. Or a rocket!"

"How's she gonna build a rocket out here, dipwad? There ain't no rocket fuel for miles."

"What? What kinda pilot doesn't carry a little flask?"

Ally just laughed at their antics. "I did drop a fishing line in the water. For all that it did."

"Whaddya use for bait?"

"Just a squishy old worm. And a toonie for a spinner. That's all I had on me."

"See!" the lead guide said as if Ally's words proved something. "I told you she was better prepared than ninety-nine percent of the guys who come through here!"

Just then, Erin screamed, "There something pulling on the line!"

One of the guides, the young native guy, leaped to lend a hand. The other guides offered nothing but tongue-in-cheek encouragement, insinuating that whatever was on the hook was all they would eat that night.

Done with her tent, one of the guides offered to get the sleeping bags in while she rejoined her friend. Back at Erin's side, she was glad to be near the fire again. Her clothes, designed for the elements, were still damp and uncomfortable in the cool evening air. The young native man noticed her shivering and called out something in what Ally could only assume was his language. Another guide, began sorting through their backpacks. Finally he joined the group by the fire, advising Ally, "I put dry sweats in your tent for you both. Sorry. We shoulda done that first."

"Thanks so much. We're doing okay, but dry clothing does sound nice."

Beside her, Erin gripped the stick Ally had tied to her fishing line. "It's really pulling. I'm afraid the line will break."

The young native guy squatted down beside her, but never tried to take over. Instead, he offered quiet encouragement and Ally watched as he made suggestions, helping her reel in her catch with a level of patience far beyond anything she could provide. She was in awe as he coached Erin, playing her catch perfectly, the camerawoman recording every move.

"I can see it!" Erin hollered. In the LED floodlights of the camera, it was easy to pick out the struggling catch in the crystal-clear water.

In a swift movement, the young man beside her leaned in, grabbing and capturing the squirming brute in his hands and holding it up for the world to see. "Muskie! She caught a ten-pound muskie with a five-pound line!"

Ally couldn't help rushing to Erin and hugging her congratulations. "That was magnificent! Wow. I mean wow!"

Ally could see the young man quietly dispatch the Muskellunge. He handed it back to Erin, making sure she had a good hold and suggesting she hook a few fingers through the gill to hike her prize up for Ally, the camera, and guides alike.

"I guess I have to cook this now?" she asked jokingly. "It's probably a good thing it's a biggie." She was still a little shell-shocked at her achievement.

"Nope," Ally said, explaining, "In my house, the provider does not cook. What do you guys say?"

The young man said he would gut and prep the muskie while the guy they called Frenchy would do the cooking. The guys joked around and finished setting up camp and prepping the fire for cooking.

Ally suggested to Erin, "Why don't you go get changed." Wrapping an arm around her, Ally pointed her toward the tent set aside for them. Now that normalcy had descended she didn't know how Erin would feel about sharing. She remembered Connie had assigned all the tents by some logical thread that meant nothing to her, except Erin was supposed to spend the night with Pam. Was she disappointed to lose her opportunity for one-on-one time with her perfect cousin? The tents the outfitter provided would accommodate four, so it wasn't like they would have been alone. Still, the idea of spending the night here and having Erin disappointed over losing time with good old Pam did plague her.

Erin turned the arm hold into an enthusiastic hug. She was floating on her fishing victory and didn't look to have a care in the world. "I'm so happy you're here with me."

Ally could love her for that alone. "Go get into dry clothes," she ordered with affection. "It looks like we get a great dinner tonight and all because of you," she added with an immense smile across her face. Erin hugged her again, then practically skipped to the tent, zipping herself inside.

Beside her, the camerawoman, stepped up, sans camera. She leaned in to give Ally a friendly shoulder bump. "I'm not sure I should let you guys share a tent."

That news threatened to crash Ally's good mood. Before she could even think of what to say, the woman began laughing.

"Oh, I knew you had it bad," she teased. "And don't worry. Connie said to let you two do whatever you like. Just get it all on camera."

"All?"

She laughed even more. "No, not all." She was still laughing as she strolled away. "S'cuse me. I gotta grab some footage of the boys cooking Erin's big catch."

Inside the tent, Erin grappled with her wet clothes. She was never the type to go without undies, but it didn't make sense to keep her wet drawers on when she had nice dry sweatpants and a sweatshirt to wear. The next challenge was deciding what to do with the wet gear. A place by the fire to hang them to dry for tomorrow would be best. Except, she wasn't sure how she felt about everyone getting a glimpse of her white cotton granny panties. *Who am I kidding? I have two brothers who've seen worse.* It wasn't the guys who were making her self-conscious but Ally—what she would think? *We're camping, not on some hot date! What the hell else would I wear?* But in the back of her mind, she worried Ally would somehow be disappointed not to see some skimpy lace number on the line. *No. She's not like that.* Finally she pushed herself and her armload of damp to soaked clothing from the tent.

Outside, one of the guys spotted her and her armload, offering to string a clothesline. That was it. She felt silly and exposed as she hung her laundry for the world to see. She was even more surprised to realize Ally was standing beside her looking seriously adorable in sweats three times her size. At least she had the bearing to pull them off, but was forced to roll up the sleeves and the legs just to walk around. "You look like a Keebler elf."

"Oooh, I'm wounded. Here I was going for the cute forest urchin look."

Erin could only laugh, then took heart to see her hang her panties too. They weren't exactly granny panties, but they too were white cotton, bottom of the drawer, and reserved for camping, fishing, and having your period-style pantaloons. The relief she felt was almost overwhelming. Ally just had a way of making things okay without saying a word. How come she couldn't find someone at home like her?

"Supper's almost ready, ladies," one of the guys called out. The camera lights switched back on, and Erin felt exposed, like a teenager caught doing something illicit.

"Come on," Ally said with a smile that seemed to erase her fears. Offering her hand, she said, "Let's go eat." Under her breath, she added, "If this all gets to be too much, just say the word, and I'll take care of this lot. Okay?"

Erin just nodded, walking hand-in-hand with Ally back to the group now gathered around the fire, including the camera recording their every move.

During dinner, Erin mostly listened. It took some time for her to get comfortable enough to share. Not normally the quiet one, she was too overwhelmed by everything that had happened. Falling in the river, she had feared for her life. The unknown hand that had grabbed onto her hand, she'd initially assumed it was one of the guides or maybe Pam. She'd always assumed Pam had her back like she did at work. But this was different. They were both out of their element here. The only difference was, Erin could admit it whereas Pam never would.

On the flight to Toronto, she had been snippy with Pam. Worried she would be this hanger-on with no purpose beyond keeping Pam informed. In a way, it felt unfair. The other queens didn't have spies. Or did they? Did Ally have someone among the women informing on everything happening behind closed doors? She assumed Connie shared certain things with her, but she shared with Rene and Pam too, so that was expected. When the camera was off, and Sandy and the guys were debating something unimportant, she turned to Ally, mentioning quietly, "I hear Rene has a spy."

"What? Like a corporate spy or something?"

"No. No. Like one of the women on the show was placed there just to keep her informed on the goings on between the women."

Ally shook her head. "I have a hard time believing she would do something like that or that Connie would agree. I mean, I get where that could help, but it sounds wrong or childish."

"Childish?"

"Like high school gossiping. I mean, if Rene wanted to know something about a contestant, why not just ask her?"

"Maybe she was worried they might lie just to get close to her."

Ally nodded at the logic. "It must be hard for her to trust. I get that part. I'm not the most...desirable or...attractive. If I were in her boots and women suddenly started throwing themselves at me, I would be suspicious too."

Erin was stuck on the part where Ally didn't think she was a desirable woman. "You don't think you're attractive?"

Ally just gave her a look, a little sad, and a little grateful. "We all have our gifts. Pam was born with good looks and charm. And she's always had that killer instinct. It serves her in the courtroom. Which, if you ever get a chance to see, you must. That woman can cut down an arrogant bastard in seconds and leave him on the stand crying for his momma. She's incredible. I would not want to be in her crosshairs. Now me, I'd never get a word in edgewise with men like that. Although I am likely to drop them in the middle of nowhere and forget to come back."

"You have a kinder side, but you're both driven." Realizing she was probably saying too much about Pam, she added, "At least from what I've seen, I think you could hold your own with her."

"It's a lot different to debate something over the Christmas table than in a court of law but you're right, if it's important, it's hard for me not to fight. I guess it's just easier for me to do so with actions, not words."

Erin grinned. "Like dropping someone off in the middle of nowhere and forgetting to pick them up?"

"Something like that. Although..." Ally smiled. "I've never actually done that, but KC and I did threaten a fire boss that we would if he didn't stop telling us how to do our job. You'd be amazed at how many guys jump into a helicopter for the first time and think if a *girl* can do it so can they."

"What do you do with them?"

"The simple fix is to let them try. A helicopter isn't forgiving or intuitive like a Cessna. It usually takes less than two minutes for them to work up a good sweat and get good and scared at how fast they lose control."

That was interesting, and very much the same as what Pam would do with a hostile witness in court; what Pam did with words, Ally did with actions. Maybe that was why she was the one to go in the water after her. When she couldn't dislodge that thought, she had to ask, "Why did you come after me?"

"Honestly, I don't know. I saw you go over, saw no one could reach you. It only made sense to try. I actually thought I could hold onto the raft and you, but man oh man that current was strong. I had no idea."

"You're telling me! First I thought I'm going for a swim then the next second I'm thinking, this is it. This is how I die."

Ally laughed, a good-natured laugh that helped Erin shake off the recollection. "Like I would let that happen. Besides, Connie would have killed me for letting a contestant buy the farm and who knows what Pam would have done."

The mention of Pam soured her mood. She couldn't tell Ally she was just here as Pam's spy or that she wasn't interested in Pam. After all, she had bypassed Ally's selection for Pam. Of course, it made sense that she would think there was something to it. How could she explain? Before she could think of anything, one of the guides interrupted.

"Sorry to break the evening up, but if we're going to catch the rest of the group, we'll need to start our hike by five a.m. That means it's time to hit the hay." He named the other guides in order of their duty as fire pickets, explaining he'd take the last spot, that way he could get breakfast started for everyone. And with those final words of advice, everyone except the young man tasked to be first sentry headed to their shelters or to find a private spot to relieve themselves.

Ally handed Erin the flashlight they had been given, suggesting she take care of nature first. "I'll wait here until you're back. Will you be okay?"

Erin smiled at her concern. "I've been going potty on my own for some time now. I'm sure I'll manage."

"Smarty-pants," Ally said, but the smile that followed was all Erin needed to realize how much the woman cared.

* * *

When Erin had stripped out of her wet clothes earlier, she had chosen to keep her wet shoes and socks. The expensive cross-trainers were now soggy, cold traps for her feet. Finally able to pull them off, she stuffed her clammy feet into the sleeping bag before deciding what to do about the tracksuit. At home, she slept in the buff simply because pajamas or a nightie made her feel constricted. In the dorm, too shy to go *au naturel*, she compromised, wearing an oversized T and her cotton granny panties. Her T-shirt was carefully packed and sitting with her gear wherever that was, and her granny panties were still wet and hanging on the line just feet from the tent. She pulled off the sweatpants and bunched them up for a pillow. The sweatshirt, while bulky and uncomfortable felt like her last line of defense. *Defense? What the hell? It's not like she's the type to take advantage.*

Erin hunkered down in the sleeping bag, thankful for the time alone. She had a feeling Ally had asked her to head in first so she would be more comfortable. But now her feet were cramping, the pain becoming almost unbearable. Ally, she noticed, had doffed her boots and gone barefoot the second they had a fire going. She admired that, but couldn't understand how she could walk around a forest floor littered with branches, pine needles, and rocks everywhere. About to sit up and massage her feet, the sound of the tent zipper opening froze her thoughts and motion.

Crawling into the small tent, Ally tossed her the flashlight. "Sorry, I should have left that with you. Did you get settled all right without any light?"

"I did. And I didn't need any light. You probably needed it more."

"Turns out there's a full moon. Once it was finally up, it was easy to see and make my way around."

"A full moon?" Not one for signs, it did feel surreal. A full moon, a tent to themselves, and the only woman she found the least bit interesting stranded with her. Trying to be polite, she rolled away from Allyson to give her the privacy to change or whatever she might want to do.

"You okay?"

"Yes. No. I'm…My feet hurt. I should have taken my shoes off earlier." She sensed Ally shining the flashlight on her, then around the tent. She unzipped the tent and disappeared with Erin's wet trainers and socks, returning quickly.

"I hung your socks and set your shoes by the fire. They may not be dry by morning, but they should be better than they are now. Remind me in the morning, if they're still wet, we can snag some plastic from the guys to line them. It's not fun but it's better than putting dry feet into cold wet runners."

"Thanks."

"Okay, now how about I look at those feet?"

"What? No. I mean, I…"

"Erin," Ally said in a tone gentler than any she'd heard before. "It's just me. I know we don't know each other very well, but you can trust me. And I want to help. I know how hard it is to sleep when your feet and legs get all cramped up. All I want to do is check to make sure you're okay and, if you let me, I'll try to dry them off and maybe give your feet a little massage to take the cramps away."

Erin was fighting her trepidation. "Why?"

"Oh boy. I've done something to upset you, and I'm a dumb lug and don't know what it is."

That admission confused her. Why would Ally think she had done something wrong? It took a second to examine everything from her perspective. When she did, she could see how things looked with her keeping her back to her and refusing her help. "I…I…This is embarrassing. It's just that I don't have any pants on. I can't sleep in big clumsy clothes. It makes me feel all tangled in knots."

"That I understand. I've never been good with nightgowns either. They always make me feel like someone's strangling me."

Erin could sense her moving around the small space, being careful not to touch her or invade her miniscule personal space. When she felt the zipper being opened on her sleeping bag she almost screamed before realizing Ally was unzipping it from the bottom and up only as high as her ankles.

"Okay, let's have a look at the damage."

Forcing herself to remain calm, she chanced a look. Ally had the flashlight in one hand and her face close enough to give her feet a careful inspection.

Finally, she asked, "May I touch them? I'd like to have a good look. Check for blisters and such."

Whimpering out a yes, she watched in fascination as Ally checked one foot, drying it with the front of her oversized sweatshirt before checking and drying off the other.

"Lucky you were wearing quality runners. Anything less might have ripped your feet to shreds. Would it be okay if I massaged out those cramps making your toes look arthritic? I mean, you must be in pain."

"I, yes, okay." Erin closed her eyes. Back in college, she had camped with her one and only boyfriend. When her feet got wet and cramped on a hiking trip, he had manhandled her twisted toes as if that was all she needed. Ally, on the other hand, didn't seem to be in a hurry or rough in any way.

"I'm going to suggest something, but I don't want you to take this wrong. Maybe I should explain?"

"Okay."

"I can do this thing with my physiology. I can warm myself up by raising my body temperature. Well, I'm not actually increasing my temp just getting my core to put out more heat. It can make my skin feel like I'm on fire, like I'm running a temperature, like I have the flu or something. Anyway, when I do it, I can share that warmth without getting cold."

Was she suggesting they get naked and share their body heat and God knows what else?

"Erin. Look at me, please."

Okay. She would set their boundaries, tell her to back off. She looked up.

"All I'm suggesting is you rest one foot against my abdomen, against my skin to warm while I work on the other. If it's too much, that's okay. Whatever you want."

Hardly what she was expecting. What the hell was going on in her head? She knew Ally. Knew her from more than this trip. She had five years of stories and complaints from Pam on Allyson always being the respectful one, so much so, Pam thought she'd lost out on plenty of opportunities to bag women her cousin would never hesitate to jump.

"That's okay. I'm sorry I pushed," Ally said while she continued to gently work the kinks out of her toes and tensed metacarpal tendons.

Erin felt shame. *Why am I behaving this way?* Ally had asked for nothing. Done nothing wrong or forward in any way, but here she was acting like the woman was some lecherous cow. Ally had done nothing but be supportive. *Fuck*, for all she knew, she would have drowned if she hadn't come to her rescue. It wasn't Pam or Rene or even one of the paid guides who had jumped in without a thought for themselves. It was Ally. Ally, who didn't want apologies or explanations. Ally who wanted her just to be her. Ally, who asked for absolutely nothing from her except maybe her share of the communal meal from her catch. "Why did you come after me? I mean, why didn't you let one of the guides jump in?"

She could hear Ally push out a breath like she was trying to sort out some heavy thoughts. "I don't think things through, I just do. I was the last person in the last boat. It never occurred to me someone else should. I'm sure Pam would have gone after you if she'd been in the right place, but she wasn't, and I was. I was sitting in stern of the last raft. I watched you go in and knew I would be the last one able to grab you. I thought I could hang onto you and get you back in the boat. If I had, you'd be camping with Pam, and none of this would be happening."

"I was scared."

"I bet. The water's cold and the river's so strong you could have been killed."

This time Erin didn't stop herself, rolling over to find Ally's naked back. "No. I was scared when you came to bed. I'm scared of how you make me feel."

Ally's eyes finally found hers, clouded with relief and confusion. "I wouldn't…"

Erin rested two fingers against her lips. "I let myself forget what I know about you and wrapped you up with Pam and Rene and all the other women who look at me like… Well, I think you know what they see when they look at me." In Ally's eyes, she could see she didn't understand. "I'm neither trophy wife material, nor do I have some great career to hold up as proof of my worth. For most women that leaves fun time girl and I, well, that's not me."

"I think you're one of the most forthright and beautiful women I've ever met."

It was said so plainly, and with such sincerity, Erin was at a loss for words. Finally, she poured out what she wanted to share. "Ally, I'm a personal assistant. I'm good at it, but it's all I am. I once thought I'd like to go back to school. Maybe get a Masters but…it just never happened. There's nothing special about me."

Shaking her head, Ally took the hand that had migrated from her mouth to her cheek and held it in hers. "Don't say that. What you do has nothing to do with your value as a human being. Look at me. I'm just a charter pilot. Pam's a senior partner with a big firm in Chicago, and look at Connie. She's twenty-two and already making a name for herself in the television industry. You can't imagine how disappointed my mother is. Thank goodness for my granddad. If he hadn't supported me, I'd be cut off and probably working at some flight school teaching rich kids to fly Cessnas for ten bucks an hour. I've done better because I was lucky. Nothing more."

With all the unspoken words tumbling around in her head, it was the action that came without thought. Leaning in Erin kissed Ally, a grazing touch that left her wanting more. Without a reason to stop or any objection, she didn't. It was Ally, ever the one to read her thoughts, who deepened the kiss, but she didn't hesitate. With permission granted, Erin was free to explore those soft, gorgeous lips.

Erin pulled the sweatshirt over her head and added it to the pile that formed her pillow. Her words just seemed to flow from some deep abiding place she hadn't know existed until just now. "I can't imagine you doing a single thing wrong." She moved in closer, taking her hand from Ally for the precious half-second it took to unzip her sleeping bag. "Don't think, Ally. Just be you."

She let Ally pull her into her arms. If the touch of her lips had been glorious, the feel of her skin, their bodies touching, entwining from head to foot was more than overwhelming and sent a wave of pleasure through her, culminating in a long sensuous moan. How could she have doubted this tender woman? The hands that had been so strong on her clammy aching feet now moved with encouraging intensity tracing her shoulders and back, pulling her deeper into their kiss, their embrace.

It was hard not to rush things, to push for more, faster, but she wouldn't risk all this for a fast orgasm. This wasn't sex. It was making love, something she realized deep within her she had never truly experienced. The excitement of attraction and the eagerness of wanting, yes, but not this slow-burning passion.

Was it a kiss that lasted and lasted, or was it kisses, she didn't know and forgot the question when Ally's hands found her small, sensitive breasts. Ally didn't just touch or caress her, she worshipped every inch as she made her way down her body. How was it so easy to read her, understand her? Did she share her thoughts through her touch? Did it matter? This, now, was all Erin wanted, needed to understand.

Halting Ally's downward progress, she teased, "You're not the pilot in command here. Tonight, I'm in charge." She pushed Ally onto her back, letting their full weight and length connect. On her, holding her, touching her, she could feel Ally's hands on her shoulders, back, hips, butt. Slow, gentle, soft and knowing. They fit one another, and the feeling was overwhelming.

Ally was a gift she had longed for late at night alone in her bed. She had wanted a love like this for so long she had almost given up hope, convincing herself that the passion she was experiencing didn't actually exist, at least not in real life.

Yet, this wasn't real life, this was reality TV.

Still, there were no cameras here, no director calling the shots. Just her and Ally, alone and vulnerable and she couldn't find a single moment that rang untrue.

Dipping her head down to take her breast in her mouth, she marveled to realize Ally's breasts weren't much bigger than her own. It was somehow reassuring and fascinating too. They were so different in some respects, even physically; Allyson was a good four inches shorter. She had never been with anyone not at least as tall as she was. Allyson's hair was short, shorter than she usually found attractive, and curly in a crisp almost military fashion. She wanted so much to run her fingers through those curls, if only she had more hands. Her skin was soft, softer than Erin thought possible. Not like silk or satin but somehow more comforting, like warm flannel. And she was hot. Her skin felt hot under Erin's hands, warming her to her extremities. Everything about her warmed her skin, her insides, her heart.

"You are remarkable," Ally gasped, "every inch of you."

Erin, between her raging desire and mounting passion, knew the words were sincere even if hard to believe. "No one's ever thought so."

A long slow moan escaped from Ally. The unpracticed words that followed found their way deep in her heart. "I feel your words, but know the truth of mine. Erin…I feel the world in you."

Erin didn't truly understand, not logically. She understood in a way she would never have in any other circumstance. She understood this was how Ally was. She understood why others didn't, why others didn't get all she had to give. "I want to be your world."

Their words fell like magic around them, flowing through their every move, every touch. Touching, tasting, believing in one another, satisfying each other became their obsession; an obsession that would last all night.

* * *

In the golden glow of the early morning light, Erin lay awake, entwined in Ally's arms and legs, aglow herself with all they were and had been together. She let reality peek in, but pushed it away, away from them, away from their possibilities; worried for all it meant.

"I feel the doubt creeping in." Ally, awake, let her know she could feel it too.

"This, us, was it…"

Ally said quietly, "What I feel won't disappear the moment we exit this tent."

Erin sighed both content and anxious. "I'm worried."

"How very strange to meet like this. I understand, and I will continue to understand, no matter what you may need to do."

For the first time, Ally's words upset her. "What do you mean, 'no matter what I need to do.'"

Allyson moved slightly, just enough so they could talk face-to-face. "You have a life far from mine. I'm not in a position to uproot and go, and I would never expect it would be easier for you either, but that doesn't change all the things I'm feeling, all the things I've been feeling since the moment we were introduced. I imagine I know your feelings, but life is more complicated than just what we feel."

"Stop talking like some self-help book and tell me the truth. Do you want something more between us than what we've just shared?"

Ally looked glad and sad all at once. "You're asking me to bare my soul. Are you sure it's what you want to hear?"

Confused, Erin had to think. Did she want Ally to tell her the truth? Could she listen if it wasn't what she hoped?

"Oh, Erin. I look at you, and all I can think about is how I want to be with you. How I want to build a life with you and how you already have a life that doesn't include me." Her eyes closed, and Erin braced for what she expected would be the death blow to all her hopes. "I could love you forever if you would let me, but I see your hesitation and know you must have a million concerns, and I feel my heart starting to break."

I could love you forever? They knew nothing about each other. But that wasn't exactly true. She knew a lot about Ally, albeit from Pam's point of view. "You don't know me at all," she said, barely able to keep the despair from her voice.

Ally nodded, seeming unwilling to say more. Finally, she said what Erin knew she'd been fighting, what they had both been fighting. "This night, last night, was the most honest and open I've ever been, felt, with anyone. That had to count for something, even with someone as logically driven as you."

What the hell made her think she was logical? None of this was logical. None of it was smart. She was supposed to be Pam's spy, not Ally's fuck buddy.

Rolling out of Ally's arms, she retreated into her sleeping bag. Staving off the cold of the early morning, cold she hadn't felt in Ally's arms. She waited with her back to her; waited for the backlash. The silence that greeted her left her confused and questioning her behavior. Was she behaving logically now? It may not seem so, but she had a life in Chicago; a good job; a boss who depended on her. She felt and heard Ally beside her, sitting up and pulling on her borrowed sweats. The sound of the tent zipper opening struck fear into her heart. *Say something. Say anything. Don't let her leave like this.*

Then the zipper closed on the tent and her heart. She listened as Ally padded off in her bare feet, followed by the distant sound of a conversation with whoever was tending the fire. The tears came so fast and hard she almost choked. Sobbing and convulsing at what she'd done, how she had just broken the one pure thing she'd ever felt. In her instant grief, she tried reassurances on herself. *It's for the best. It's not what I need. It's not the right time. It wouldn't have worked.* None stemmed the tide of tears.

* * *

Ally, shell-shocked and mute, joined the guide and the camerawoman who sat by the fire, morning mugs in hand.

"Hey early bird," the camerawoman called. "We have coffee, and I think your clothes are dry, maybe even your boots."

Ally nodded, accepting an aluminum mug of coffee. Unwilling to trust her voice, she took a sip of the scalding brew, never mentioning her distaste for the drink. This morning she would be a coffee drinker. *Might as well.* In her mind, nothing else made sense either. She found a place to sit and parked herself, hoping the others would think her still half-asleep and not pester her. Luckily, Sandy the camerawoman and Charlie the young native guide were in a deep conversation Ally couldn't follow and was not inclined to try.

Ally concentrated her efforts on watching the forest as the nocturnal life bade its farewell and the sun began to rise. Today would be a difficult day. For the life of her, she couldn't understand what she'd done wrong. Had she said too much, too little, the wrong thing? At the edge of losing control of her emotions, she did what she always did, concentrated on business.

In a few weeks, Triangle Airlines would be all theirs. Would they change the name? Her granddad wanted it to become Parker Airlines, but old man Pringle argued for continuity. What were KC's thoughts on the matter? She had contended that most people these days associated the triangle with the LGBT community, not the Golden Triangle it was named for.

What would Erin say? She pushed all thoughts of Erin from her mind, but knew down deep she could never actually do that. Did she love her? *Yes.* Was it too soon. *Yes.* Was it misguided? *Maybe.* But it was what it was. If they never met again, she knew Erin would always have a place in her heart. Would she write her love letters? *No.* She understood it would not be received in the vein of her intention. Would she send gifts? Maybe a birthday gift. Something small and silly to say no hard feelings. Or would she fall prey to sentiment and send something terribly personal? That was more in line with the type of mistake she would make. Letting go was hard, but what if the thing she needed to let go of was something she'd never really had? *I could love you forever.* Why on earth had she said such a thing? They made love. They connected on a level she'd never experienced. *And yet, I was wrong to say so. I was wrong to hope. Now all I can do is concentrate on what I can do. I can fly. I can run a business. I should be happy with that.*

As hope soured, she drank the bitter coffee she disliked and recited checklists for her aircraft. The practice stilling her mind of all the shards of hope slicing her heart to pieces. *Seat belts, on; flight controls, free and correct; throttle, closed; landing light, off; engine anti-ice, off; hydraulics, on; fuel valve, on-guard in place; altimeter, set; instruments, static at zero; battery, on; caution lights, engine out—transmission oil press—low rotor rpm; caution lights, press to test; fuel quantity, check; collective, down; rotors, clear...*

CHAPTER SIXTEEN

Week three had been long and torturous for crew and participants alike. The biggest upset was the elimination of Rene. No one had seen that coming. Connie had attributed it to Allyson's renewed interest in getting to know the five women she had chosen in the last ceremony. What she didn't admit, and what no one would ever learn, was Rene's confession that among the six women she had selected and was getting to know, she could not consider a single one she would want to marry. They had talked candidly and privately, and Rene admitted she would rather take her chances next season than pretend to fall for someone, anyone, this time around.

While the contestants cast their final vote for the last two queens they most wanted to be with, Connie arranged to have three separate cameras record the votes. That way no one except for her and Rene, not even the crew, would have the big picture as to which two queens would make the final round. The original concept she had pitched would have taken the queens down to one final choice, but after the loss of Virginia and her investment dollars, she had decided to only take it down to these last two. Now it looked to be up to Ally and Pam to deliver results. One of them had to get down on one knee, or she'd never get renewed.

With both queens in until the end, Connie had a better chance one would propose. Without a proposal, she knew the series would come under fire from the network, and that would be it. She needed a win and was betting her sister or cousin would become serious enough about one woman to take things to their scripted conclusion. If not, she was counting on her relationship with them, and their investment, to pressure them into a proposal for now. She would pull the same stunt they had used with the first edition of *Joe Millionaire*, getting the lead to propose and then announcing after the show aired that things just hadn't worked out and the engagement had been called off. She was counting on being able to persuade one of them, if not Pam, then Ally. Ally had always been there for her. If Pam wouldn't bend the knee, she was counting on Ally to get down and propose to someone, anyone, just as long as she got a proposal out of this.

They had shared dates, played sports, gone on tours, and camped out with the contestants. All that was left was for the two queens to choose their three finalists. Tomorrow, they would begin three days of half-day dates. Finally, each would have an overnight date. Connie had to be careful who she chose for that last night. She wanted it to be someone the audience would cheer to see together with her chosen queen, a favorite, but that was hard to gauge in production. And she didn't want to alienate the actual woman Pam or Ally might be interested in, but she needed some upsets too.

Of course Pam would have no problem bedding her second choice and then getting down on one knee the next day for someone else, but Ally would be a problem. At least Ally lived close by. It would be easy to send a crew into the city with her and to film them at her apartment. Pam was a problem. They didn't have the money any more to hire a US production crew, and they couldn't send their crew into the states without work visas, even to film just one night. Following Ally's advice, she called their grandfather and asked permission to stage Pam's three days of personal treatment in their ancestral home at the estate in Highland Creek. He had chuckled and approved, letting her know he would be happy to disappear for a few days and let Pam have the place to herself. Her aunt Patricia was in residence, but he promised he would convince her to join him on a little impromptu getaway. Perhaps Quebec City and the Château Laurier. She loved it there. Or he'd offer to take her to Milan for a little shopping. That, he was sure, would take care of Connie's need for the house and Pam's desire for a little privacy.

Now all she needed to do was sort out just who Pam and Ally would choose as their final three. That would have to wait. For now, she had the final face-to-face for each contestant. They would have ten minutes alone and on camera with each queen. Once all eighteen contestants had cycled through their on-screen time with the queens, they would vote for the one they wanted to be with. She'd set it up so the voting would take place in the three locations where the private meeting would be held. That way, no one could compare the results, except her and maybe her editor. She assumed some would be surprised when Rene was eliminated, but that was to be expected. Upsets were good as far as reality TV went.

It took a gruelling six hours to film the one-on-one sequences and the elimination vote. When Connie finally joined everyone in the ballroom, she could see they were tired. Determined to make this scene work, she sent the contestants off to change into their designer duds, explaining she needed time to prepare the three queens for this scene. Once the room cleared, she pulled out chairs for Rene, Pam, and Ally. "Are you guys ready to film this last scene?"

"When do we get to see who voted for whom?" Pam asked.

"Never, you brat. The voting is confidential. All you get to do is stand there and smile or frown if you're eliminated. Now here's what I expect you each to do…"

Ally stood on the spot marked with an X in gaffer tape. She just wanted to get this over. Already it felt like the longest three weeks of her life, and she wanted her life back. She felt her part had been a clusterfuck from the start. Not that the production was disorganized or anything, it was just that she knew she was nothing more than window dressing for Pam's big moment. At least she would be eliminated tonight and could leave this whole fiasco and get back to work. It would be hard. Her heart still felt completely stomped on and shredded to bits, but once she was back at home she could concentrate on work and wouldn't have to see Erin ever again. *Erin.* What the hell had she been thinking? The woman was smart, poised, beautiful. Women like that never went for her unless they knew about her family, unless they were clued into her financial success. And those weren't the kind of women she wanted to share her life with. She wanted a partner. A confidant. An equal in heart, mind, and soul. *A pipe dream.* She scolded herself for her lapse in judgment, but honestly, she had thought, had truly believed that Erin had felt the same.

* * *

Connie watched as one by one the women entered the ballroom and took their place like a choir, situated on one side with Ally, Pam, and Rene standing center stage. Tommy was back with mic in hand, ready to announce the two queens who would remain. Tomorrow morning they would have time to play by the pool with the two remaining queens, not alone, but as a group. It would be time for the women to strut their stuff for Pam and Ally because they would then select the three contestants they were most attracted to. That was a conversation she would have to have with Ally and Pam but later, after they had this scene in the can and Rene said her farewells.

"ACTION!"

Tommy began, "It's been four weeks since our queens chose just six women they wanted to get to know and an amazing six weeks in all, with high-flying antics to romantic getaways to life-threatening drama. You've just watched the women vote for their final two choices. They've had time to get to know each of the queens and spend time with their favorite. Now it's time to learn which queen is their Queen of Hearts." Tommy continued his scripted dialogue, explaining how the two Primaries with the most votes would continue and how they too would soon need to cast their votes in an elimination round that would reduce the number of women competing for their hearts to just three each. "That's right. Only three contestants each will remain. Who will go home we can only guess at because tonight the choice is not that of the queens but the women who will eliminate one, bringing us closer to learning who will truly be the Queen of Hearts. Ladies, are we ready to let these hopefuls know who it is you favor?" They nodded and offered encouragement as directed.

Dramatically, Tommy moved to his second mark, placed strategically in front of Rene, Ally, and Pam. "Are you three ready to learn who our wonderful women have fallen for?" He looked first to Pam, then Ally, and finally Rene. On cue, each gave her scripted permission to proceed. "When I call your name, please step forward and take your place as the final two queens competing for the love of one of these amazing women." He paused for effect while the cameras focused on the tense faces of the three queens. "With the most votes, our women have chosen… Pamela."

There was applause and a certain amount of revelry from the contestants, all of which the cameras caught, and Connie would carefully edit in later.

"Pam, please join me," he invited her, and with a breathtaking smile she walked to the place marked on the floor. "How do you feel knowing you're the favorite among these ladies?"

"I'm overwhelmed with joy. All I can hope is that I live up to their expectations."

Allowing another pause for the cameras to move to the next position, he waited for Connie's cue, explaining, "As much as we have come to love and respect our two final queens, we know there can only be one Queen of Hearts." Looking dramatically to Rene and Allyson, he waited for Connie to cue that he could continue. "Rene, Allyson. You two have had quite the ride. Rene, you shared your love of car racing, and Ally, your passion for flying, but in the end, the women have made their choice, and only one of you can continue. I will say the vote was close, closer than expected. Still, only one can proceed. Are you ready to hear which of you that will be?"

Rene answered first, as Connie directed. "Tommy, I have loved every minute here and these women, I never expected to meet so many interesting and sexy ladies. No matter what the verdict, it's been my pleasure to take part in the *Queen of Hearts*."

"And you Ally. How are you feeling?" Tommy asked on cue.

"I'm nervous, but as Rene said, I've had the time of my life. In my work, it's rare to meet any women, so my time with so many smart and beautiful women as those gathered here, has been a gift I'll always cherish." Contrary to Connie's direction, it was clear she was delivering these words to just one of the eighteen women standing carefully arranged for the cameras.

"The second queen selected tonight is… Allyson! Rene, I'm sorry, but you are not the Queen of Hearts. I must ask you to say your goodbyes and leave Glendennon Castle."

They watched as Rene nodded her understanding then walked first to a stunned Ally, giving her a hug and shaking her hand in congratulations, then to Pam. She waved to the women and exited out the grand entry where another cameraperson was waiting and would follow her out to her car. Once she was out of sight, Tommy called on a confused and overwhelmed Ally to join him.

Stepping clumsily to her mark, she looked more like someone who had just been eliminated, not the other way around.

"Ally, I must say, you look a little shocked. Are you surprised to be chosen by our women?"

"Surprised? Tommy, I'm downright…" She stopped herself from falling on a well-worn expletive. "I…I'm beside myself. I had no idea there were enough women who had taken an interest in me to keep me in the competition. I'm…thank you," she said, looking thoughtfully at the contestants. "I'm honored and hope I can live up to your expectations."

"Now I know you and Pam are cousins. Do you feel any rivalry coming into this final round?"

"I guess I should, but I don't. Where my heart is concerned, I can only try to be open and honest."

"Pamela, why don't you join us?" He waved for Pam to stand beside Ally. "Now tell me truthfully, are you feeling any competitive pull with Allyson here?"

"Oh, Tommy. What a question! I know Ally's right about one thing. The *Queen of Hearts* is about finding love, true love. In a way, this competition has given us so many opportunities and the flexibility to make choices that fit us both. I just hope when it gets down to selecting our final three women, we aren't competing for the same one."

"Do you believe the way the women voted tonight will influence your choices going into the final elimination round?"

"Not at all. First, we don't know how they voted. Both Ally and I will have to depend on our hearts to steer us in the right direction. Honestly, I've grown attached to many of the women in this room. Going into next week's elimination, I already know the three women who have the greatest chance of taking my heart forever."

"And you, Ally. Are there three women dangerously close to winning your heart?"

"Tommy, these women are all unique and who wouldn't fall for any of them. But three? No, at this moment there is only one I have my heart set on. But…this isn't like other shows. It's not just me getting to choose. Each woman gets her say, gets to choose if I'm right for her. She could prefer Pam and why wouldn't she. It's not a one-way thing, and I can only hope my heart finds the right woman for me."

Ally tried to listen as Tommy prattled on. It was all she could do not to fixate on Erin in her stunning cocktail dress. Her long legs and carved calves made her mouth water to be with her again. The dress she suspected was too short for Erin's tastes was stunning, but it was the woman wearing it that took her breath away. Trying not to give herself away or make Erin any more uncomfortable in her presence than she already was, she turned her full attention to Tommy and Pam and the conversation flowing around her. *All I have to do is get through the week. I'll be eliminated in the final round, and Pam can have her day, or night or whatever. Just as long as I'm out and I never have to see Erin again, there's a chance I'll survive. That's all I can hope for now.*

CHAPTER SEVENTEEN

Connie let them sleep in. Of course, sleeping in was a relative term with her. A PA had awakened Ally at eight thirty and ordered her into pool attire, with instructions to get her ass down to the patio by nine. Tired and a little cranky, she had done as she was told, dressing in a suit with boy shorts and a tank top. When she reached the ballroom where the buffet was set up, Connie grabbed her, ordering her to switch out the tank top for a T-shirt she was carrying.

"Is this mine?" Ally asked in confusion. Connie was holding up her Cabbagetown Boxing Club T. Except someone had cut down the crew neck to a deep V and removed the sleeves. At least they had sewn the edges so it didn't look like she was wearing a ripped-up shirt. She would never do that, not even with her workout wear which was what this T-shirt was for. She started to pull it over her suit when Connie stopped her.

"No, take the bathing suit top off and wear this instead."

"I…Connie, that's a bit much for me." The T-shirt was a tight fit. Good for a sweaty workout but not for hanging out by the pool. It would show off just a little more than she was comfortable sharing. But Connie pointed out the French doors to where Pam was laughing and joking with several women. She was wearing a skimpy bikini. Ally wasn't surprised. Pam had always been proud of her body, even a bit vain.

Groaning, and turning her back to the few women still milling around the buffet table, she tore off the bathing suit top and pulled on the T. "There! Now can I have a blessed cup of tea or am I supposed to throw in a table dance too?"

Connie grinned. She was long used to Ally being a grump in the morning. "Get your ass outside. I'll have someone bring you some tea and maybe a leg to chew on, you brute."

Ally groaned for effect. She did love the kid, but man oh man, Connie was going to owe her big for this. She walked out on the patio, noticing the cameras and how the lounge chairs had been arranged into two very separate groups. Before she could decide which set was for her, Mary, the overtly fresh woman who had crossed her personal boundaries during the first-week regatta, was at her side and didn't waste a second claiming her prize. Ally had been saved from her advances when she set her sights on Rene. Now that she was gone, it looked like Mary was hedging her bets on her.

Allowing Mary to direct her to the loungers set out for her, Ally quietly removed her hand from her ass, and taking a seat, stretched out her legs to prevent Mary from sitting on the end. Across the patio, she couldn't help noticing Erin's eyes on her. She was so caught in her look, she almost missed Mary cocking her leg like she intended to straddle her. Grabbing the leg in motion, she smiled decisively. "Geez Mar. I haven't even had my first coffee!" That sent the woman scurrying off to bring her a cup.

Another woman, this one from her group, laughed at her move. "She doesn't even know you don't drink coffee!"

The woman beside her added, "She would if she'd taken half a second to get to know you." Of the five women who had spent time with her over the last week, Teresa and Bobby Ann were the only ones who had bothered to join her. *I guess that tells me everything I need to know about who is interested in me.* "Please, please, please don't let her get that close again."

Teresa was giggling while Bobby Ann moved two loungers closer to Ally. "There, we'll each cover a flank, but you're on your own if she comes at you in a frontal assault."

"Spoken like a true tactician. Thank you, both."

They gabbed and talked about last night's ceremony with Ally, generally making her feel better. One of the caterers delivered a full pot of tea and all the accoutrements. Not sure what to do with the tray, Ally asked her to set it on the foot of the lounger. She hoped Mary would get the hint. As far as she was concerned, this was the woman's last day at Glendennon Castle. She had no idea who Pam wanted for her three finalists, but Mary didn't even come close to making Pam's list, and she certainly wouldn't be on hers no matter how fresh she got. When she returned, coffee cup in hand, Ally was kind but frank. "Why don't you go enjoy the pool and the amenities." Her message clear—this is your last day so enjoy it.

Beyond angered, Mary heaved the cup at her. For a moment it looked like the coffee mug would hit her square in the head. Ally wasn't sure if Mary was a bad shot or she had ducked fast enough, but the resounding sound of china hitting the patio stones behind her was enough to stop all conversation.

Ally stood. Never one to back down from a fight, she was stunned by the level of vitriol that sprang from the woman's mouth. The camera crew, of course, caught the whole thing while Connie and two of the PAs wrestled with Mary, pulling, then leading her out. Across the patio, she noted Erin's look. She didn't hide a smile. Was she pleased the woman was angry with her? It was all so confusing.

It didn't take long for the place to right itself. As conversations were resumed, a few other women strolled over to ask Ally what had brought on Mary's assault. Thankfully, Bobby Ann came to her rescue.

"Turns out Mary doesn't like tea."

A few laughed, and that was that, at least for them. Sitting back, she finally got to pour her tea. The first sip was like an instant tonic of pure relief. Confiding in Teresa and Bobby Ann, she admitted, "For a second there I thought she'd follow that cup with her fists."

Teresa, a little shocked by it all, was reluctant to understand that women could be as badly behaved as men. Bobby Ann, however, had seen it before. "I dated a woman like that once. I'll be honest, she was a tiger in the sack, but boy oh boy, there was no talking her down when she got angry. It's no way to have a relationship."

"Please tell me she didn't hit you?" Ally asked with concern. "I mean, I know it happens, but why? I just can't figure why."

"Once," she admitted. "After that, no amount of great sex could lure me back."

"Good for you," Ally said. She noticed the camera crew had followed Connie and the PAs has they hauled Mary out. Looking around and trying to relax, she spotted Erin's eyes on her again. She would look away every time Ally caught her eyes, but she still kept looking.

Bobby Ann too, picked up on Erin's continued interest, asking, "Just how many women have you pissed off?"

"It's my superpower."

Teresa, quieter and more reserved than Bobby Ann, almost spewed her coffee all over them. She swallowed hard, releasing a snorting laugh before clamping her hands over her mouth.

"Better hide," Bobby Ann advised. "Looks like your superpowers are in full swing."

Storming out from the ballroom, Connie marched to her side, practically manhandling her from the lounger and dragging her back inside.

Clear of the French doors and any view from the patio, she couldn't keep the act up and began laughing harder than Ally could remember her ever doing. Finally under control, she hugged Ally. "I don't know what the hell that woman thought she was doing but fuck me, this is going to be a great show!"

"You liked that, did you? I just admitted to my two, and my only followers, that pissing women off is my superpower."

"You." Connie shook her head, leading her from the ballroom and up the stairs to the classroom used as her production office.

Ally hadn't been in this room since the first day when they were hanging 8x10 photos of all the participants. Now the whiteboard was rearranged, but all the photos remained. Rene's pic had a red X through it and had been moved to the sideboard where the X'ed out photos of the eliminated contestants hung along with Virginia's, the first queen out. On the main board, Pam's and Ally's pics were on top and the group of contestants still vying for their queen clustered below.

Connie grabbed Mary's picture and moved it to the other board, offering Ally the red marker. "Care to do the honors?"

"Oh no. I'll leave all the X'ing to you, boss."

Without a second's hesitation, she crossed out Mary. "Good, that takes care of that bitch. If I'd known you could get a woman mad that fast I would have put her back in your group last week."

"Trouble?"

"Even Rene said she was a psycho bitch. I've been looking for a way to ax her since day one so thanks for that."

"As I said, it's my superpower."

"Is that why Erin's so pissed at you?"

Ally colored, but didn't answer. What could she say? We made love, and I professed my affection, and it upset her enough that she hadn't said a word to her since? What she needed to gain her forgiveness she wasn't sure. Ally's lack of comprehension was a recurring theme with all her relationships. Of course, she had never felt like this for anyone else. Still, it was how things went for her when it came to women. It was probably the only reason she and KC had never gotten together. They respected each other too much to fuck it up with sex.

"Okay, so you're not talking either." Connie stood with her arms crossed. "Well, you just did me a biggie, another of several, so I won't beat you up, but I have it on good authority there might have been a spark between you two, but if you're not interested…"

"Who said there was…a spark?"

"Oh no. I'm not tattling. The point here is I need to know who you plan on eliminating tonight, and I need to know if there's a chance you want time to turn things around with Erin."

"Why?"

"Oh Ally, Why, why, why? That's not the right question, and you know it. Stop acting obtuse. It doesn't suit you. Now tell me, is there something between you two?"

"No." It was a simple statement, and the truth of it renewed the ache she had been trying to ignore.

Connie sighed, but didn't give up. "Okay. Let me put it this way. Would you have liked there to be something between you?"

Ally couldn't answer. If she said no she would be lying, if she said yes, Connie wouldn't let up until she had every torrid detail.

"Sit!" Connie ordered. She might be eighteen years younger than her cousin, but she was the director, and she was clearly in charge. "I see we'll have to do this the hard way. So, let me tell you what I know. One, you jumped in the Ottawa River rapids when no one else did. Two, you hung on to the woman as if your life depended on it. Three, you pulled out all your fancy survival skills to care for her until rescuers could reach you. Four, you retired to a tent alone, where I have it on good authority you made love for most of the night. Five, and this is the one I can't figure out, you stormed from that tent in the early dawn, and the two of you haven't shared as much as a single word since. And six!" She was really on a roll counting off her evidence. "You two still can't keep your eyes off each other, even if you can't be alone in the same room."

Ally sat silently brooding. What could she say? How could she explain? When Connie's stink eye started to burn, she pushed past the shame to try. "Connie, I… She… It…"

"Oh my God! You're in love with her!" She started pacing around the room, her clear glee the opposite of what Ally had expected. "This is perfect, just perfect." She was talking more to herself than Allyson. Grabbing a handheld radio from the table, she called for a PA to ask Pam to join them in the office. "Ally, this is friggin' perfect. Oh man! Never in a million years would I figure you would be the one to fall, this is amazing!" she sang out.

Not amused by Connie's ecstasy, Ally had to toss some water on this fire before it truly got out of control. "Ah, Con, I think you're forgetting something. It doesn't matter how I feel if the woman hates me. Fuck. They all hate me."

Stopped in her tracks, Connie backtracked to where she was sitting. "Al, I know you must be hurt, but I don't think you see the big picture. Yes, she's upset about something, but from where I'm sitting she's still plenty interested in you. We've still got time to turn this around. All you have to do is pick her to be one of your final three. Whatever went wrong, you'll have time to talk about it, maybe even get past whatever the problem is."

"Right. I can see it now. I'll call her name, and she'll walk right by me again. Let's face it. Even if she is interested in me, which I'm sure she isn't, but let's say she is, how can I compete with Pam? Fuck it. Even I would pick Pam over me."

"I don't think you have to worry about that this time. Please Al, just trust me on this and tell me you'll pick her."

"Pick who?" Pam asked as she walked in.

Connie smiled like the big bad wolf. "Ally was just telling me that she wants to pick Erin to be in her final three."

Pam soured on the spot. "No damn way! Erin's in my final three, and that's it. End of discussion."

"Pam, come on! You know you aren't interested in her, and I think there's a chance there could be something real between these two."

"Real?" Pam chortled her disbelief. "Please, that would never happen. Besides, I already said I need Erin so no deal."

"Stop it!" Connie warned. "You're being a brat."

Ally didn't know what was going on, but she had caught a look between the sisters. "I'm sorry Pam. I didn't know you were attracted to her."

Pam threw back her head as if she would laugh uncontrollably.

Ally was sure this was one of her stage theatrics for the courtroom and wondered why she was suddenly getting the treatment. She listened and watched as guarded words and looks flew back and forth between the sisters. "Will someone tell me what's going on?"

"Nothing," Connie insisted, but neither she or Pam would look her in the face.

"Are you in love with her?" she asked Pam, sincerely hoping the answer would be no. The response she got was nothing she would have imagined. Pam started to laugh.

"God damn it, Pam!" Connie warned again. "Enough!"

"Forget it. Look Con, the jig is up. You might as well tell her, or I will."

"Tell me what?" Ally was afraid to hear the answer. Were Pam and Erin lovers? Were they involved before the show even began?

Grabbing her older sister by the arm, Connie looked desperate to put an end to whatever was going on, but Pam would have none of it. Shaking off her grip, she turned her anger on Ally. "You can't have Erin because she isn't a contestant. She's my assistant, you dumb ass, and here to keep me informed of what the other women are saying and thinking. So no. You can't have her. You can't touch her, and more than anything, there is no way I'll let a smart girl like her get mixed up with the likes of you."

Ally's face, hot red, looked as if Pam had slapped her. The shock, the confusion, it all came tumbling down on her. If she hadn't already been seated, she would have fallen down. Like a goalie who'd taken one too many head shots, she stood, wavering slightly, then pushed out of the room and straight out the front door. If she could have run, she would have and kept on going. Instead, she stumbled down the stone steps, almost into the shrubs, falling to her knees. She threw up the tea and the few bits of fruit she'd managed to get down, then followed with dry heaves. She heaved again then got to her feet and tried to run. Stumbling, she fell, crawled, stood again, stumbled and fell over and over until she reached the Huey. She was in no shape to fly but could take refuge with the only female who had never let her down.

Crawling into the back of the helicopter, she curled up on the cold steel floor and cried, just cried.

CHAPTER EIGHTEEN

Erin knew she had to talk to Ally, needed to desperately. She needed to apologize, needed to explain, but first and foremost, Ally needed to know the truth. Yes, she liked her, was attracted to her, could even admit she had feelings, deep, deeper than she could understand, but that didn't change why she was here. If they were to have a chance, regardless of this stupid show, she needed her to hear the truth of why she was here, and now, before the truth slipped out. It would be just like Pam to let her cover slip if she thought she could use it to her advantage. She didn't think she would do it vindictively, but like she was a shark in court, once that competitive edge crept in there was no telling how she would react.

Erin had been waiting on the patio with everyone else, ignoring Pam's parade of "Oh, look at me," and waiting for Ally to show. When she did, she was pleased to see there wasn't a crowd of women vying to be at her side the way they fluttered to Pam. It also broke her heart. Ally was just as much the catch as Pam, maybe more so. She was certain she knew enough about Allyson now, not just from the stories she'd heard but from her own experience with the woman to know she wasn't the type to step out on her partner. Pam, on the other hand, didn't exactly have a great record. She knew Pam was zeroing in on two or three women but a proposal, if it happened—she doubted it would ever culminate in a wedding much less a long and happy marriage. It just wasn't in her DNA.

When Ally finally showed, she knew immediately she was tired and hurt. *I did that.* She needed to find a quiet moment where she could approach Ally and ask for a few minutes to talk. Watching Mary cock her leg as if she wanted to piss all over her prize and claim Ally as all hers—it had made her cringe, but she wanted to applaud the way Ally handled her. She couldn't guess what she said, but at least the woman had scurried off. She had started to walk in that direction when Pam hooked her arm.

"Not in the mood to swim?"

"Maybe later. Once I've digested my breakfast."

"Oh sweetie, you should be like me and skip the whole damn thing. It does wonders for your figure."

Startled by the comment, she was clueless to understand it. Was her boss saying she was fat? And what if she was, which she wasn't. She was healthy and fit and the exact right size for a woman of her height and age. Not like some of the walking skeletons fawning over Pam for an ounce of her attention. Before she could think of what to say, a commotion on the other side of the patio brought the world to a stop.

Mary was back and had, for who knows what reason, thrown a full cup of coffee over Ally's head. Or had she been aiming for her? The long unbroken line of obscenities that followed brought the attention of all the women, the camera crew, and the director. Suddenly Connie and her helpers clamped onto Mary and began hauling her out. That didn't stop the litany of accusations flowing from her angry mouth. *Oh, Ally!* At that moment, her heart broke for her lover and friend. *Lover?* That word stuck in her mind, and it was all she could do not to run to her side. For once she was thankful for Teresa and Bobby Ann. Bobby Ann especially. She had a feeling that woman could fight the devil herself and come out without a scratch.

When things began to settle, and Pam resumed presiding over her court, she knew she had to make her way over. She caught Ally's eye a few times, but for some reason felt she had to wait for her to signal it was all right to join them. Before she could make her intention clear, Connie was back and had hooked Allyson by the arm and pulled her from the patio. Stunned that anyone would pin this on Ally, especially the intrepid Connie Coen-Parker, all she could hope was that the whole thing was for effect and it did have the women speculating to beat the band.

With her chance to talk gone, she decided to join Teresa and Bobby Ann. She had a feeling these two would be the ones rewarded with final selection by Ally, if for no other reason than their willingness to stand guard with her. Walking across the patio, another thing dawned on her: she wanted to be the third in that group, wanted to have time with Ally. Even if it was divided with those other two good women, at least it would give them the time to learn more about one another if it didn't provide the time she craved to explore what they had started.

Erin had just reached the two women sitting in loungers when a PA asked Pam to join Connie in the production office.

"There goes our second queen," Bobby Ann said, as Erin reached them. "Hey, Erin! Want to join the crazy club?"

"Will there be any more flying coffee cups?"

"Not from us, but if it's important to you, I'll see what we can do."

"Uh, no. I'm good, but that was something."

Teresa, always the quiet observer, smiled her welcome. "Always room for a normal person," she said.

"Tell me about it," Bobby Ann added, pulling her lounger aside to make room for Erin. "Might as well park it. You and I can sit here and gab or watch the Pam Show."

"Nothing there to interest you, Teresa?"

She smiled, but it was Bobby Ann who answered. "T's writing a novel. She'll bury herself in her work in about ten seconds. So that leaves you and me to figure out what's going on."

"Well, my guess, one of the PAs is helping Mary pack her bags, and another has called a cab."

"For sure, her ass is outta here and none too soon. What I can't believe is that Rene actually picked her to stay past the first elimination."

Erin nodded, settling into the deck chair Ally had vacated, asking Teresa, "You're writing a novel? That sounds so exciting and hard."

She nodded, pulling out the notebook she carried religiously in her oversized bag.

"It's top secret," Bobby Ann explained. "Me, I've got money on a romance featuring a strong female lead who charms all the women then leaves their hearts broken." She nodded toward the other group of women who had been buzzing around Pam and now looked lost without her.

"Okay. Bobby Ann, I have to ask. You're not like any of those social climbing wannabes. Teresa, you too for that matter. Why would you sign up for this circus?"

"As our writer-in-residence is busy penning her opus, I'll answer for us both. Teresa needed time away from her work to finish her manuscript and a month of hanging out at a posh castle and getting free food and booze was a lot cheaper than a writer's retreat. As for me, I guess I did it for a lark. Actually, a few friends challenged me, and I love me a challenge. Truthfully, I didn't expect to last this long. How about you?"

"Pretty much the same. My boss kind of twisted my arm," Erin said, sticking to what was the truth.

"I hear, yeah. So, I can see you're not interested in Ms. Perfect Pamela. Or have I read you all wrong?"

Erin couldn't help the smile, "Guilty as charged," she admitted, then thought to ask, "What gave me away?"

Bobby Ann smiled, letting her know she was okay with what she was about to share. "I've got this feeling you would rather be over here at the nerd table. Hanging with the cool kids doesn't seem to be rockin' your world."

There was no denying the charge. "Ally seems so...I don't know, *normal* doesn't sound right."

"I know what you mean. Can I ask another question?"

"Why not. Might as well go right down the rabbit hole."

Bobby Ann laughed at that. "I like you, Erin. I have a feeling you're good people, so I'll lay it out for you. I like Ally. I like her a lot."

She could feel a challenge coming on, and her heart began to hurt more than it already did.

"T here likes Ally a lot too, but not nearly as much as she likes that damn book she's writing. Me, I love the woman, but I wouldn't walk down the aisle with her. Now her business partner, that KC woman! If I could get my hands on her, I'd never let go. I know that's terrible to say, but it is what it is."

Erin was stunned. Here were the only two women who showed an interest in Ally and neither was truly interested in her romantically. "So, why the show? I mean, it looks to the world like you two can't wait to get your hands on her."

"Ally's fun, and she's nice, way nicer than that lot over there. I guess I'm feeling a little protective and T, well, look at her. Head into whatever it is she's writing. Ally respects that and she's cool with her real objective. I have a feelin' we'll all be friends for years to come. Now my question is, what are you going to do?"

"Is this the protective part of you kicking in, or are you just worried Ally's third pick will be her Yoko, and break up the band?"

Bobby Ann laughed. "I knew I liked you! Come on. Let's leave T to work on her script while we grab another coffee and see if we can pick up any gossip from the crew on what exactly is going on with all the Parker women holed up in the office."

Erin followed Bobby Ann, relieved and just as curious as her to know what Pam, Ally, and Connie were discussing that required them to close themselves in for as long as they had.

CHAPTER NINETEEN

No one had seen hide nor hair of Pam or Ally all day. Now gathered in the ballroom, set to record the final elimination ceremony, the women seemed on edge. The whole place did. The crew, Connie, even Tommy Proulx looked nervous, and the man did this sort of thing for a living. Just like all the earlier eliminations, they were grouped to the side and all done out in designer dresses and a few suits. The camera crew shot something called B Roll while Tommy and Connie stood well off to the other side of the room discussing who knew what. Finally, the camera crew moved to the place they had been for the other ceremonies and told Connie they were ready. Except there were no queens present. Erin could only assume Connie wanted them to make an entrance. She knew Pam would love that, love the attention. Ally? Not so much.

It was another twenty minutes of standing around and wondering what to do before they heard the tell-tale sound of a helicopter landing, and it was coming down on the back lawn, maybe right on the patio. Curious, most of the women, who had been enjoying the champagne, took the opportunity to move to the closed French doors. This landing explained why the doors were closed. If they had been open, the whirlwind caused by the machine would have ruined a lot of perfectly coifed hair. Walking to one of the French doors with Teresa and Bobby Ann at her side, Erin was surprised to see the network traffic helicopter land, the big emblazoned Channel One Traffic unmistakable on the side.

"Is that KC?" Bobby Ann asked.

"It must be," Erin said, adding, "the big helicopter is still out front, so I don't know who else it could be."

"Well, this is getting interesting. What do you think, T? What does your writer's brain make of this?"

"It would explain why we're so late getting started. Doesn't KC fly the evening traffic report?"

They watched as Connie rushed out to the helo the moment the blades came to a stop. The pilot climbed out of the machine, pulling off her helmet and tossing it back inside. It was KC, and she wrapped a sisterly arm around Connie, who led her in via the poolside and not the ballroom doors.

"Something's wrong," Bobby Ann speculated.

Teresa, forced to leave her notebook in the dorm, was more attentive than usual. "I didn't think Ally was bothered by that whole incident with Bloody Mary."

"No. I don't think she was either," Bobby Ann agreed. "Any guess?" she asked Erin.

"Not a clue but at least whatever's happening, you may get a chance to flirt with KC. That's gotta be something."

"Oh yeah!" Bobby Ann said with a grin. "Still, something, as they say, is afoot."

Teresa groaned. "Okay, Sherlock. How's about you go suck up to Sandy and see if she has any idea what's up."

Sandy, the lead camera, was busy keeping busy.

"Hardly. She's the one who can't keep her eyes off you."

"Really?" Erin asked, surprised by that. The things you learn when you put more than one lesbian in a room. Taking a page from Bobby Ann's book she challenged, "Go on, T! We need answers, and you have the inside advantage. Go!"

* * *

KC walked with Connie to the indoor pool, where Ally was sitting alone. She looked better than she had sounded when she'd called that morning. "Hey, Al. You okay?"

She nodded, but still didn't trust herself to speak without breaking down. One of the crew had spent an elaborate amount of time with makeup and concealer, hiding her swollen eyes and red nose. She looked good, or at least normal, but KC knew better.

"Con, why don't you go get Pam's dumb ass ready to go. I'll have a little pep talk with my buddy and meet you…where do you want her?"

"Main door to the ballroom. As soon as I see you guys there, I'll call Action." Turning to Ally she promised, "We're all ready. All you have to do is walk out, take your mark and say your three names. Tommy knows the score. He's not going to pull you in for a one-on-one. So, no worries, you've got this."

Allyson just nodded, but didn't make eye contact. That had Connie worried. Still, KC gave her a signal that she would handle things and she was confident she would.

Once she was gone, KC pulled a deck chair over next to Ally. "Fucking women, eh? You can't live with them, and you can't shoot 'em."

That cracked the slightest smirk from Ally. Not because it was funny, it was just KC's fallback whenever she had woman troubles.

"So, big bad old Pammy played you…again! Fuck, that bitch gets under my skin. I probably woulda killed her by now, but I have a feeling I'll need her to bail my ass out one day, so it's a no-win, either way."

Ally nodded.

Wrapping an arm around Ally's hunched shoulders, KC was quiet for a few minutes. An eternity for KC. "Listen, I was goin' to tell you. After that flight you took up to Petawawa with PP3, I don't know what you said, but that boy's really trying to straighten out his act. Oh, he's still an ass, but he finally understands he's not the boss's grandkid anymore, and he only has a job as long as we're happy with him. It's night and day. So, kudos. Really... Ah, what else... Oh, I got a new tow bar from DeHavilland and topped up the spares. And I worked out a new training rate with Flight Safety for our pilots. I found an old girl, retired from Ward Air, to keep the in-flight crews trained and laid down the law with the ground crew to follow procedures and stop trying to do anything they're not trained for, but I gotta tell you. We're going to have to ease up on the one-man, one-job thing. We just don't have the manpower like the big guys to cover all the bases. What I'm thinking is we create a specialist position that has all the ground jobs covered and work our guys up to that level. Then when we schedule, we can make sure we have at least one full specialist on and three generalists. How's that sound?"

"Better," Ally finally answered. "Good."

"Single-word answers. Well, that's an improvement. I'm glad, I was worried you'd be pissed I was treading on your territory, but hell, you're here and what the fuck."

Ally smiled and nodded. "Thanks, buddy. Sorry you got stuck holding the bag."

"Ah, it's nothin' you haven't done for me. Remember that time I chased that crazy bitch out west? I thought she loved me. Turned out she was just lookin' for someone to move her pot."

"Least it's legal now."

"Now, but could you imagine back then? We woulda been fucked. Forget jail time. We woulda lost our operating certificate."

"Naw. You figured it out in time. Not like me."

"Hey. Stow that shit! You're not some doe-eyed dumb kid. You fell for a girl—a nice one the way I hear it. Looks to me the big issue is Pammy. As usual. I don't get her crap sometimes. I mean she has everything—looks, hot bod, she's made her name in criminal law, and Connie says she rakes in a cool million a year, not to mention what goes to the partners. Fuck, I'm living in Port Credit because I can't afford to buy in the city and you're only doing okay because your gramps unloaded the Admiral on you. Fuck, between the hours you put in with the hotel, our air charters and now the airline, I don't know when you sleep."

"I delegate. It's all that's saving my skin."

"Hey, I get that but take a bow, kiddo. The Admiral was a big loser before you took over and we both know there isn't a helo charter company in the country that can afford to stay in business these days with the way drones are taking over. Fuck, if they ever figure out how to haul a Bambi Bucket to fight forest fires, that'll be the end of helicopters. Maybe even the air traffic contract we have. I don't know how you pulled it off. CBC can't afford a helo, and even Global is in renegotiations with their traffic helo. That A-Star of theirs looks good, but she's even more expensive to run than our baby."

"We should reach out to them and offer to carry their crew in the back while you report for Channel One up front."

"Fuck me, that's brilliant!"

"It's just an idea."

"Yeah, and it's your ideas that have kept us in business. So smarten up and get this fucking show done and come back to work. This isn't you, letting some bitch fuck you around."

"She's not a bitch! Don't call her that."

KC nodded, the grin on her face giving away her tactic. "So, you do like her?"

"Yes, I fucking like her!"

"Whoa Nelly!" KC tried a calming tone. "I was just seeing if she was really someone special to you."

"She is. Was. But…"

"But you won't cross Pam? Am I right?"

"Connie asked that I respect what she's doing and…What else can I do?"

KC nodded, thinking. Finally, she said, "I like the kid, and this is her show. You agreed to play it her way when she schemed you into taking part, so I get you're in a pickle here so here's what I'm gonna suggest. Play it Connie's way. Go out there and name three of those babes, whichever three she said. Finish the week and get back to work. Then and only then, reach out to this Erin. Maybe write one of those brilliant letters you do and lay it out for her. My bet is she's feelin' just as fucked by this whole thing and you gotta remember somethin' else. She works for Pam. Not everyone has family to fall back on like you and me. I bet she's not just feelin' the pressure from good old Pam What if she's worried 'bout losing her job?"

Ally turned to her, looking into her eyes for the first time. "I never thought…"

"Of course not. Don't beat yourself up. Like I said, we always had the option to bounce home to family when things got tough. Not everyone can. She may be feeling caught in a hard place, like fifty nautical over Superior, with the chip detector blowin' alarms."

Understanding KC's metaphor, Ally took a deep breath and stood. "You're right. I'm ready. I'll play this the way Connie wants and then we're goin' home to kick our new airline into serious contender gear."

"Now we're talking." KC was on her feet and walking Ally down the long corridor that wrapped around the ballroom. She couldn't help asking, "By the way, what kind of school has a ballroom?"

"The kind that's supposed to turn out debutantes."

"Hmmm… Well, buddy, I gotta say, they fucked up on that score where you're concerned."

Ally laughed, finally starting to relax. "You got that right."

CHAPTER TWENTY

Erin paced in the dorm while Denise stood vigil at the window overlooking the comings and goings at the grand entry below. Charlotte, the third of Pam's group, was still fussing with her luggage. Last night after the ceremony, they had spent an hour saying their goodbyes to the women who were eliminated. With the bus strike still on, the production team had rented a party bus, a stretched Hummer with plenty of room to take those leaving into Toronto or out to Pearson International.

Last night Erin had prayed that Ally would pick her to be one of her final three, but she hadn't, and with the wildcard option to choose any queen if selected, she had no choice but to accept or reject Pam's invitation to join her. In her mind, she knew it was for the best. She had come here to be of assistance to Pam. That, after all, was her job and she had agreed to it. In her heart, she ached to be with Ally, if for no other reason than the chance to explain.

"The limo's here," Denise announced.

After a light breakfast without the two remaining queens present, they had been shuffled off to the dorm to pack and wait. They had already watched Ally's group and their camera team climb aboard her helicopter and take off. In the circular drive, the production vans and crew were busy leaving with all the equipment they needed during their stay at Glendennon Castle. Erin knew it would be just minutes now before a PA was sent to fetch them and make sure they were leaving the dorm as they found it. Mother hen Denise had taken it upon herself to inspect the room and adjoining communal bathroom and declared them fit to leave. All that was left to do was get Charlotte squared away.

"Here," Erin offered. "Let me help you get those closed." Charlotte must have packed everything she owned. It took her sitting on each of the three matching suitcases to get the zippers closed around the bulky bags. She didn't know which of these two women Pam had her heart set on. Denise for sure would be a perfect housewife, managing her home and their social affairs with ease. Charlotte, on the other hand, was a complete disaster in that department, but she was arm candy, and Erin knew how much Pam would adore that kind of woman.

"I wonder what her house is like?" Charlotte asked.

Erin didn't want to burst her bubble and confide that they would be spending these last few days at the Parker Estate, the home they grew up in, but not where Pam lived and worked. She did wonder what they would do with all the time scripted to be spent introducing the women to friends and associates. In a way, she suspected Pam had had a hand in that. She had no idea if anyone back in Chicago knew she was taking part in some reality TV program. Certainly none the other senior partners. Everyone knew Connie was her sister, so Erin assumed that Pam believed this would take care of the family introductions.

Would her parents fly in to attend the scripted family introductions? If they did, she knew Pam would omit her from the event. The Coens had met Erin many times and didn't look to be the type of people willing to play along with the subterfuge.

Although Pam's mother was desperate for her daughter to find a suitable spouse, so who knew.

There was a knock at the door; then a PA let herself in. "Car's ready, ladies. Grab your bags and let's go."

She didn't look to be in the mood to help with the luggage, so Erin grabbed one of Charlotte's extra bags while Denise grabbed the other. Charlotte ran to the bathroom for one more check of her hair and face, forcing them and the PA wait.

"Come on Charlotte," she ordered, "let's not keep Pam waiting."

Those were the magic words needed to kick Charlotte into gear, and she grabbed her purse, her oversized carry-on and stumbled to manage her remaining suitcase. Rolling her eyes, the PA captured the last bag and carried it while she propelled Charlotte toward the door.

It didn't take long to get settled into the limo. Charlotte's bags, of course, were a problem which was solved by loading them in the production van heading to Highland Creek. Sandy and her camera gear were already in the limo, making it a cozy fit. Erin, understanding the stakes for Pam, took it upon herself to sit up closer to Sandy and the assistant director who would be running the shoot at the Parker Estate while Connie traveled with Ally and the group heading to someplace called the Admiral. Evidently, Allyson lived in a hotel. In her mind, Erin imagined her crammed into some drive-in motel turned residential rental like those places long swallowed up by the suburbs, too close to attract motorists, too far from the core to attract visitors. She knew it was silly to think that way, but couldn't imagine any other scenario for a woman on a charter pilot's salary.

When Pam arrived, Denise and Charlotte made room for her in the center of the rear bench. Erin tried hard not to roll her eyes and sat quietly while the camera rolled. As the AD asked questions, Pam was required to repeat them or work them into her answers, allowing the editors to later edit the woman's voice from the scene. They got a brief history of the Highland Creek estate, learning the land had been in the family for five generations. Her great-great-grandfather had built the place, what Pam called the center block. Over the years he and then his son and then Pam's grandfather had added to the home, expanding it to suit their social status and the ever-growing family. She talked about growing up there, with Ally and her mother in residence, until both girls were packed off at age twelve to Glendennon Castle School for Young Women.

Listening to Pam's story of a charming life, Erin was not so gullible as to believe everything had been as perfect as Pam let on. Pam spoke affectionately of her grandfather, her mother—a young widow, she alleged—and her aunt, Ally's mom, the scandalous divorcee. Growing up sharing a room with Ally had been about ensuring they formed a bond the mothers hoped would serve them in adulthood. And they were close, judging by all the stories Pam had shared. But the reality of the last few weeks did make her question Pam's loyalty to her cousin.

Part of her was excited to see where these two women had grown up and she had hoped to meet "the old boy" as Pam referred to her granddad. Except, Pam was explaining, he was off on an adventure with her aunt Patricia, Ally's mom, and wasn't expected back this week. After all she had heard about the wily old timer, that was a disappointment. When his granddaughters were young, he had coached them in finance and law with the hope they would one day take over the family holdings. And while Pam had indeed taken up the law, she had turned to criminalistics as her focus, not tax law. And Ally, Ally was her own person, striking out to follow her passion for aviation.

Pam had often complained that Ally had let him down even when her own rebellious self was sitting five hundred miles away in her law office, presiding over criminal offenders instead of finance. Ally, she said, could still analyze a spreadsheet better than a team of forensic accountants and in half the time. Still, it was aviation that had called to her and Erin was proud to know she had stuck to it, even if her success couldn't be measured by financial gains in the same way as Pam's career.

Dwelling on it, Erin did wonder if it was just another sign things between them didn't have a chance. After all, she was an admin assistant, a good one, but still. After her rent and the necessary wardrobe she needed for work, it didn't leave a lot to spare. After moving to Chicago, she'd sold her car and started taking the "L" so she could afford healthcare. Pam had tried to get full health coverage pushed through for the admins, but so far the partners just didn't see fit to agree. She hated men for that. How was it a guy could buy two suits for a hundred bucks? She was shopping the outlet malls and still couldn't find as much as a skirt and jacket appropriate for the standards of her workplace for under two hundred. And what about shoes? Women were supposed to have all sorts, to match every outfit. She had three pairs of good quality pumps she kept looking good only because her grandfather had taught her how to apply polish and remove salt stains. Most of the other admins cycled through the discount shoes that tore their feet to shreds and fell apart in a month, all to fit the company dress code.

Pam pointed to the sign they were passing: *You Are Entering Highland Creek.* "Here we are."

"I don't see any houses," Charlotte observed.

Smiling that pompous proud smile that sometimes irritated Erin, Pam clarified, "You won't. All of this is ours. Well, we have eight hundred acres gifted to the University of Toronto to expand the Scarborough campus, but all in all, it still belongs to the Parker family."

Sandy checked to make sure the PA sitting up front beside the driver was shooting footage of their drive in, then turned her attention back to them as the limo slowed and turned into an almost invisible drive, camouflaged by huge sugar maples in full leaf. On each side of the drive, two great stags carved from stone were almost swallowed by the foliage, their backs alive with thick green moss.

"These old boys," Pam explained, pointing out the statues, "represent our family name. We can trace our lineage back to Queen Matilda, who in ten-eighty-three named a Parker the first Royal Forester. In case you don't know it, Prince Philip, Queen Elizabeth's hubby, is the current Royal Ranger, so it's no slouch job."

"Wow," Charlotte said. She, as well as the others, were seriously impressed.

Erin couldn't help but wonder what they would think of the house, which she'd seen in plenty of pictures, including the one hanging in her office. It depicted the elder Parker with his two tween granddaughters dressed in their lower school uniforms, alongside a family friend, a young man attending a private college associated with the Parker family. Pam loved to show that photo off, asking visitors if they recognized the young man also in uniform, a young Prince Andrew, the Duke of York.

They rounded the long forest road, emerging in what Pam called the park. It was a fifty-acre manicured and traditionally landscaped front lawn. Beyond it was the family home, a sprawling Georgian manor almost as large as Glendennon Castle and certainly as breathtaking, perhaps even more in its upkeep and magnificence.

This is where the family lives and Ally's stuck in a hotel room downtown? Erin's respect for Allyson's determination to follow her calling spiked beyond what she imagined possible. She listened as Pam shared stories as the car slowed and the house grew ever larger. Finally, near the front entry, Erin had to admit, even knowing what to expect, she was overwhelmed. The manor was beyond extravagant. So this was what old money and a long legacy looked like?

"Welcome home, everyone," Pam offered as the limo came to a soft, silent stop.

As they climbed from the car, a uniformed, elderly butler and two much younger maids opened the big doors and stood waiting to greet them. Pam, of course, they knew and welcomed home formally. The butler rattled off the guest arrangements and looked to be ready to escort them in when the camera crew finally emerged. He looked aghast, stuttering at Pam, "Miss Pamela, this is highly irregular. Mr Parker said nothing about you having…tradespeople accompany you?"

Pam laughed it off, taking his arm affectionately. "Oh Jarvis, these are my guests and should be treated as such."

He eyed the camera crew suspiciously, especially since they looked to be filming the encounter. "Highly irregular, ma'am."

Pam smiled. "Just like me."

"Very well, ma'am. I've set out refreshments in the library. Mr Parker advised that you will be using it as your…'Base of Operations.'"

Pam was about to lead her guests inside when the production van finally rounded the corner to the park. "Perfect, there's the remainder of my party."

Jarvis looked to be having an aneurysm. "Miss Pamela, really? You hardly expect me to allow a trades van to enter here? They certainly can't park where guests might glimpse their…"

Pam shrugged, apologizing to the assistant director. "Okay, have them park by the service entrance. But they are my guests too. Is that understood?"

His consternation was more than evident. Still, he acquiesced. "Very well, ma'am. I will direct them to the Highland entrance. Once they arrive, I will show them to the library."

When it looked like Denise would grab her own luggage, he looked as if he might faint. Pam ordered her to leave it. Her amusement at his reaction helped to defuse Denise's embarrassment for her faux pas. Encouraged then, Denise offered casually, "Come on girls. Let's get inside before Mister Jarvis here has a coronary."

* * *

By the time they landed at the Billy Bishop Airport on the western end of Toronto's island chain, Ally knew three things: Karen, the woman who had been chosen instead of Erin, was a puker; Teresa's only salvation in life was writing; and Bobby Ann had a thing for KC. That was all fine. She knew she would never bend the knee for any of them. Not like she wasn't attracted to these lovely women, but realistically, they weren't Erin, and that was all she needed to know. How she wished Rene had won the elimination vote.

With Connie's eyes on her and the camera rolling, she helped Karen from the helicopter, repeatedly telling her not to be embarrassed. Lots of people had a hard time getting used to flying in helicopters. She even told them about the time both she and KC had upchucked on a flight so rough their chopper had sustained structural damage. That didn't help, and she decided this was a "less is more" kind of situation. Luckily for her, KC had just landed from her morning traffic patrol. She had arranged for one of the shuttle buses that delivered passengers from Union Station to the airport to haul them over to the Admiral. She wasn't enamored of the idea of having these women and the crew invade her home, but Connie hadn't given her much choice. Besides, Pam had already laid claim to Highland Creek before it even occurred to her that she could take her guests there. She could have insisted they double up. With eighteen bedrooms, they had space, but Pam wanted to play keeper of the castle, and no way was she getting in on that.

KC trotted up to join them, explaining, "No need to go street side. I got permission for the bus to roll in here."

She watched with interest as Connie helped get the gear unloaded, and sparks flew between Bobby Ann and KC. Ally almost laughed. *One down and two to go.* As she stood holding up the still-weak Karen, the bus rolled through the airside gate and KC waved it over to where the Huey was parked. She needed to get the aircraft cleaned, and right now. She was pretty sure Karen had made good use of the air sickness bag, which KC quietly grabbed and disposed of, but if she missed even a little, the sun and the warm day were all that was needed to bake the smell of vomit into the cabin.

Once they began loading onto the shuttle bus, she trotted back to the Huey. KC, just as experienced, had read her mind and joined her by the big side door, jumping in and sniffing around. "I think we're okay, but I'll get our new cabin guy to give it a good wash out and pull out the utility seats so we're ready in case we get a charter."

"Like that'll happen."

"Hey, where's the optimistic Ally who flew outta here weeks ago to go save the day for the kid?"

Ally groaned. "Still banging my head against a wall. And don't ever let me do something that stupid again."

KC was chuckling as Bobby Ann joined them. "Is it bad?"

"Nah," KC reassured her. "We'll have one of the kids hose her down. She'll be as good as new in an hour or two. Well, not new but good anyhow. So…" Chatting up Bobby Ann, she asked, "How was the flight in, barf and all aside?"

"Not bad. I could get used to traveling like this. Sure beats the hell out of my Charger."

"You've got a Charger! Oh, man I've been looking at them and oh wow. Still, I kinda wish I could afford a Classic Mopar."

Bobby Ann's smile was gorgeous. "Oh boy, you and me both!"

Ally shook her head, turning to see Connie storming her way to their side.

"Let's get a move on, ladies! It looks like Karen needs a bed and the guy driving the bus says he needs to be at the Royal York by eleven."

Checking her watch, she knew they had plenty of time but understood Connie's need to get things back under control. "KC, I hate to…"

"I got this buddy. You head out with the gals and don't forget I'll be joining you guys after my last traffic report." She added this reminder more for Bobby Ann's benefit. "Oh, I've got those financials you wanted, Ally. Any chance you can find ten to have a look-see?"

"I'll make time," she promised, hooking Bobby Ann's arm for effect and tossing her business partner a wink. "We'll see you around eight, then?"

"I'll be there with bells on."

"One day I'm gonna tell you what that means."

"Whatever," she tossed out with a wide grin, her smile meant for Bobby Ann, not Ally.

The longest part of the drive to the Admiral Hotel was the five-minute wait for the car ferry and the three-minute crossing of the hundred and fifty-meter channel. Two minutes later they pulled up in front of the cube-shaped, five-story, silver-glazed building. The driver helped them get their luggage and gear to the curb, then continued on his way. While this was a hotel, there were no doormen per se, but one of the desk clerks, recognizing her, rushed to help them in.

"Welcome home, Captain Parker. We're so happy to see you have returned and with your guests. Everything is set up as per your instructions. Let me take care of your bags."

"Just help us get them upstairs…"

"Of course, of course."

They dragged all their gear toward the busy lobby. There were far more people than one would expect for a hotel this small, especially at ten in the morning. Ally knew they were lined up out the door for Starbucks, not the front desk, and skirted around them, heading straight for the elevators.

Connie immediately ordered her PA to get in line and grab coffees for them all. She copied down their order on a Post It note, then joined the line.

Ally winced. *Coffee drinkers, oy.*

"What's the plan?" Connie asked.

"The front desk will bring your keycards up when the rooms are ready. I'm assuming you want us all to head up to my apartment first."

"Yeah, I do, but I want to shoot your arrival. Can you hang here for five while we get set up?"

Ally gave her a look that said, like I have a choice? But Karen, still leaning against her, didn't look like she could wait.

"Okay, I'll take Karen with us. We can interview her later about her first impressions. Come on kiddo," Connie said. Taking the sick and weak Karen by the arm, boarding the elevator with the remainder of the production crew, she called to her PA, "Deb! Meet us in 501." Then she tossed Ally one of the crew's two-way radios as they crammed their cases of gear aboard the elevator along with everyone's luggage.

Ally blew out a hot breath, trying to decide what to do with her guests. It was summer in the city, and the harbor was alive with all sorts of activities. The Admiral was only one of two hotels on the south side of Queen's Quay with the Hilton at the far end of the harbor. In between, the old wharf buildings had long been converted to galleries, shops, and seasonal restaurants. The docks were lined with paddle boats, tall ships, and ferries available for daily rentals and harbor tours. "I know what we'll do. Metro PD's marine division is housed just behind us. I know Bobby Ann will get a kick out of seeing their cedar strip runabout. If a Mopar lights your fire, wait till you get a load of the twelve-cylinder Packard engine they're running."

Bobby Ann, a true motorhead, almost swooned at the prospect, and Teresa looked to be at least amused.

The marine division boathouse wasn't open to the public, but they knew Ally, always remembering that she and KC were quick to offer free air support during a crisis, and immediately welcomed them in. While Bobby Ann drooled over the long, sleek and highly polished lines of the Packard powered runabout, which had seen more than seventy-five years in police service and still looked brand new, Teresa peppered the young constable giving them the tour with questions about the modern rescue boats housed alongside.

Enjoying Bobby Ann and Teresa's pleasure, Ally was disappointed when the handheld radio squawked to life. "Sorry, guys. Duty calls."

Leading them back into the hotel and upstairs, she used her passcode to open the digital lock. Technology sure made life easier sometimes and had saved her from having to knock on her own door. Inside the entry, she waved the other two in. "Welcome, welcome. Please make yourselves at home."

Stopped dead by the extravagant view, an unbroken panorama of the Toronto harbor and island chain, neither woman moved.

"Guys, you can come in. It's safe."

It was Bobby Ann who voiced their incredulity. "Holy smokes, Parker. You live here?"

Ally, confused by their confusion, finally understood. To them, contestants and crew alike, she was just a lowly charter pilot. Tired of the subterfuge, she wasn't interested in playing anymore. "Guys, I may be just a pilot, but I'm still a Parker. Now come on in and make yourselves at home. Besides, if you're this impressed with the foyer, your heads'll explode when you see the rest."

"There's more?" Teresa said. Evidently, her estimate of life with a pilot had immediately escalated.

"Oh, my good novelist, you have no idea." While the camera recorded every aspect of their astonishment, Ally was running low on patience and had to paste a smile on her face. Connie had wanted to see their shock and awe, and it looked like she wouldn't be disappointed on that score. "Please follow me, and I'll give you the five-cent tour. Obviously, this is the foyer." She pronounced it in the French fashion more suitable to her education. "Those stairs lead to the rooftop terrace. I think the plan is for us to have dinner up there tonight with a few friends of mine." She pointed to a hallway to the right. "The guest bedrooms are that way." Pointing to the left, she explained, "The master suite and my office are this way. And if we continue toward the view, you'll find the living room, dining room, and the kitchen." The entire space was open concept with the living area taking up the entire southeast corner of the floor, while the dining room area and long ornate bar, which fronted the kitchen, occupied half of the southwest. Together, the space was larger than the entirety of most suburban homes. "Any questions?"

They looked shell-shocked.

"Oh boy. Connie?" Ally called, wanting her cousin and the show's director to handle the situation.

Standing beside her camera crew, she did what directors do, ordering, "Okay guys. Come in and look around. I bet you're both more than a little surprised and I would be too." Connie led them to the living area, backing her way there, circling her crew around the visitors to capture them as they stepped up to the floor-to-ceiling and wall-to-wall view.

While Connie shot the expressions on Bobby Ann's and Teresa's faces, peppering them with questions from behind the camera, Ally headed for the long bar to make herself fresh iced tea. She spooned tea leaves into the brew basket then filled the reservoir with filtered water. Grabbing the glass jug that went with the machine, she topped it with ice before turning on the machine. While it spit and hissed, pouring hot tea on the ice to instantly cool it, she sliced lemon and tossed in a few wedges. While it finished brewing, she listened to Connie explain how Allyson had learned of the hotel's demise and approached their grandfather with a plan to redevelop the property as a boutique hotel. He'd wanted a full proposal, including a business plan and full financial forecast, which she provided. He'd liked what he saw and partnered with her to acquire the property. His only demand: that she take up residence to be sure the establishment was run to the family's standards.

"The last owner took this entire floor for himself. Probably one of the reasons it wasn't doing well," Connie explained. "Ally was intending on keeping just a quarter of the space she now has, but Grandad thought this was more appropriate. So, there you have it."

Bobby Ann, the boldest of the lot, moved to her side, the fixed panoramic view all she could see, and gestured to the vast windows. "Do these open?"

"No," Ally answered. "It's one thing I wanted to change but the bylaws wouldn't allow it. Evidently I'm too close to the airport to have either a balcony or windows that open. That's why I had the staircase put in and the rooftop terrace added."

Before she or anyone else could comment, the doorbell chimed. Connie excused herself to let her PA in with their coffee order. Bobby Ann, still bolder than the rest, said what Ally imagined the others thinking. "You were right to keep mum on having a place like this. Could you see what some of those women would have done if they suspected you were doing as well or better than good old Pam?"

"It was the one thing Connie and I discussed before production started. You two and Karen are here because you're nice and you've been good to me. No matter what happens, I think I can count you each as friends."

"Not more?" Bobby Ann asked.

She had a twinkle in her eye and Ally grinned. "I think you have a thing for pilots. I can tell you, my closest friend with wings does play down her success too, much the way I do." That was all she would say about KC. If Bobby wanted to know more she needed to ask KC herself.

Bobby Ann wrapped her arms around Ally's neck giving her a hug and whispering, "Thanks for understanding."

"I think that's something we have in common."

* * *

Erin had been hoping for some quiet time after their refreshments, but Pam, of course, had other ideas. She had sent them to change into the provided riding gear—fancy English habits, not boots and jeans like average people would expect. They would spend the day at the stables. Who the hell had stables, and a herd of thoroughbreds, in this day and age? Parkers, obviously. Pam had sometimes mentioned a horse she loved and rode as a girl, but Erin had missed the full implication. She had learned over morning refreshments that the Parkers raced and bred thoroughbreds, and remembered Pam complaining about Ally trying to screw up horse bloodlines by introducing Paints to the line. Later in the stables, they were introduced to one of the offspring of such a pairing, and she had to admit Ally had a point. The young stallion was magnificent. His coat was a sleek black like his sire just two stalls down. but mixed with blazes of brilliant deep red.

"This is Blaze, as we call him. He's our newest contender," the groom explained, adding, "our trainer just started him at the track this year. He's already amassed an impressive purse."

Erin had no clear idea what that meant, but assumed it more than proved Ally's idea valid and profitable.

"He should be on the track, not here," Pam declared.

"The vet and our trainer were concerned about his stress level. He's home for a holiday before we trailer him to Knoxville."

Pam nodded, but didn't comment. Erin knew that expression. It meant she didn't have a counter argument and knew enough not to draw attention to it.

"He is beautiful," Erin said. "I guess I can't say beautiful for a boy?"

The groom smiled. "He doesn't mind at all. Unlike most men, this boy is happy with the compliments. And you should see him in the breeder's paddock before a race. Proud as a peacock, this one."

The groom moved with Pam who passed him by without a comment, and Erin knew she wouldn't say another word. She never did when she was wrong. That was Pam, and knowing it just underlined how much she wanted to talk with Ally—to talk, listen, explain. How was it that she missed her so much? Last night, she'd awakened in a sweat, aching for Ally, wet and excited, and it was all she could do not to search out the wing of the castle where the queens were in residence. Maybe she could find a phone in the house and call her. She had spotted one in the library. But she didn't even know her number. She debated just coming straight out and asking Pam. The temptation to reach out was as strong as her feelings. How could it be like this after such a short time and why the hell had she pushed her away?

At last night's elimination ceremony, she'd watched Ally as she named her three choices. Deep inside she'd prayed Allyson would name her, but looking at her, seeing she never once looked her way, she knew it wouldn't happen. When Pam called her as planned, she debated just walking to Ally's side, begging her to reconsider but Pam had laid down the law with her in a secret and emphatic face-to-face. Pam needed her. Needed her to watch and learn which of her two final choices was truly the one. She knew it was Pam's way but wondered how it was she could tell who had developed feelings for Pam but Pam could not? Was it the litigator in her who wouldn't or couldn't trust what she saw and heard to make her own choice? Or did she just not trust anyone? Whichever it was, the truth of Pam's actions saddened her. It was all she could do not to scream at Pam to just trust her gut.

Part of her hated Pam for putting her in this position while another repeatedly reminded her she had agreed to this. Agreed to this role. Accepted it as part of her job. No matter how she felt and for whom, Pam was her boss. And when all was said and done, she still had to go home, still had a job to return to, a job where Pam was in charge.

* * *

Ally, a master at the barbecue and a disaster in the kitchen, stood vigil over the steaks on the grill while Bobby Ann set the table, Teresa flipped the salad and KC regaled them with high-flying tales. Their adventures always sounded much more fun coming from her. The woman could spin the most routine of sorties into harrowing acts of bravery, the stuff of legend. To her own recollection, they both had been young and stupid, and lucky enough to get away with their mistakes. As the camera rolled, she could only hope the FAA or Transport Canada didn't take her too seriously and decide to investigate. Thank goodness for Granddad's team of legal beavers at the ready to defend any and all misdeeds committed by the Parker clan. Adding in her own caveats, she said lightly, "Just know, no animals or humans were hurt during the commission of our youthful indiscretions."

Even stoic Teresa was enjoying the fun. "I love the part about circling the water tower to read the town name so you guys could figure out where you were."

"Oh, that's nothing," KC scoffed. "Did Ally here ever tell you about our first year flying fire patrol? She was in a spotter plane, an old DeHavilland Otter, and gets her ass good and lost in the smoke and realizes she's gonna run outta fuel long before she can reach the base at Longlac."

"Where's that?" Bobby Ann asked.

"As far north as you can drive before you run outta roads. To give you an idea of the distance, it would take less time to drive to Miami from here than it would to drive up there. Anyway, old Ally's here's in a real pickle. Almost outta go-go juice and no way to make it home. Now I woulda declared an emergency and let ATC help me out, but Parkers don't think like the rest of us, and she's sittin' on a bigger pair then anyone I know."

"What did you do?" Teresa asked, intrigued.

Ally just smiled, piling the steaks on a plate, finally admitting, "Something stupid."

KC, always the storyteller, explained, "Your girl here decides she needs gas and if you can't reach a place to get aviation fuel, why not mogas."

"Mogas?" Bobby Ann asked. "I assume that's motor gas, as in for cars?"

"You got it. Anyway, Ally heads for highway 11. That's the Trans-Canada Highway. Spots a gas station, lands that big bird on the highway and taxies up to the pumps and tells the bug-eyed kid working there to fill'er up! Can you imagine?"

"Oh, my lord!" Bobby Ann was flabbergasted while Teresa looked more bemused than amused.

"You can't do that?" Teresa asked.

"Think about it, T. KC's talking about a fairly big plane, not some little Piper. What would you think if that American Eagle commuter plane we flew in on landed on the I95 and rolled into the service center?"

"I'd think they lost their mind."

Laughing, KC agreed. "That's pretty much what the kid thought. Someone did call the cops, but Ally here was off the ground long before the Northwest Patrol could catch up."

"Lucky for me, the young man working there wrote my tail number down wrong. He was either watching out for me or dyslexic. The Provincial Police knew I did it, but without proof, they couldn't make a charge stick."

"You guys!" Bobby Ann teased. "I love these stories, and I'm so glad you two didn't get yourselves killed. It sure sounds like you came a little too close more than once."

"Hardly," Ally said, passing the plate of grilled steaks to Bobby Ann. "The most dangerous part of flying in the far north are the black flies, mosquitoes, and low time pilots. Which, I will admit, we once were."

"It sounds like you approve of that sort of thing?" Teresa stated simply, but KC took offense.

"Hey, writer girl. It may sound like we were ass—"

"KC!" Ally warned, not wanting her notorious expletives to be recorded as the camera team, with Connie at their side, caught everything.

"We were acting juvenile, okay—but flying sixteen-hour days, seven days a week, working our butts off to make sure really good people didn't lose their homes and animals and their lives, it's grueling work. No one can handle a job like that for long, not to mention the emotional toll the fires take on you. You think you know what we're talking about, but you haven't listened to a forest cry after a fire. If you did, you would never question our antics. It's the only way to cope."

Teresa was not moved. "I assume you're talking about people or animals who have lost their homes or habitat. That's sad but…"

"No! Tell them, Al."

For the first time that day, Ally looked as bad as she had after learning of Erin and Pam's betrayal. Desperate not to choke up she stalled, gulping down her unsweetened iced tea. Finally, she took a deep breath, explaining, "After a fire, the forest, the trees…you can hear what sounds like screams of pain. It's the sound of moisture escaping the charred remains and if you ever thought trees were just things without a soul, those screams, which go on for days, sometimes weeks, will change your mind. You don't just hear the screams, you feel them, and even the toughest of the guys break down. It changes you, changes the way you think about life. Nothing is insignificant afterward, nothing. Maybe a Buddhist monk could explain it better, but after the first time I experienced it, I cried for days. Not tears of sadness, but hard, falling down sobs. Maybe it's why we still work the fires every year."

"We take turns every fire season," KC explained quietly. "This year we'll probably have to hire someone to take the Huey up for us, 'cause we're so busy down here, but for all the work and the shitty conditions and pay, we'll always find a way to help."

Recognizing this was a good time to shift the conversation, Connie interjected from behind the camera, "Bobby Ann, why don't you tell us about your interest in cars? Not many women, even today, get involved in souping up cars for the track."

Ally was able to enjoy her supper and listen as Bobby Ann regaled them with her tales of growing up with three brothers and a dad all into heavy metal—cars, not the music. She talked about working in her dad's custom speed shop and learning the ropes. It made for lighter conversation and Ally could only thank her for the effort.

With the focus off her for now, her mind automatically slipped back to thinking of Erin. She had battled herself all night, tempted to just march down to the dorm room and demand an explanation. Why had they made love if her only intention had been to guard Pam's back? Why had she not simply explained her situation? She could understand that Pam may have warned her to keep that fact under her hat but why not come clean when things heated up between them? Question after question, and she had lain in bed broken and twisted inside, every inch of her aching, not just from the heartbreak, but from wanting her. *Erin, how do I get over you?* She had wanted to choose Erin to join her—so much so, she was ready to defy Pam's warning and Connie's plea just to stick it out. Never did she imagine this whole scripted fantasy thing would deliver a match who would take her heart so completely.

Listening passively to Bobby Ann and KC flirt was a fun distraction. Much more so than having to cope with Teresa who, while slightly interested before now, now looked to be fighting her desire for all Ally had and her distaste for all she was. Because Teresa's expectations of her had changed, Ally knew she would have to tell her directly, and hopefully off camera, that she wasn't the one. Ally had more than enough women ready to lower themselves to be with her for the opportunities she and her family name could provide. *No, Teresa. You have been kind and interesting, but it's not gonna happen.*

Once supper was over, Teresa returned to scribbling away in her notebook while Ally cooked up dinner for the crew and

Karen who was starting to feel better. KC and Bobby Ann, inseparable, cleared the table and reset it. While the crew dug in and enjoyed their meal, Ally opened a bottle of wine for her and Teresa, and uncapped two Sleeman's Honey Brown Lagers for KC and Bobby Ann. She carried the beer and her wineglass to the outdoor couches and got comfortable, stretching her jean-clad legs and plunking her bare feet on the coffee table. It was time to relax. The summer breeze neutralized the day's heat and made for perfect viewing weather.

A Dash-8 on approach to the island airport flew low across the harbor on a direct path for runway two-six. Out of habit, she checked her watch, and Bobby Ann caught the fact that KC did the same. "Okay, you two. What's up with that? Every time one of those commuter planes comes in you both check your watches."

KC didn't answer, which in itself was strange, and Ally knew she had to say something. She was about to obfuscate and call it a habit or a pilot thing but KC, sitting across from her delivered an imperceptible nod.

"It's not just any commuter aircraft. They're ours."

That confused Bobby Ann, and she asked, "You mean you own that plane? I mean, I suspected something when you flew us up north for the rafting adventure but…"

"No, Bobby," KC interrupted. "We own the airline. It's the only one operating out of the island, and we bought it almost six months ago. Next week we'll announce the change of ownership."

"Holy smokes, guys! I suspected you two were doing better than you let on but… Holy smokes and congrats. Oh my God, now I get why you needed to hire a pilot to take over flying the fire duty thing up north. You need to be here to fly the traffic thing and run the airline."

Ally applauded how quickly she connected all the dots.

She turned to KC, sitting across from her, asking simply, "Will you keep flying the traffic patrol? I mean I get the idea you like to do that?"

"I do, but it's taking a toll now that I've been doing the reporting and flying. I have to be in the air by six in the morning, and I'm rarely back down before nine, and then I have to do it all again starting around four."

"Yikes. When do you find time to run the airline? I mean that's massive. I've been watching those—what did you call them, Dash-8's? come and go all afternoon. How many planes do you have?"

"Eight so far," Ally answered. "Right now we're in review mode, watching and observing how things are currently running and who is contributing and who, well, isn't."

"Even so, I watched my brothers run my dad's shop into the ground, and they were working their tails off." Bobby Ann was from Buffalo, which had been hit hard long before the 2008 recession and suffered deeply from the housing crisis.

KC set her bottle down, sitting up to add her two cents. "Things are a little different up here. Our laws prevented the kind of thing that happened to you guys. We're an oil-rich nation, so we weathered the storm, but it was fucking hard to sit up here and watch what you guys were going through."

"Yeah but I always hear about how bad the taxes are."

"Thirty-two percent of my gross annual income," KC said with a nod. "But it covers everything, health care, old age pension, the armed forces, highways, airports, you name it."

"Geez!" She snapped her empty bottle on the table, "All that and great beer too. Sign me up!"

With a wide smile, KC said suggestively, "I was hoping you would say something like that. Which brings us to the tricky business I know Ally here would never ask." She looked over at the group still engrossed in enjoying their supper, and checked to make sure Teresa wasn't too close before leaning in and motioning for Bobby Ann to do the same. "How would you feel about getting engaged to my buddy here?"

Bobby Ann looked like she would choke. Ally jumped up to get her and KC another beer each. When she sat down again Bobby Ann and KC were sitting with their heads together in deep conversation. Ally topped up her wineglass, then stretched out again, letting them have their private talk. She knew exactly what the conversation was about but had elected to let KC handle it. She was a damn good negotiator, and on the plus side, had a personal stake in what would happen next considering her attraction to the fun-loving and intelligent woman sitting with them.

When Bobby sat back, she had a wicked smile on her face and a spark of insight in her eyes. "You're really up for this? I mean, we'll have to carry this at least until the show airs and maybe until the season is out."

Ally nodded. "It'll give Connie what she needs and, well, I get the idea you might like hanging out?"

The wicked smile was back. With a wink for KC, she moved closer to Ally, wrapping an arm around her shoulder. "God, I like the way you two think."

* * *

Erin was beside herself. She couldn't sleep without thinking about Ally. She had tried to broach the subject of calling her just to talk, but Pam had been Pam, shutting her down and laughing at her persistence. After her second sleepless night, she decided she would simply sneak into the library. Surely directory assistance had her number, or maybe it was already programmed into the phone. She couldn't have imagined good old Granddad memorizing everyone's number unless he had a cell and used that to call his grandkids. When she did finally get away from the group to slip back into the library the desk phone was gone. The hovering butler, Jarvis, explained he had been ordered to remove all the house phones. "To comply with the rules of the competition," he told her. She wanted to kill Pam. Kill her and stuff her piece by piece into the crap they had mucked out of the stalls that morning.

Tomorrow, Ally and her group would join them at the Parker Estate for the final ceremony. Today, Pam had gone into town to select engagement rings suitable for each of them. They would be displayed for the cameras before the ceremony, and the audience would have a chance to see just which one she thought suitable for each woman. If Pam decided she was ready to propose to either Charlotte or Denise, she would carry that ring into the ceremony. She knew Ally was probably doing the same thing, picking out a ring she would present as she asked someone else to be her bride. The thought was killing her. Would it be such a terrible thing to let her have a five-minute call with Allyson?

Erin sulked all day, deciding this was not what she signed up for. The only thing keeping her from complete mutiny was the prospect that Pam would fire her ass. Then what would she have? A return airline ticket to Chicago, no job, and a completely broken heart. The worst part was knowing tonight's schedule was the overnight date. She didn't know if the director would name Charlotte or Denise to spend the night with Pam and didn't care. It was the thought of who Ally would choose to entertain. She couldn't and didn't want to erase the image of Ally in her arms, Ally naked and making love to her, with her, wanting her. Only now that memory was tainted by the image of another woman taking her place. She didn't care who that woman was, just the thought of it was killing her.

Jarvis, seeming more attuned to her plight, poured her a glass of single malt. "That is from Mister Parker's selection. I believe it will numb your malaise, Miss Erin."

She accepted the drink, but didn't trust her voice to speak.

"The other ladies are enjoying the afternoon by the pool. Would you not rather be with them?"

"No sir."

"Hmm, I see." It looked as if he was about to leave her to her thoughts when he said, "It's not my place to ask, but I have been with the Parkers since Miss Pamela and Miss Allyson were very small children. I do care for them and have taken a keen interest in their careers, and interest in that of young Constance too. May I ask, are you the Miss Erin Bogner, Pamela's assistant at the firm?"

That caught her by surprise, and suddenly she found a spark of hope. "I am. I'm not part of the competition. I'm not supposed to say so, but I think you already know that."

He nodded appreciatively. "And Miss Ally, I take it you have had the opportunity to meet in the course of things?"

Seeing her chance, she pounced. "I did, and it's Ally I need to call. I know Pam wants to follow all the rules but I, but…"

"I see. Well far be it for me to interfere where Mister Parker's grandchildren are concerned." He turned to leave, and all Erin's hopes looked to be leaving with him. At the door to the library, he wavered. "Miss Pamela is not expected back for some time. I would be remiss if I did not mention the telephone is sitting in the top drawer of the desk. Miss Allyson's number is programmed on speed dial, number nine."

Stunned, Erin sat immobilized, then raced to the ornate oak desk, pulling the phone from the drawer. Was this really such a good idea? She didn't know. Then decided she didn't care.

* * *

Ally stood leaning against the outdoor café railing at the Colonade on Bloor Street, the two large bags from Brooks Brothers dumped at her feet.

"There you are," Pam called, impatiently. "Connie's setting up for you…" She shook her head at the shopping bags. "Two hours and that's all you have to show for it! I thought at least you would have found some decent footwear." When Ally didn't immediately answer or offer a retort, she asked with more concern, "What's happened? Did KC dump one of your precious whirlybirds in the lake?"

"What?"

"Good God, Allyson. You get denser every year. Please tell me you have a pair of shoes stuffed in those bags?"

"I…no. I'm fine with my Blundstone's."

"Ugh. I swear you're like a caveman. At least let me take you over to Browns and get you something plainly respectable when Connie's done shooting your segment in Cartier's."

"Are you done there?"

"Of course, and don't even think of pulling a ditto and rushing through the whole thing. This segment is important to Connie."

Ally was in no mood for Pam's bullshit. She'd always been on the pretentious side, but it was getting old and more than that, wearing on her nerves. "Where are you going?"

"Well, since I'm here and my dollar goes so much farther, I thought I'd head next door to Michael Kors then Prada. Oh, I have to stop at MAC too, and I want to hit Holts for some basics. Can I pick anything up for you?"

Ally shook her head. "I'm happy getting my gitch at the Bay."

Now it was Pam's turn to feign shock. "I swear KC has been a terrible influence on you. I don't know which I find more shocking, your use of the word gitch to describe your intimate apparel, or the fact you shop at the Hudson's Bay."

"You know, you get worse and worse every year. And just so you know, I happen to like the Bay."

Pam rolled her eyes, then waved off any retort. "Go pick out your engagement rings. I'm going shopping. Get inside and take your time. I plan to take mine." She spun around on her Alexander McQueen heels and Ally watched her march her skinny ass into Michael Kors.

Inside Cartier's, Ally followed Connie's direction, letting the representative introduce himself and lead her up the circular stairs to the private sales room dedicated to serving clients like the Parkers. While the stylish young man went through the whole presentation schtick, Ally tried to pay attention.

She hadn't been expecting a call, at least not from Erin. Putting aside the fact that Jarvis, bless his intrepid soul, had broken the rules and Pam's orders to prevent it from happening, she wasn't sure what to think, what to feel. After all the heartache and crying, the longing and desire, was it possible that Erin cared? It was easy to imagine her in the family library, drinking Granddad's scotch and baring her soul. That view from his library had been enough to send more than one woman into her arms and declaring her everlasting love. But Erin didn't say she loved her or anything like that. She said she was sorry. That she never imagined she would meet anyone, fall for anyone, especially under such circumstances as these.

"CUT!" Connie called, pulling Ally aside roughly, a look of impatience plastered across her face. "What the fuck, Ally. We don't have the place all day. I need you to work with me here. I get you're not into this, but I can't have you looking like you're ready to bury your best buddy! Now either get in the game or... Oh Geez! You're not going to cry on me..." Aware there was more behind the sudden rush of emotion, she pulled Ally out of hearing range. "What's going on? Did Pam say something stupid to..."

"Erin called me."

That stopped her instantly. "Ahh, guys..." she called to her crew. "Five-minute break and Deb, can you go grab the makeup bag?" The crew filed out, one by one, down the stairs while the clerk locked away the extravagant display of diamond engagement rings and followed suit.

Connie inspected her. "Are you okay?"

"I...I don't know. I mean, I feel relieved, confused, and upset all over again."

"Can I ask what she said?"

"Pretty much what I just said, 'I'm relieved, confused, and upset.' Oh, and she was sorry for the subterfuge, she has feelings for me, which she never expected."

"Holy cow!"

Ally tried not to bite her lip. "I want to believe her, but I'm also freaked out that she's sitting at Granddad's while she's saying this."

Nodding, Connie had to ask, "Worried she might be another money grubbing bitch like Janette?"

Ally nodded, but didn't trust her herself to say more.

"Okay..." It was Connie's go-to word. "Okay, tell me this. If she wasn't at home and saying these things, what would you be thinking?"

It was all she could do to hold back the tears, while at the same time a crooked smile crept across her face. "I...I would say, she, it was real, what we shared, what I feel, that she feels it too."

"And what about that gut of yours? It's never failed you in business or flying for that matter. What if Erin was an airplane..."

"Really?"

"Cut me some slack here, I'm working to a deadline. Just think about it logically. Forget the house and all that stuff, what does your gut say?"

Ally rocked back and forth weighing what she did know, what they had shared long before Erin set foot in the Parker home. "She doesn't know anything other than I'm a charter pilot with a wealthy family. Even Pam is cautious about sharing the details of just how comfortable the family is and she sure as hell wouldn't bother telling anyone, much less her assistant, how well I'm doing."

"That's true. She's way too jealous of your successes. And she's been a total bitch with Erin since learning you two were into one another and that was before she figured out you two slept together. I won't be surprised if she downright threatened Erin's job over this. It must have taken some serious balls for her to call you. By the way, how the hell did she pull that off?"

"Jarvis."

Connie nodded. "I always loved that guy. Boy, that alone should tell you something."

Nodding, she had to agree. "Still, do you think..."

"Ally, for me you have always been the voice of reason. I know this has been killing you. Fuck, when I found you bawling in the chopper, my heart broke for you. If there's a chance, even a little one, don't you want to find out?"

Ally closed her eyes to think, but the image of Erin forced her to open them. How could she not remember the feel of her in her arms, the scent of her hair, the touch of her skin? "If I'm wrong..."

"And if you're right?"

She smiled. "If I'm right, Pam's head will blow." She mimed an explosion with her hands, adding "Kaboom!" Connie laughed as her equilibrium returned. "You're right. It's worth the risk just to see Pam's face."

Giving her cousin a big hug, she counseled, "Now just remember, that's my big sis you're talking about. Also, secretly, she could do with a big serving of crow these days. I swear she gets worse, year after year. Now, the big question is how do you want to do this?"

Ally nodded as she pulled together a plan. "Here's what I'm thinking…"

CHAPTER TWENTY-ONE

Everything was set. The crew, along with the household staff, had decorated the garden, adding to the already well-designed and discreet lighting with decorative torches and well-placed spotlights. In the few places where flowers were not in bloom, huge arrangements had been added. Candles floated on the lily pond, and all the seating had been removed to make the three areas where the stars of the final show, the queens and the host, would stand. This wasn't how Connie had originally scripted the finale, but with the loss of Virginia on the very first day, or more importantly, her investment in the production, corners had to be cut. Still, this would actually be better. Instead of taking each queen to her own finale or eliminating either Pam or Ally, the show would seem a showdown, setting one against the other to see which if not both would go all the way and get down on one knee and propose.

The tension was high in the house as Connie led the six remaining contestants through their rehearsal, showing them their marks and preparing them for the night ahead, but it was not nearly so palpable as the pressure between Pam and Ally as host Tommy Proulx led them through their rehearsal. Ally was silent and stone-faced while Pam was full of herself and quipped at her cousin with ease.

Before the contestants joined the two remaining queens in the garden, Connie shot the ring choice scene with Pam. She hammed it up, picking one then another, then the last, changing her mind several times. Connie knew this would be a hard scene for Ally and simply recorded a static display of the three rings she had chosen at Cartier's and left the selection to the last moment when Ally would take the stage, so to speak.

Connie had a bad feeling, a premonition Pam would let her down and forego the proposal in favor of asking her choice to commit to getting to know one another more. Or Pam might yet surprise her. There was no telling with her big sis. She always had a plan. One that no one, not even she herself would see coming. It was what made her such a success in the courtroom and a pain in life.

Connie knew she could count on Ally, but whose hand Ally would ask for was still a mystery even after yesterday's revelation. She had spent her overnight date with Bobby Ann. Connie couldn't for the life of her guess what was going on with them, but the two looked happy together as the cameras followed them through the evening, departing when it was time for them to retire for the night. She had filmed them walking hand-in-hand to Ally's master suite. After that, she had packed up her crew and headed to Highland Creek to join the other crew, compare notes and plan out the following final day of production.

With the rehearsals complete it had just been a matter of waiting till evening to shoot the final sequence. Now tensions were high as she took supper with the crew and the six final contestants. She had ordered Pam and Ally sequestered separately to be sure Pam didn't trounce what was left of Ally's nerves or heart. The last thing she needed was an all-out fight between the cousins and goodness knew they were on the brink. Lifelong friends, having grown up together, there had always been healthy competition between the two, but Connie had never imagined their relationship could get this bad. She also had to question what the hell was driving her big sister. Pam could be an arrogant ass at times, but lately she was over the top. She'd have to talk to their mom about it or maybe Granddad. Connie worried for her, but right now her priority was getting this program into post-production. The network was already airing promos and had scheduled the first episode for next week. They were freaking out that she hadn't delivered it to them yet, but she couldn't finish the final edits until she was sure she had an ending, a big ending, and a down-and-out fight between Ally and Pam was not the one she wanted to shoot.

After dinner, she slipped outside to be sure everything was perfect. She caught Sandy and a few of the crew smoking a doob. Normally she would have gone all Rambo on their asses but fuck it, it was legal now, so she joined in, hoping a few drags of pot would calm her frayed nerves.

This had to work. Her reputation, her savings, and Ally's and Pam's investments were on the line.

Ally paced the library. She started to pour herself a finger of Granddad's scotch, then thought better of it, choosing the Bombay Sapphire and adding tonic. She paced herself drinking it, knowing she couldn't handle much and she couldn't get drunk. She didn't want to let Connie down and she sure as hell wasn't going to propose to anyone while she was half in the bag.

KC, at her side for moral support, didn't hesitate where the scotch was concerned. "I gotta hand it to Pops." It was her nickname for the elder Parker and one he got a kick out of. "He sure does keep the best hooch in his house."

That made Ally laugh, remembering their first contract flying in Newfoundland. "Oh my God. Do you remember that Screech?"

"Newfie Screech. Oh fuck, I thought we would die! I have never had a hangover like that but man oh man what a night. I could not live there full time. Fuck, those people sure know how to party and have fun…"

"I know, great folks, great fun, but God I was so worn out from that trip I thought we'd need a month just to recover."

"More like a month drying out. Man, they can handle their booze, and did they ever get a hoot out of us. I thought my family was wild but nothin' like those folks. I thought the Aussies were bad, and even what's his name spends half his year there."

"Russell Crowe," she furnished. "Remember his band was playing at the pub? It's like partying in Ireland, but with cheaper booze. Even the accents are almost the same."

KC raised her glass. "Here's to hot babes with funny accents, and the stamina to party all night and get up the next day and go to work."

Ally clinked her glass. "I am so glad we're too old for that."

"Hey, speak for yourself!"

She laughed, for the first time in days. "Have I told you lately…"

"What, that I'm an ass or the best pilot in town?"

Ally topped up KC's scotch and waved her over to the old nail-head chesterfield. "You're my best friend and the second-best pilot in the world."

KC groaned, but accepted the compliment. "Speaking of which, we're gonna have to train someone to cover me on the traffic patrol, you know, just in case."

"I do, but I think we should bring in two or three pilots. We need one, probably two to handle the fire contract for the Huey and yes, I think we need to consider having you only cover the morning or afternoon report. I think we need to take over the management of the airline. Those financials you brought tell me it's in the details where we'll get screwed."

"I was thinking that too, but I had to run it by you to be sure. We seem to have a lot of fat cats sitting on their hands collecting big bucks for a whole lotta nothin'. I was thinking about something, though. Maybe we should go the West Jet way, and empower the employees. Make it their job to take care of the little things. Well, make it everyone's job."

Ally nodded emphatically. "I like that. We'll have to create a bonus structure or consider handing over a share of ownership.

Either way, if the employees feel like they have the power to make things better for the passengers, everyone wins."

"Agreed," KC said, clinking her glass with Ally's again. It was that simple with the two of them, and what had made their partnership so profitable. "You know, I was thinking. Instead of recruiting pilots to fly the helos why don't we look for aircraft maintenance engineers who have some flying experience or are hot fired to learn to fly? Most of the crap we run into is attitude from the AME's about working all night when the pilots are sleeping—like they don't get how tough that part of the job is. We could hire two for the fire contract and work them in shifts, you know, one week on maintenance and one week flying."

Considering the suggestion, she nodded. "It doesn't give us much time to get them trained but you're right about it solving most of the personal fights that go on when people are pushed like they are during fire season. Maybe we need three. That way we can rotate them out for breaks and reduce the risk of burnout."

"It'll cost us more but, hell, if they're low time or if we're footing the training bill, we could pay them the minimum. Of course, they could screw off to a better paying job once they get some time in and there goes all our investment."

"Maybe not. We could use a training contract, you know like the airlines do. If they quit before a certain time, they have to pay all the training dollars back."

"That would be a hell of a bill, but I get it. There's no better incentive to stick with it and make it work than a fifty grand training bill hanging over your head."

The library door opened and Deb, Connie's PA, walked in. "How are you ladies doing? Ready to rock?"

KC was on her feet, "We are definitely ready for that. The show, well that's another thing. Ally?"

Returning to the drink cart, Ally set her half-empty glass down. "Good to go."

While KC slipped outside to find her seat beside Jarvis, the household staffers and the production team members not currently operating cameras or monitoring sound, Ally joined Pam waiting by the garden entrance for their introduction. Their marks were chalked on the patio stones, and they were ready.

Pam, looking as nervous as Ally, turned to her, wrapping her arms around her cousin's neck. "I'm so sorry for the way I've been acting these last weeks. Sometimes I just get so competitive. Truth be told, I've always been jealous of you, Al."

"Jealous of me? Why the hell for?"

She shook her head, hugging Ally again before confessing, "You're always so calm and cool. Even your flying. It's like nothing's a challenge for you. You see something, you do it. Even when Aunt Patsy freaked that you wouldn't go to business school and get your MBA the way she wanted, even when she threatened to have Granddad cut you off, you just did what you knew you were meant to do. I didn't get that before, I didn't get that flying isn't something you do but part of who you are. I'm so sorry."

"Never apologize, never explain. Just be who you are. I live by that, and I wish you would too."

She nodded, giving Ally another hug. "No matter what happens tonight, remember I love you."

Ally returned the hug letting some of the tension fall away. "I love you too, you pain in my backside."

"There's my girl!" Pam was laughing as was the PA who joined them, "Shush now, you two. It's time." She rechecked their wireless mics and the sound transmitter packs taped to their backs. "Okay, you're set."

From the garden, they heard the assistant director call, "All quiet on the set. Let's get this in one take, folks."

For once, it sounded like everyone had shut their traps, and the same woman called to Connie that the lights were a go, the cameras a go, and the sound on the various microphones.

"ACTION!"

Tommy Proulx stepped to his first mark. "Welcome to the finale of *Queen of Hearts*! Yes, folks, this is it. We began twelve weeks ago—" He was referring to the timespan the show would take to air, "—with thirty wonderful women vying for the love of our Queen of Hearts, but unlike other programs, this one has a twist. Instead of just one beautiful and eligible bachelorette to choose, we introduced four. And, we gave our contestants the power to pick and choose just who interested them most. As you recall it didn't take long to eliminate our first hopeful for the title *Queen of Hearts*." He paused; Connie would edit in highlights from the first ceremony and a clip of Virginia's Roll Royce leaving Glendennon Castle.

"Once our contestants narrowed the pool it was time to really get to know the remaining three hopefuls. Rene Santos-Dumont, our tech millionaire and racing mogul…" He paused again. Another clip of Rene's arrival in her supercar would be added here.

"Our next hopeful was the gorgeous defender of the people, Chicago's hometown girl, Pamela Parker with her stunning arrival by helicopter!" Again, he paused.

"Then, we had a real upset. Just when we thought we'd seen everything, our pilot extraordinaire, Allyson Parker, doffed her helmet and joined the women on the front lawn of the gracious Glendennon Castle, our home for this past twelve weeks." Pause.

"It was a wild ride while our women got to know our three hopefuls. They raced cars with Rene. Enjoyed the finest restaurants and toured award-winning vineyards with aficionado Pamela, and escaped to private beaches only accessible by a helicopter piloted by our Allyson." Pause.

"The women standing here tonight survived the first elimination by our queens, enjoying outings with their favorites, culminating in a most exhilarating and thrilling rafting trip down the always breathtaking Ottawa River: an expedition so treacherously exciting, one of our women would have been lost except for the bravery of our queens!" The highlights of this part were already cut and would look like Pam and Rene were part of the rescue attempt with Ally going overboard after an unidentified contestant, and Pam planning the rescue and coordinating from their base camp, and Rene leading the rescue party. Yes, it was a fiction, but it made for good reality TV.

"After that harrowing experience, our women flew home to face a true test, the final elimination of a queen hopeful. It was a nail-biting moment for all three of our queens, but in the end, the women wished Rene safe journey and sent her home." Pause. "But with so many women and so little time, they were soon set for another elimination. This was a difficult decision for our two remaining queen hopefuls as they pondered just who would warm their hearts. Their final decision: Pamela chose the delicate Charlotte, steadfast Denise, and brave Erin, while Allyson asked high-spirited Bobby Ann, creative Teresa, and unwavering Karen to stand by her." Pause.

"CUT! That was perfect, Tommy." At this point, Connie would insert the opening credits. Then the program would cut for the commercial break. "Okay women. This is it. Take your marks. Everyone, try to relax." She nodded to the assistant director who checked off all technicals as ready. "ACTION!"

"Welcome back to the *Queen of Hearts*. It's time to join the final six women vying for the heart of one of our two queen hopefuls. Before we call on Allyson and Pamela, let's check in with our women and see how they're faring."

Moving to his next mark, Tommy picked up a handheld microphone for the women not fitted with the wireless mics. Starting with Ally's group of three he began with the least favored to win Ally's heart, Karen. "It's been a long twelve weeks, Karen. How are you holding up?"

She smiled as rehearsed then answered as practiced. "I've had the time of my life. Allyson is so sweet, and I just loved spending time with her."

"I understand flying is not your favorite thing?"

She blushed. "I'll admit, it's a challenge for me, but one I'm sure I can overcome."

He moved on without comment, just a smile, knowing Connie would edit in some part of her discomfort during the last helicopter ride and Ally's kindness and soothing words afterward. "Teresa, tell me about your experience?"

"Tommy, it's been outstanding. Honestly, I have learned and experienced more in these last weeks than I could have imagined."

"I understand you're a budding novelist. Is that something you believe Ally would favor?"

She smiled pleasantly, if disingenuously for the camera. "I know it is. And she's provided so much content. I think I could write a dozen novels just drawing on her flying experiences alone."

Stepping to Bobby Ann's side, he smiled. "Bobby Ann, I understand you are just as adventurous as our Allyson, only more ground-based."

She laughed, much more genuinely than Teresa. "Souping up cars does not compare, but what a ride! I've had a wild time, and Ally is just the best. I adore her and all she does."

"High praise from our women, all hoping to catch the eye of Allyson." He paused again, then moved to his next mark when Connie gave him the nod. Starting with Charlotte, he asked, "You picked Pamela right from the start. Please tell us why?"

"She's amazing. So poised and smart. And I just love her command of the world and the work she does to help the wrongly accused."

He patted her shoulder, moving on to Erin. "Erin you're from Wisconsin, and we learned early on you work in the legal field too. Since you know the legal life, was Pamela's career a plus or minus for you?"

"Honestly, it's difficult. I know how hard lawyers work, especially the best of the best, as Pam is. What she does is important, and you have to accept the job with the woman. Like Ally, it's not what she does, but who she is."

Turning to the last contestant, and Pam's favorite, Denise, he asked, "You're standing here with these other incredible women. Tell me, do you think you're cut out to live the life of a high-powered attorney's wife?"

"Balancing careers in a relationship is always work. Compromises need to be made, but with love and understanding, there is always room to make things work."

Seeming unsatisfied with her answer, he asked, "What about that career? Tell us, if Pamela were to ask for your hand, would you put her career first or your own?" It was a fair question, just not the one she had rehearsed. This was an answer Pam wanted and had asked Connie to add at the last moment.

Denise did not look pleased, but plastered a smile on her face as she said, "In the end, the best marriages are built on honesty and being true to ourselves. I wouldn't be the woman Pam wants to marry if I neglected my own needs or my own career."

Tommy smiled and moved back to make his final remarks before introducing Ally and Pam. While they listened from inside the garden entry, Ally and Pam exchanged a look. Both women were bothered by the remark, especially since Denise was between positions and seemed to be floundering in her so-called career. They both knew their careers were part of them and mattered as much to them both as being Parkers.

When Tommy called Pam, Ally nodded, blowing out a hot breath and signaling her confidence with a thumbs-up.

Pam nodded to the signal; then she walked out as if she hadn't a care in the world.

"Pamela, welcome, welcome," Tommy said as Pam stepped up to his side, stopping expertly on her mark.

"Thank you so much, Tommy. I'm very excited for this night and if it's okay to admit it, a little nervous."

He grinned for the camera. "Well, of course, sweetie. Tonight is a big night for you, these women, our audience and of course Allyson, who, as we have mentioned before, is your first cousin. Tell me, what was it like competing against family?"

"Oh Tommy, this has been an adventure from the start, but as far as competing, I feel we are here first and foremost to find that perfect someone."

"Now, you and Allyson have very different careers, and live in entirely different countries, but what was it like growing up? Did you see much of each other?"

"We did, more than you would expect. We grew up in this house, even sharing a bedroom and attending all the same schools until college and our careers took us in separate directions. We may be very different women but at heart we're both Parkers and Parkers are resilient and loyal to one another."

"I understand your family has a long history. One you can trace back to good old England. Can you tell me about that?"

"It's not unique, but we pride ourselves on our name and motto. The Parker name was granted to our ancestor in the year ten-eighty-three by Queen Matilda as Royal Keeper of the Park. That role today is held by His Royal Highness, Prince Philip, the Duke of Edinburgh as the Royal Ranger of Windsor Castle. Our family motto, which Ally and I take to heart is, Loyalty is Our Reward."

He practically swooned. "Heady stuff and a royal connection too! No wonder you attended a castle for high school. What was that like?"

"It was absolutely amazing to have Allyson there with me. I don't know if Ally has told you, she was the school lacrosse star. I was a bookworm and her greatest fan."

He smiled and paused as scripted, then added, "Let's call Allyson out and hear what she has to say about your confession that you spent your high school years buried in books. Allyson?"

Ally stepped up to his other side, having to shuffle a bit to make her mark.

"Here she is, lacrosse star and daring pilot. Before we talk about your experience over the weeks culminating in this night, tell me, was Pamela the bookworm she claims to be?"

Ally couldn't hold back the grin. "The first thing you need know about Pam is she has an eidetic memory. She only needs to read a thing once to know it by heart so, buried in the library? Not so much. Of course, she's modest. She was captain of the debate team—the undefeated debate team, I might add. She was also a cheerleader and our school's most popular girl. I, on the other hand, was short…of course, I still am, plus awkward—oops, still guilty on that too, but having Pam as my popular and gorgeous cousin made life much easier, and oh did I mention she had all the girls after her then too?"

Tommy almost snorted at the off-script comments. "Tell me about these last twelve weeks. Did you feel you were competing against Pam for the love of these amazing women?"

Choking, Ally looked over to where Erin was standing with Pam's picks. She blew out a visible breath, admitting, "Yes and no. I think we have different taste when it comes to our affections, but we do overlap in the ideal of true love."

Tommy, excited, almost clapped. "Now, I'm not going to ask more on that as it's time for a break. When we return to the *Queen of Hearts*, we'll welcome our representative to tell us about the engagement rings you have each selected."

"CUT! Perfect. Okay, guys take a breath and relax. Don't move from your marks, but please shake off some of the tension you're carrying in your shoulders. Some of you are starting to look like linebackers for the Argonauts."

Connie ordered her crew to check and recheck their equipment. She wanted to get this right. It would only be fresh once, so there was only one chance to get it done. While they did their thing, she moved around the garden-turned-set, double-checking everything and everyone. Finally, she stopped beside Ally and Pam, telling them both, "You'll take turns doing this with only one of you on camera. We start with you contemplating your three rings as a set, then looking over each ring separately. I've got the shopping sequence edited and the close-ups of the rings already. It's just a matter of you taking a moment to contemplate each ring. We know each was chosen for a specific woman, but the audience doesn't know which, so when you pick up the ring you want, if you pick up a ring, it'll be all suspense until you either propose or ask your choice to get to know you better."

Out from the direction of the service entrance, two production assistants carried what looked like a backdrop or screen. She spotted them and showed them where to set it. Once she was satisfied, she turned to Ally and Pam. "When Tommy calls on you, take your time. Look the rings over carefully, even pick each up as if you may be reconsidering. Finally, if you decide on one, remove it from the box and hide it in your hand. Then and only then, I want you to walk around the screen, and stop on the mark just like we practiced. Try to breathe and wait for my nod. If you miss it don't panic and backtrack, Ally," she added, knowing who was the most nervous. "You will move to the last mark in front of the group. Yes, all six women will be standing as just one group for this part. So you can't miss that final mark. If you're going to propose, do it in whatever fashion you see fit. Especially you, Pam, since you're in a dress."

The beautiful and expensive designer dress Pam had purchased just yesterday did not look suitable for kneeling much less anything but standing and looking gorgeous. Ally on the other hand had selected a suit from Brooks Brothers that screamed her name when she tried it on. It was neither masculine or business-y, and fit the occasion perfectly. "Okay. Any questions?"

Looking terribly nervous, they both shook their heads.

"Guys, you've got this. Remember, this is your future you are wagering on, and your hearts. I want the real deal, no matter what. Got that?" she said, accentuating her words and making sure they both understood by repeating herself, "Remember that, no...matter...what."

Connie moved back beside the camera crew but didn't take her seat; no one was in their chairs anymore, the tension was just too high. She nodded to her AD who ran through all the checks.

"ACTION!"

Off script, Pam moved to Ally's side, hugging her before returning to her mark and beginning her wavering over her three chosen engagement rings. Finally she chose one, removing it from the box and palming it carefully. She turned to Ally again, pausing as if looking for support.

Ally nodded to her, tempted to give her another hug, then, throwing all instruction out the window, did just that. Pam was shaking up a storm and looked as if she would cry on the spot. "You've got this," Ally said quietly. "Stick to the advice you gave me and follow your heart."

Pam nodded, then walked past the screen to take the mark Connie wanted her to hold on, while the camera grabbed a closeup of her nervous and contemplative face.

Jarvis, more astute about Pamela's needs and the complexities of being a lady, had placed a small stool in front of her next mark and a PA had quickly covered it with a black cloth. It would be almost invisible to the cameras unless she chose to bend a knee.

When Connie finally nodded, Pam was visibly shaking as she walked to her mark. Hitting it squarely, she seemed to almost forget her purpose, standing frozen in front of the six final contestants.

Connie gave her a moment to collect herself, knowing the tension and delay would play out perfectly on TV.

The tensions heightened further as she stepped forward, resting a bare knee on the draped stool and holding out the ring for the cameras and audience, plus the women, to see.

Knowing she could only shoot this once, Connie had cameras everywhere including one honed in on each of the six women she had moved to stand in one group.

Pam offered a smile that would sway any jury in its authenticity. "I never imagined this would happen to me. I thought I would go through this, have some fun, meet some amazing women, and go home much the way I arrived, single and determined to stay that way." She paused again, taking deep breaths. Then she said, "I don't want to go home alone and no matter what the future holds you have changed the world for me. Seeing and experiencing life through your eyes has brought the fun back and the wonder." She swallowed hard, asking "Will you marry me, Charlotte?"

Charlotte, all a-quiver, burst out in joyful tears before throwing herself into Pam's arms. It was all she could do to keep her balance.

Connie let them have their moment, just as surprised as the other women and crew. She was careful to check out the expression of the others, especially Denise and Erin. Erin looked surprised and delighted, the smile on her face betraying her fondness for the two together. Denise, on the other hand, looked like she would start a fight. Perfect. *More food for the audience.*

Finally able to get to her feet, Pam turned to the cameras as practiced and with Charlotte's hand shaking so hard it took some work, placed the ring on her finger. Charlotte held it out for the world to see, then returned her arms to their place around Pam's shoulders. She was rewarded with a kiss capable of setting fires.

Before anyone could step forward to congratulate them, Connie held up a hand to remind everyone they were still shooting. She let the two carry on in each others' arms for several minutes then called for quiet again. She didn't call cut but did move Pam and Charlotte to stand beside Tommy, who looked beyond cheered.

The main camera panned back to Ally who stood looking immobilized by fear. Quietly, Connie encouraged her; she could edit the audio later to remove her voice. "Okay Ally. It's up to you now. Just follow your heart."

Swallowing visibly, she stood looking at the rings. When she had chosen them, only one mattered to her, the perfect three-carat diamond ring sitting in the center of the table. Her hands were trembling so much she had a tough time getting it from the box. When she finally had it in her hand, she held it so tightly her knuckles were turning white. Trying to breathe, and to remember Connie's instructions, she almost stumbled when she turned from the table. She couldn't look at the women grouped together. Instead, she looked to Pam for support. The tears of joy she saw there were real, and gave her the confidence to keep going. Forgetting to wait for Connie's signal she started for the next mark in front of Teresa, Karen, and Bobby Ann, and the remaining Erin and Denise. Realizing she'd missed the mark, she almost backtracked, then remembered Connie's warning not to do that.

Now in front of the five remaining women, she stood frozen. It was if she couldn't remember her instructions or words or anything. She forced herself to be calm, reciting the Huey's takeoff checklist in her head. She was tempted to do it, again and again, but pushed the compulsion away. Determined not to choke, she swallowed hard, and taking Pam's example, drew in several deep breaths. Finding her voice, she said, carefully and not to any one of them in particular, "I fell in love with you the day you walked in. I didn't understand it, want it, and goodness knows, I was sure you never would either."

She wanted to rub her face; the makeup was irritating her, the bright lights in her face distracting; even the people watching her were making her feel as shy as if she were back in high school. She chanced a look to Pam and got a comforting nod. "I don't know what it is about you. I feel you challenge me, you have made me work harder, think more, and believe more than I ever imagined possible."

Ally couldn't think of any better words. Maybe she should have written this out or practiced it, but all anxiety fell away the moment she got down on one knee. She still couldn't bring herself to look at her, so she closed her eyes to see her face. "I have never wanted anything in my life as much as I want to spend it with you." She opened her eyes and held out the ring. "Will you marry me… Erin?"

While Bobby Ann grinned up a storm, Teresa and Karen exchanged looks. Erin, still standing beside the angry Denise, stood riveted.

Understanding her disbelief, Ally looked to her, adding, "Erin, you are the woman I want to spend my life with."

Finally seeming to understand it was her, she was the woman Ally wanted and had asked for, Erin moved toward Ally as if afraid Connie was about to call CUT. Those last few feet an eternity of miles until their tear-stained eyes connected. Still looking unsure, as if she had heard wrong, Erin stopped, almost formally, before her. When no objections rang out, Erin's hands moved to sit carefully along her collar. She stood, looking, silently asking. With the evidence of Ally's words written on her face, she threw her arms around her neck and held on. They stood there for the longest time, their joint snuffles the only sound to be heard.

Unable to take that as answer enough, Ally had to ask, "Does that mean yes?"

Erin answered without hesitation, the tears falling unabashedly, "Yes, Ally. That means yes!"

Bobby Ann, standing directly behind them prompted joyously, "Put the ring on, come on you two!"

There was fussing and crying and finally the ring was on, but Erin had no intention of wasting time showing it off. Back in Ally's arms, she kept repeating "Yes…yes…yes…yes." They didn't kiss long, both of them so stuffed up from tears they could hardly breathe.

Bobby Ann, clearly overjoyed too, couldn't help herself and stepped up, wrapping her arms around the two. Once she left her mark, Pam and Charlotte did too. Even Tommy rushed in to join the group hug.

Connie, beyond happy for them, had her hand clamped over her mouth, afraid she'd do something stupid like call CUT when she wanted to record every second of an ending she could not have scripted or predicted in a million years. She knew she should pull Tommy out to finish his dialogue and start the post interviews but why ruin the moment? Her sister had found a woman she wanted to marry and Ally, Ally was deeply in love and had done what she worried she would never have the confidence to do.

Beside Connie, Jarvis set a hand on her shoulder. "You have done what even Mister Parker worried would never happen. Bravo Miss Connie, or should I say, brava?"

She smiled at him and took his hand. "What the hell," she said, dragging him forward, and the two of them offered their heartfelt congratulations. Even she couldn't control the tears. It would take hours to get everything and everyone back on course to finish the rest of the shoot.

So, what, she decided. I can clean the rest up in post.

EPILOGUE

Allyson all but tripped trying to get all the luggage in the door. "Good God, Pam! How much stuff did you bring?"

"Oh, those are just Charlotte's. Don't give me that look! She has to see what my bridesmaid dress looks like before she can decide what to wear."

KC and Bobby Ann, cuddling on the couch, offered to help. "Come on babe," KC said. "Let's get all this stuff in the guest room."

While they began moving bag after bag, Ally had to ask, more than a little frustrated, "Looks like you brought everything but the kitchen sink—except you seem to have forgotten my bride?"

Pam laughed, heading straight for the bar and pouring herself a glass from the wine Ally had just opened. "Settle down. With all this luggage, we had to take two cabs. She and Charlotte are right behind me."

"Ignore her," KC offered, stopping between trips to the guest room. "She's been like this all day."

"Yep," Bobby Ann said, adding, "we've been threatening to lock her out on the roof and let the snow cool her mood."

Pam just smiled. "Oh you lovesick fool. Well, worry no more. Your bride will arrive momentarily and," she paused to sip her wine, "wow, this is good."

"Pam!"

"That's it!" KC said. "Come on Pammy, grab an arm. Someone needs a little snow time."

A knock on the door stopped all plans to dump Ally in the two feet of powder that had been building over the last few days. Winter was making its presence known with steady squalls bringing down tons of the white stuff.

Tripping over the last bag, Ally found herself falling this time. She looked up from the floor to see Erin's curious expression and Charlotte stepping over her as if this was all normal.

Erin bent down to help her up and managed to slip on the wet floor and toppled down on top of her.

Ally pulled her tight, deciding then and there that she had no interest in letting go.

"Oh boy, here they go," KC said, walking with Bobby's hand in hers as they returned to the couch.

Pam offered her wineglass to Charlotte. "Here, my love. You must be parched from the drive."

"I've never seen so much snow!"

"I have," Erin said as she found her way back on her feet, then helped the red-faced Ally up too. "It reminds me of home," she added, wrapping her arm around her neck and pulling her close for a long overdue kiss.

Ally was finally able to ask, "Is that a good thing?"

"It's a perfect thing, my beautiful and maybe nervous bride."

Ally smiled. "Between the snow and KC's constant razzing, I wasn't sure you'd make it."

"That bad, huh?"

"KC and Bobby Ann just threatened to lock me out on the roof!" she whined, but with a grin.

"Forget them, honey. They can tease all day, but I'm here. You can count on me. Always."

Bella Books, Inc.

Women. Books. Even Better Together.

P.O. Box 10543
Tallahassee, FL 32302

Phone: 800-729-4992
www.bellabooks.com